D1348458

0727 847643 2100 FB

THE SEVENTEENTH STAIR

W.M.
RESERVE STOCK

THE SEVENTEENTH STAIR

29. APR. 1995

Rosalind Laker

WOLVERHAMPTON LIBRARIES

JFR

0727 847643 2100 FB

B 0947 LBC   RA

This first edition published in Great Britain 1995 by
SEVERN HOUSE PUBLISHERS LTD of
9–15 High Street, Sutton, Surrey SM1 1DF,
under the Rosalind Laker name.
First published 1975 by Macdonald and Jane's,
under the name of Barbara Paul.

Copyright © 1975 by Barbara Paul
All rights reserved. The moral rights of the author have been asserted.

British Library Cataloguing in Publication Data

Laker, Rosalind
  Seventeenth Stair. - New ed
  I. Title
  823.914 [F]

  ISBN 0-7278-4764-3

To Daphne and Ted

All situations in this publication are fictitious and
any resemblance to living persons is purely coincidental.

Typeset by Hewer Text Composition Services, Edinburgh.
Printed and bound in Great Britain by
Hartnolls Ltd, Bodmin, Cornwall.

CHAPTER ONE

In the over-furnished drawing-room Rosella Eastwood closed the door behind her, before moving, with a rustle of underskirts, towards the light of the window. The letter she was opening had come with the afternoon post. It had been a long time in transit, but Martinique was far away from Kent and ships were often delayed by storms and other disasters. Her fingers eagerly unfolded the sheets of paper, covered by her elderly French guardian's elegant but rather shaky hand, and she sat down on a horseshoe-backed chair to read them.

The sun, penetrating the lace curtains, threw a spider-web pattern over her, casting shadows into the drapery of her skirt, highlighting the rich wheat-colour of her glossy hair which she wore in heavy coils drawn back on her well-shaped head. She was young, lithe and slender, taut with longing for life, desperate to escape from the wholly feminine establishment of the Seminary for the Daughters of Gentlefolk, which had kept her confined too closely and too long. She hardly dared to hope that the letter would contain a satisfactory answer to the impassioned plea for liberty that she had written to André Cadel, reminding him that three years had passed since his last visit to Europe to see her, and that she was no longer a child but a woman.

The letter began with a wry comment on her reference to the passing of time. He was painfully aware of the fact, he wrote. Daily over the past eighteen months or more he

1

WOLVERHAMPTON
PUBLIC LIBRARIES

had found the climate of the island was no longer treating him kindly. The need for a change of environment, to say nothing of a visit to his Parisian doctors, was long overdue. Without doubt his days abroad were over, and it was certainly high time that her future was discussed and settled. Therefore he had booked a passage aboard a steamship that would be leaving at the end of the month.

Breathless with excitement she read on to the end, when she sat back in the chair with a long sigh of satisfaction, gazing unseeingly out of the window at the stretch of lawn and garden with the blossoming orchard beyond. She was to meet her guardian, André Cadel, at the very grand Hôtel du Louvre on the rue de Rivoli, which he always made his *pied-à-terre* whenever he was in France. She knew it well, having spent holidays there in the past. No promises had been made, but it seemed almost certain that André Cadel planned to buy a house in Paris and she would reside there with him. She closed her eyes on the thought, clutching the letter to her. It would be the first real home she had ever known. Something she had always longed for. And in the city that had always enchanted her.

The creaking of the door made her straighten up.

'Oo, there you are, Miss Rosella!' the young maid exclaimed in soft Kentish tones. 'I've been looking everywhere! Madame Delagranges wants to see you in her study.'

'*Merci*, Lucy.' Rosella rose to her feet. She was not surprised by the summons, having guessed that the principal would have received a letter from André Cadel by the same post.

It was a strict rule of the seminary that French was spoken by the pupils at all times, and as conversation was forbidden with the servants, most of whom were local folk, it was rare to hear English spoken within the precincts, except snatches that drifted from below stairs or chat overheard between the gardeners.

Madame Delagranges, a shrewd, intelligent French-woman, had been employed in her youth as governess to the children of a minor member of Empress Eugenie's entourage. She had been wise enough to foresee the upheavals that were to beset France, and had crossed the Channel to open the school in Kent. Her staff consisted of poor but well-bred fellow countrywomen, to whom she entrusted the education of her English pupils. The waiting list for places was always full. Academic qualifications were not in demand for the daughters of well-to-do gentlefolk, but Madame Delagranges offered her pupils the chance of an exquisite French accent and a fluent knowledge of the language, both of which were social assets beyond price, putting up the stakes in the marriage market. When, to Madame Delagranges's great good fortune, the Empress settled in exile in Kent, not far from the seminary, she successfully captured the Royal lady's patronage and was able to raise the fees even higher.

Rosella had been in Madame Delagranges's excellent care for as long as she could remember, and had grown up to be comfortably bi-lingual. Had the seminary offered anything less André Cadel would have sent her to some educational establishment in France, instead of allowing her to grow up in the country where she had been born. Rosella had no close relatives. Her English father had died before she was born, and after her birth, which had been difficult and complicated, her mother had lived only a matter of weeks before following her husband to the grave. So André Cadel, to whom her mother had been distantly related, had bestirred himself at his white mansion overlooking his sugar plantations in Martinique, and had travelled half-way across the world to ensure that an orphaned infant was placed in good hands, to be properly reared and suitably educated.

3

Since that time André Cadel had come in and out of her life at infrequent intervals, smelling deliciously of cigars and crisp linen and the hint of eau-de-Cologne. His hair and goat's beard were frosty white, his sun-weathered face bronzed and stern and unsmiling. Her affection for him, although blended with respect and a great deal of awe, was deep-rooted and binding, for he represented all she had ever known of family ties.

Hurrying along the corridor that led to the principal's study, Rosella met a flood of younger girls emerging from a sewing class. She spoke to one, complimenting her on a sampler that was finished and ready for framing, before continuing on her way. At seventeen Rosella was of average height and softly curved with a slender waist. Her face was arresting, particularly her eyes which were dark amber flecked with gold, and her mouth was quick to smile.

She reached the study and tapped on the door before entering. Madame Delagranges, a straight-backed, full-bosomed figure in tight purple bombazine, with a cameo brooch at her throat, was seated at her desk, her spectacles in her hand. An opened letter, unmistakably from André Cadel, was lying on the blotter in front of her. She was not an unattractive woman, and her black hair was enhanced by a single silvery quiff that grew wing-like from a point on her forehead. All her movements were dignified and composed: good deportment was a matter of importance to her — and to her pupils.

'*Bonjour,* madame.' Rosella curtsied politely.

Madame Delagranges acknowledged the greeting and with a sweep of her spectacles indicated a chair. 'Be seated, Rosella. I see by the letter in your hand that you have already received the news that I was intending to impart.'

'I have indeed, madame,' Rosella said happily, sitting down to face her.

4

'So you are going to leave us at last.' Madame Delagranges regarded Rosella with a kindly eye. In her opinion Rosella should have gone out into the world long since, although she would have missed the girl's help in taking the younger children for singing and music during the last eighteen months when there had been nothing left to teach her. She had no fear about the girl's future. Monsieur Cadel was a true gentleman of old France, and Madame Delagranges was convinced that he would launch his ward into the proper Parisian circles. She had come to know him well over the years, for although one of the staff had always accompanied Rosella to Paris he had never failed to return the child himself. Over a glass of wine in the study he had asked questions about her progress, satisfying himself that all was well.

'You've always been very good to me, madame,' Rosella said, 'and I've been as happy at the seminary as was possible under the circumstances, but naturally I'm over-joyed at the thought of joining my guardian in Paris. I've had a growing feeling during recent weeks — ' here her voice quivered on the fear expressed at last ' — that I was never going to see him again.'

'Foolish girl!' Putting on her spectacles Madame Delagranges glanced over the letter in front of her. 'Now let's see what arrangements are to be made. Monsieur Cadel wants you chaperoned all the way to Paris as you have been in the past. A chaise from the Hôtel du Louvre will be awaiting you at Calais when you disembark from the steam-packet.' She looked up with a smile. 'I think Mademoiselle Dupont can be spared for a few days to accompany you.'

As it happened Mademoiselle Dupont was to be denied an impromptu visit to her native France. A mysterious bout of fever attacked a number of the staff and over half the pupils. Although the sickness was of very short duration it took everyone several days to recover. Rosella, who had helped with the nursing, was lucky enough to escape the fever, not so Mademoiselle Dupont and on the day of her departure Mademoiselle Dupont was still not fit to travel. Nor was there any other responsible person available to make the journey with Rosella. Had Madame Delagranges not been taken ill herself she would never have allowed Rosella to leave for Paris on her own, but her head throbbed and her body ached with the fever, making it impossible for her to offer any determined protest. When the door closed on the girl who had been in her charge since early childhood, Madame Delagranges prayed fervently that all would go well.

Rosella felt liberated. To travel without the rather dreary Mademoiselle Dupont was a bonus beyond her wildest dreams. She enjoyed handling her own tickets and passport, and was attentively assisted at every turn. The wind blew strongly off the Channel and the crossing on the steam-packet was obviously going to be rough, but an obliging steward found her a seat in a sheltered spot and put a rug over her knees. She took one last look at the white cliffs of Dover already moving away, and then turned her head to watch for the grey line that was France loom up on the horizon.

As arranged, the chaise was waiting with four horses and two uniformed postillions, and Rosella was helped inside and her luggage stowed away. She had brought little in the way of clothing with her, for her guardian had written that she must be fitted with an entirely new wardrobe suited to every occasion. This generous offer she had taken as another indication of his intention to let her live with him in Paris.

With a clatter of hooves and a rumble of wheels the equipage moved forward across the cobbles. Rosella settled back for the long journey that would last the rest of the day and all through the night. Her thoughts naturally turned to her guardian and the reunion that was to come. She was longing to see him, looking forward to this new life in Paris.

Stops on the journey were few. She slept all through the dark hours, waking only when there was a change of horses. She was fully awake soon after dawn, and wild with excitement at the thought that before long she would be in Paris.

Although the day was dull and overcast, it did not dampen her spirits. And when towards noon the clouds lifted, and she was able to see the Triumphal Arch and the windmills high on the hill of Montmartre, her joy knew no bounds. There was a short delay at the custom-house where an official checked her luggage to ensure that no municipal duty needed to be levied on any goods she was bringing into Paris, and then the chaise was on its way again.

It was all endearingly familiar. The white plastered houses, tall and humble, the shutters faded. The grandeur of the boulevards where the trees threw out new green lace and the magnificent buildings rose high on each side. The shops and coffee-houses busy with people. The traffic. Cabriolets, curricles, calèches and coaches mingled with horse-buses, horse-trams, and commercial vehicles of every kind, the clatter of wheels and clopping of hooves mingling with the shouts of street traders. The flower-sellers made bright splashes of colour with the baskets they humped on their arms or rested on a convenient step.

Rosella eagerly watched for the Hôtel du Louvre as the chaise carried her along the rue de Rivoli. There it was, facing the great palace itself: far from being overshadowed by its close proximity, the hotel had a heavy façade of columns and caryatids that gave it a grandeur of its own in keeping with its setting.

The postillions brought the equipage smartly alongside the steps up to the entrance, and it was almost impossible for Rosella to wait those few seconds before the chaise door was opened. She managed to alight decorously without any show of ankle, in a manner that Madame Delagranges would have approved, and mounted the marble steps, her feet light with anticipation.

Entering the crimson and gilt lobby she looked around quickly, expecting to see the frock-coated, top-hatted figure of her guardian rise stiffly from one of the many plush-upholstered seats that were half-hidden by potted palms. But there was no sign of him among the throng of people who were coming and going. Hesitantly, still glancing about her, she made her way across the chequered marble floor to the reception desk where she was greeted by one of several clerks busily on duty.

'*Bonjour*, mademoiselle.' His hair was brushed flat as paint and his breath smelt faintly of tobacco beneath the disguising scent of a violet cachou.

She gave her name. 'You will find that accommodation has been booked for me by Monsieur André Cadel. He is expecting me. Would you please send word to his suite that I'm here.'

'Certainly, mademoiselle.' The clerk checked the booking. 'Two suites were booked by letter from Martinique, and they are ready, but Monsieur Cadel has yet to arrive.'

She stared at him in dismay, touched by a chill of misgiving. 'Is there no message for me?' she enquired anxiously. 'No letter?'

'Nothing at all, mademoiselle.' He pushed the register towards her and held out a quill pen. 'If you would kindly sign your name I'll arrange for you to be shown up to your suite.'

An under-manager came forward with a swirl of coat-tails to lead the way up the curve of the wide staircase, snapping his fingers surreptitiously at the porters carrying her trunk and other baggage. Half-way up the stairs Rosella paused, her gloved hand resting on the banister rail. She looked down with a vain rush of hope at some newcomers streaming through the glass doors of the hotel, thinking that no matter what had delayed her guardian he must be on the point of arrival and could appear at any moment. But he was not among them.

She was about to continue up the stairs when her scanning gaze rested on a tall, well-dressed man lighting a cigar as he turned away from the reception desk. She could not see his face because it was hidden by the wide brim of the shallow-crowned hat that he was wearing. Unaccountably her mind's eye registered the height and supple spareness of him. He possessed the kind of languid grace of hard-muscled limbs that would make him equally at home in a saddle or the riggings of a ship. In another second Rosella would have turned away, but he happened to lift his head while shaking out the flame of the match. His dark, extraordinarily piercing eyes met hers and held them with devastating impact. She had a lightning impression of a strong, square face, a straight nose with nostrils powerfully curved, but thin and arched, and a wide mouth, incisive, stubborn, sensual, that was already quirking into an outrageous, challenging smile. Hastily she tore her gaze away and continued up the stairs, but she knew that he was still watching her through the curling smoke of his cigar. Resolutely she avoided the temptation to glance back.

Rosella had never occupied so grand a suite before, and it offered further proof of her guardian's awareness that during his absence she had grown into a woman. A maid was waiting to unpack, but she sent her away for half an hour, wanting to be alone for a little while. Inexplicably her spirits had lightened. At any moment a page could

9

come with the message that André Cadel had arrived. His ship must have been delayed somewhere. Or else he had taken longer over the journey from Marseilles than he had expected. A perfectly simple explanation would be forthcoming. Of that she was sure.

She untied the ribbons beneath her chin and tossed aside the little silk-trimmed hat. Going across to the glass doors that opened on to the balcony, she pressed down the handles and flung them wide. The spring sunshine streamed down on her and the noise of Paris assailed her ears like a pleasantly discordant overture. It made her feel that she was standing on the threshold of a great adventure. Everything was about to begin. Even love was waiting for her somewhere in the sun and shadows of this exciting city. She set her hands flat on the stone parapet and leaned with straight arms to look down into the wide sweep of the boulevard below.

The stranger from the lobby was stepping into an open landau drawn up at the hotel steps. She saw him settle himself on the seat, cross one leg over the other. Perhaps sensing her gaze, he looked up quickly and those challenging eyes met hers again. Swiftly he raised his hat with his gloved hand, but she withdrew instantly into the room, and closed the doors. Nevertheless, she stayed by the windows and watched the landau with its fine, high-stepping horses disappear from view in the direction of the rue St. Honoré. A little smile played on her mouth. The incident had reawakened poignant memories of someone else. Someone not at all like the dramatic-looking stranger. Someone with a special place in her heart, whom she had met once in France a long time ago during a holiday with her guardian. He had been no more than a youth then, but now he would be twenty-three or -four. She spoke his name aloud. 'Sébastien de Louismont.'

But at the sound of her own voice speaking his name

10

other memories, dark and unhappy, rose up to cloud the brief moment of happiness she had known with him. She shuddered away from them, remembering against her will a grey château that she never wanted to see again. It was as well Sébastien had gone out of her life. Like the stranger in the landau.

Determinedly she put both men out of her mind and rang the bell to summon the maid to unpack.

CHAPTER TWO

Rosella spent the following day at the hotel, reluctant to move outside its doors in case André Cadel should arrive and find her absent. To while away the time she purchased some fashion magazines and a couple of novels, as well as a particularly daring book that Madame Delagranges would never have allowed her to read. But it was hard to settle down to reading when all Paris throbbed and vibrated outside the windows of her suite in the clanking of wheels on tram rails, the continuous clop of hooves, the shouts, the noise, and once the sound of a woman singing as sweetly as a thrush for *sous* on a corner near the hotel.

Again and again she put her reading matter aside and went out on the balcony to watch the tangled flow of traffic, the breeze bringing a potpourri of aromas blended from horse-sweat and heavily scented flowers, leather and garbage and garlic and the occasional whiff of onion soup, all peculiarly belonging to Paris. From her vantage point she was able to see that the trees along the Rue de Rivoli were not all the same height: most of them being replacements for those cut down for the barricades during the siege of less than a decade ago, not yet come to their full glory. She was touched to the depths of her sensitive nature by this poignant reminder of the city's past sufferings amid all the show of wealth and prosperity that abounded in this most fashionable of cities.

A hotel messenger, who had been sent to the shipping company's office, returned with the information that the

12

steamship from Martinique had docked slightly behind schedule due to bad weather, and this piece of information did much to ease her mind. Obviously her guardian, tired by the voyage, had decided to rest for a while in Marseilles before journeying on to Paris. Naturally, he would see no need for haste, assuming that she was being safely chaperoned by one of the seminary's dull but reliable members of staff. It simply would not occur to him that she might be on her own in the city.

Rosella consulted his letter again, although she had read it many times since it had first reached her. He had arranged a draft upon Rothschild's bank in order that she could use a suitably increased allowance as she wished, but he considered it of utmost importance that she should be fitted out with a suitable wardrobe for every occasion *without delay*. The emphasis conveyed by these two underlined words made her decide that instead of waiting around in the hotel for another day, she would spend the time carrying out his wishes in the thoroughly enjoyable pastime of buying new clothes. Drawing a chair up to the escritoire in her drawing-room she started to make out a list of all she would need.

Knowing her guardian's impeccable taste, she launched herself on a shopping spree that took her to one of the most exclusive fashion houses in Paris. With some trepidation she entered its portals, painfully conscious of her church mouse drabness, but she need not have worried. The *directrice* rose from her seat at an exquisite Louis XIV writing table at the head of the sweeping staircase, and came to greet her most charmingly. She was well accustomed to fitting out rich young *mademoiselles* fresh from their convent schools, although it was not often that one came on her own. When a few discreetly phrased questions brought the name of Monsieur André Cadel into the conversation, the *directrice* summoned forth her most experienced *vendeuse* to take charge of the young customer.

'This way, if you please.'

The *vendeuse* ushered her into a long room glittering with chandeliers and furnished with silk-upholstered chairs. Rosella had enough French blood in her veins not to be surprised that her guardian's name was known to the fashion house. There must have been private occasions during his sojourns in France when he had needed to make gifts of furs or gowns to some female of his acquaintance. But it was no business of hers. In fact, it simply served to prove that she had been right in the selection of the place from which to choose her new clothes. She took a seat and gave herself up to the pleasure of viewing the lovely garments in a host of colours and wonderful materials, which were displayed to her. She discovered that bustles were at their peak in an extravagance that delighted her, and never had fashion been more feminine in an abundance of ruffles and lace, flounces, ribbons, flowers and berthas.

On the whole she knew what would suit her, but the *vendeuse* tactfully restrained her from selecting an evening gown in a deep rose velvet. 'It *is* your colour, Mademoiselle Eastwood, but the fabric is too voluptuous and is not considered quite – er – proper for a young girl.'

Rosella was willing to be advised, wanting her guardian to be proud of her, and the last thing she desired was to cause him the slightest embarrassment. 'Do you mean that in velvet I might be mistaken for a *demi-mondaine*?' she enquired with innocent frankness.

The *vendeuse* drew in her breath slightly. 'Let us say that it is entirely suitable for any matron to wear, but at your age it would not be correct.' With an almost imperceptible little jerk of her authoritative chin she indicated that the offending garment should be borne

14

quickly away. 'A silk tulle in the same shade perhaps?'

In the fitting-room Rosella tried on the evening gowns, the calling costumes, dresses for every hour of the day and for every occasion. Some fitted her perfectly and would be delivered at the hotel within the hour, but others needed some minor adjustment or she decided to have them made up in another colour or material.

She shopped for three days. In addition to the dresses and coats, she bought a riding habit and even a full-skirted bathing costume with long matching bloomers in white-braided black alpaca, lace-trimmed underwear, negligées of gossamer silk with falling ribbons of cherry and apricot, shoes and high-buttoned boots and dancing slippers with rosettes, purses, fans, and ribbons for her hair. Her hats arrived in striped boxes from various milliners, and amid clouds of billowing tissue paper she tried each one on again before the looking-glass of her dressing-table, thinking that there was nothing in all the world like a Parisian bonnet.

André Cadel would approve her purchases. Of this she was certain, even though, in spite of a sizeable accumulation of her allowance at the banks, she would have spent every franc by the time the bills were settled. She certainly had no intention of letting him subsidize her allowance. He had been more than generous over the years, and she was looking forward to giving some measure in return by doing everything in her power to run his home well and efficiently, nursing him back to health if that were possible, and making his declining years as easy and comfortable as it lay in her power so to do.

But then she would pull herself up. Suppose she was jumping to conclusions in assuming that he intended to keep her under his roof? Another thought struck her. So alarming that her hands faltered in adjusting the lilac-trimmed bonnet that she had put on, and she saw her reflection grow pale in the looking-glass. Suppose he was intending to settle her into a marriage of convenience with some man of good family and background, whom *he* would consider suitable! Was this the reason he had deemed it important to cast away her dull schoolgirl clothes and array herself in a new finery without delay?

She rose quickly from the stool on which she had been sitting and took a few paces up and down the room, her hands clasped nervously. Why on earth hadn't she considered such a possibility before? She had been too dazed with joy at the prospect of joining her guardian in Paris, her days of loneliness behind her, that she had given no thought to any alternative arrangement he might have in mind. It would be a natural conclusion to his responsibilities for him to see her safely wedded and off his hands for ever. And he would think it right and proper to select a husband for her with little or no thought for her opinion on the matter: young French girls did what their parents and guardians thought best for them. Such marriages were everyday affairs. But she couldn't -- no, she wouldn't! -- marry a man not of her own choice!

She slept little that night, dread of an unknown future adding fuel to a nagging fear that she had been suppressing but had found herself unable to dismiss. In the dark hours she faced it squarely at last, and now it threatened to overwhelm her. She had seized upon the shopping spree to keep her unease at bay, trying to convince herself that the feeling of foreboding, which had hung over those last months at the seminary, had been without grounds. But something was wrong. Terribly wrong.

As soon as it was light she dressed and went downstairs. A few early travellers were about and the reception desk was fully manned.

'Monsieur Cadel still hasn't arrived,' said one of the reception clerks, anticipating the question that she had asked so many times, but she had something else to ask.

'How could I find out if there's been any kind of accident on the road between Marseilles and Paris? A diligence overturning. Or a crash between vehicles that has resulted in injuries to the passengers concerned.'

'Leave it to me, mademoiselle,' the clerk said briskly. 'I'll have enquiries made at the appropriate coach station and other sources.'

By breakfast time she had learned that, although a number of mishaps had occurred on the road from Marseilles over the past few days, there was nothing that could have involved her guardian. Where was he then? Why hadn't he written to her? Or sent a messenger?

She spent the morning in the Louvre, looking at its many treasures, but all the time her mind was concentrating on how to locate her guardian.

Finally she gave up the pretence of an interested spectator, and took a seat in one of the rooms, to sort out her thoughts. To whom should she turn? To the police? But her guardian would be furious if a *gendarme* turned up to question him while he was on private business.

Yet it was as though André Cadel had vanished into thin air. She shivered, raising her head, and saw for the first time that she was surrounded by stuffed bears and wolves and every kind of wild beast. Each one was snarling in terror and rage, as at the moment of violent death and the glass eyes looked alive in the reflected light of the windows. She sprang to her feet and rushed from the room, but her mounting fear seized her in a nightmare grip that was slowly tightening.

When she returned to the hotel the clerk, to whom she had spoken earlier that day, was watching out for her. 'Perhaps I should have mentioned it the first time, but a gentleman called again this morning asking to see Monsieur Cadel.'

So she was not alone in her waiting! Somebody else had

17

been informed of the expected date of her guardian's arrival in Paris and was eager to see him. 'What was the caller's name?' she enquired swiftly.

'Monsieur Philippe Aubert.'

It meant nothing to her. She had never heard it before and could only assume that the gentleman was one of many of her guardian's business acquaintances.

'Did you tell him that I was staying here?'

'I did indeed, but you were out and he could not wait. He left a letter for Monsieur Cadel.'

'Let me have it,' she said firmly. 'I must be in charge of my guardian's affairs until he comes.'

In her room she tore the letter open expectantly, certain that it would contain an address that she could contact, but it was a note scrawled in haste on the hotel's notepaper, the handwriting strong and vigorous.

Sorry to miss you this time, old friend, but I have already delayed my departure to the villa and there are urgent matters awaiting my attention. I am on my way to catch the train to Orléans, and shall not be returning to Paris until the autumn, but in the meantime I hope to offer you and your ward some country hospitality, which will be a small return for all I have received in Martinique under your roof. My cordial good wishes.

Philippe Aubert.

She lowered the letter and put a hand to her forehead. If only she had not gone to the Louvre that morning! She could have confided her anxieties to Philippe Aubert and sought his help; instead, she was left with a brief note that gave no clue as to his ultimate destination or even where he had been residing in Paris. It seemed as though fate was set against her on all sides.

It was an effort to change for dinner that evening.

Rosella felt weighted down by worry, gripped by the nightmare that was growing more terrifying every moment, and she resolved not to leave the hotel again in case she missed anyone else who might call.

She had finished putting the final touches to her hair when a tap came on the door. 'Entrez,' she called out.

It was a maid. 'There is a visitor to see you, mam'selle. Monsieur Bataillard.'

'Show him in!' Rosella crossed the floor quickly to meet the stockily-built, grey-haired man who entered the room and bowed to her. He was dressed in sober but distinguished travelling clothes, which were a little crumpled and dusty as though he had come far and in great haste.

'Mademoiselle Rosella Eastwood?' he enquired, his expression very grave. 'I am Monsieur Cadel's lawyer. Forgive this intrusion without warning, but I have this minute returned to Paris and I have come straight to you. I am the bearer of sad news, I am sorry to say.'

She stood ashen-faced, knowing what he had to tell. 'My guardian is dead,' she whispered.

He inclined his head in regret and sympathy. 'That is so.'

She sank slowly down on to a chair, all strength sapped from her. 'Why wasn't I sent for? Why didn't you let me know he was ill?'

He took hold of another chair and drew it forward to sit facing her. 'That was not possible. Monsieur Cadel died on the voyage home and was buried at sea.'

'At sea!' she echoed in anguish.

'I was on the quayside to meet the ship, as instructed from Martinique. Monsieur Cadel had planned to discuss certain outstanding business matters of special urgency with me on the way to Paris. I saw the doctor on board, who assured me that everything had been done to try to save him, but my client had suffered a severe heart attack and did not recover consciousness. Naturally I had to see to his effects and complete all the formalities involved before carrying out the instructions given to me some time ago – which were to go straight to England and inform you before anyone else that he was dead. He knew that French newspapers were delivered to the seminary and, although it was unlikely, he wanted no chance report on his death to catch your eye before the facts had been laid before you.'

'Do you mean that you have been all the way to Kent and back again?' Her lips felt stiff and wooden.

'That is correct. I was not aware that you were in Paris until I arrived at the seminary.'

'You must be exhausted by all your travelling.' She switched her mind with effort to the rules of hospitality, getting up from her chair to press a bell. 'You must have some refreshment. A little wine perhaps? Some food?'

'A glass of wine would be most welcome. That is sufficient. And you should take some yourself, if you will permit me to advise you. You've had a great shock and I have much to tell you yet.'

It was only a matter of minutes before the wine was brought and served. During that time Monsieur Bataillard made some inconsequential remarks about the weather and his journey, but to Rosella it was obviously a pause in which to give her time to gather her strength. He had said he had much to tell her. There had been an ominous ring to those words. What was it she had to face? Surely nothing could be worse than the news he had just broken to her.

They both took a sip of wine. She noticed that her hand was shaking and hastily set the glass down on a side-table, fearful of spilling it. 'Well, Monsieur Bataillard?' she prompted, the numbness of shock enabling her to appear fairly composed. 'What is it that I am to hear?'

20

He spoke slowly, watching her carefully. 'I have to tell you that Monsieur Cadel was more than your guardian. Much more. There are ties of blood and family that you have never suspected.'

She stared at him in bewilderment. 'What do you mean? I have always known that my mother was distantly related to him.'

His expression did not change. 'She was his runaway daughter — his only child.'

Rosella sat forward, gripping the rounded ends of the chair-arms. 'Dear God! Is that true?'

The lawyer gave a deep nod. 'He was your grandfather — and you his granddaughter. His *natural* granddaughter.'

It took no more than a second for the significance of this last remark to sink in. 'What are you saying?' she demanded in a low, hoarse voice, stunned by disbelief. 'Was I not born in wedlock?'

'I regret to say that you were not.' He made a gesture towards her glass on the side-table. 'Drink a little more wine. It will help you.'

Obediently she put the rim of the glass to her lips. The wine ran over her teeth inside her mouth and she had difficulty in swallowing it. Her throat felt closed up. With great effort she managed to whisper questioningly, 'My father — ?'

'Unfortunately your English sea-captain father, John Eastwood, was an unprincipled rogue. When his ship put in to Martinique he managed to engage your mother's affections, and finally persuaded her to leave with him for England. He went through a form of marriage with her, but he was married already. Then he deserted her in a portside hovel at Plymouth a few weeks before you were born. When she realized she was dying she sent an appeal to André Cadel, begging him to forgive her and to take

21

care of his only grandchild. To avoid your being touched by the taint of scandal, Monsieur Cadel decided that you should grow up in England, believing yourself to be his ward. No doubt he intended to tell you all this himself when the time was right, or perhaps it was always his intention that you should know nothing about it until after his death.'

'What happened to my father?' Rosella asked dully, putting down the wine-glass. 'Is it true that he died before I was born, or was that a fabrication made up to deceive me too?'

'It is perfectly true. His ship was wrecked in a storm off the Cornish coast, and his body was washed up on the shore several days afterwards.'

With a shuddering cry she covered her face with her hands. 'If only I'd known that I was André Cadel's granddaughter! I loved him dearly, but never felt I belonged to him in any way!'

'He did what he thought was best. Such a scandal would have wrecked for ever any chance of your marrying into a family of standing, to say nothing of the misery you would undoubtedly have suffered through knowing the true circumstances in childhood. Do not think harshly of him. Proof of his affection for you is in his will. You are the main beneficiary.'

She raised her head and stared at him bleakly. 'I don't understand.'

'He has left you the Château de Louismont.'

The lawyer thought the girl would faint, for she went white to the lips, but she recovered and shook her head vehemently. 'No! No! I don't want it! I won't have anything to do with that horrible place!'

'Mademoiselle!' he protested incredulously. 'It is one of the grandest châteaux in the Loire valley. The money you inherit with it will allow you to live in luxury there for the rest of your days.'

But she shook her head again and spoke with difficulty, torn by emotion. 'I spent a holiday in it six – or was it seven? – years ago. My guardian – ' She paused and corrected herself. 'My grandfather took me to it during one of my visits to see him in France. He thought it would be good for me to spend some time with a French family while he travelled around on business, and he wanted me to be friends with the children there, three of the four being about my own age, their father his distant cousin. Mine too, I suppose, although I wasn't aware of it at the time. But never once did I suspect that the château belonged to my grandfather. I thought it belonged to them.'

'Then if you know the château, why have you this aversion to it?'

Her eyes were dark and deep and tragic. 'I spent the unhappiest six weeks of my life there!'

'But that was a long time ago. You were a child. No more than ten or eleven years old. You were left among strangers, lonely and homesick, I expect. Things will be very different now.'

'How different?' she asked stubbornly. 'Aren't Pierre and Marguerite de Louismont still living there with their brood of children?'

'Madame de Louismont is now a widow. The younger of her two daughters is married, but lives in the neighbourhood.'

'That would be Sophie. What of Louise?'

'She still resides with her mother at the château, and Jules de Louismont is also there for several months of the year. Sébastien, being the elder son, runs the estate.'

'So I'll be as much an intruder now as I was then!' Rosella swung herself to her feet, hands clenched. 'I'll not accept the conditions of my grandfather's will!'

'You are forgetting that the de Louismonts are the intruders now – not you,' the lawyer pointed out. 'It is your home – not theirs any longer.'

She rounded on him angrily. 'I cannot turn a family out of a place where they have lived all their lives!'

'They have been fortunate to occupy it for three generations. It was only due to your great-great grandmother marrying a Cadel and escaping with him to Martinique during the Revolution that their branch of the family was able to move into it as custodians.'

'Do they know the château has been left to me?'

He gave a shake of his head. 'Not yet. As I told you, you are the first to know everything.'

'Then I'll make it over to the de Louismonts as a deed of gift! That could be arranged.'

'Indeed it cannot! Please sit down again and listen to me.' She obeyed, but he could tell by the expression on her face that he had a fight on his hands. 'Since the château was first bequeathed by the nobleman who built it several centuries ago, it can only be passed on to a member of a younger generation. You are the rightful owner, whether you want the château or not. Moreover, it was your grandfather's wish that you should take up residence without delay, which was little enough to request in return for all he has done for you.'

She could not answer him. Was she to deny the wish of the only person in the world who had cared anything for her? She knew she could not. And the lawyer had cunningly phrased his words in such a way to ensure that she could not.

'Your grandfather also stated in his will that there was to be no wearing of mourning garments,' the lawyer continued. 'He told me once that he'd had to endure a whole year as a young boy clothed entirely in black with mourning crepe tied on his hat. It gave him an aversion to all public show of mourning that never left him, and he wanted to spare you from all that when the time came.'

'But he must have made such a ruling when I was still a child!' she exclaimed. 'That shows how long ago the will was made and why he wanted me to move into the château without delay. He thought that Monsieur and Madame de Louismont could be trusted to look after me. He never knew how much I'd disliked being there.'

'It is true that you were still very young when Monsieur Cadel decided the château should be yours, and no doubt he resolved that you should live there for the reason you suggest, but although he made a new will less than eighteen months ago he made no change to his request that you should take up your abode there without delay.' He rose stiffly to his feet. 'It is my duty to see that the wishes of the deceased are carried out. I'll settle your hotel bill this evening and order a carriage to be at the door by noon tomorrow. I'll read the will to you before we depart for the château where I shall explain the circumstances to the de Louismonts. The will is no concern of theirs. Your grandfather left them nothing.'

Rosella saw how wearily he eased his shoulders before reaching for his hat. The poor man had journeyed far on her behalf and it was extremely discourteous to abuse him for her grandfather's decisions.

'Is it necessary for you to travel with me tomorrow?' she asked. 'I can make the journey on my own. In fact, it would be far better for me to face them alone as the new owner of the château. You could follow in two or three weeks' time. By then the de Louismonts and I should have resigned ourselves to each other's company, and you will be able to iron out any arising problems that might not show themselves in the first few days.'

He studied her with narrowed eyes. 'Am I to understand that you have no intention of giving them notice to leave?'

'That is right,' she answered firmly.

He looked grim. 'I hope that I shall be able to make you reconsider such a foolish decision when we meet again.'

She gave him her hand. 'Thank you for your advice and all you have done for me already.'

She closed the door after him and sank against it, her forehead coming to rest against the panel. All her grief welled up in her, eclipsing all thought of the château and what might await her there. She was never to see her grandfather again. Never to hear his voice. Never to walk with him again in the *Bois*, or to talk long and deeply in the sheltered evenings. He had slipped away from her into a cold and lonely grave. He who had loved France had been denied a last glimpse of it.

Sobs racked her. She moved into the bedroom and flung herself across the bed. There she wept until her pillow was soaked and her handkerchief a screwed-up, sodden ball in her clutching hand. Her cheeks were still wet from rivulets of tears long after she had fallen into an exhausted sleep.

When she stirred it was already morning. Hastily she rang the bell and summoned a maid to pack for her. When she had bathed she put a *peignoir* over her underclothes and breakfast was brought to her, but she could eat nothing. A cup of coffee was all she could manage. The maid asked her which travelling costume she would wear.

She answered without hesitation. 'The scarlet taffeta and the ruched and feathered bonnet to match it.'

She knew she must establish herself from the moment she stepped inside the château. It would be disastrous to make a meek appearance and let them think she could be bullied and teased and tormented as she had been in the past. The de Louismonts were like tigers. Not the wild free beasts of the jungle, but the caged and embittered creatures that must be faced with an upended chair and a spike. She would confront them in a flamboyant outfit to keep them back and at bay.

There was only one of them whom she did not fear. That was Sébastien. But how would he react when he heard that the child he had once befriended had returned as a usurper to claim the roof from over his head?

She was ready and waiting when Monsieur Bataillard arrived. He read the will to her, and afterwards they discussed many matters arising from it. Even without the château and its lands she had been well provided for, and again she begged the lawyer to try to find some loophole to remove her from its ownership, a request that he noted without offering hope or approval. Then it was time for the porters to carry her trunks from the suite.

She adjusted a veil to hide eyes still swollen from the night's weeping and went slowly downstairs at the lawyer's side. They reached the equipage drawn up at the hotel steps.

'It will not be long before I visit you at the Château de Louismont,' he said. 'I hope to find you reconciled to your new abode.'

'Never!' she declared vehemently.

He regarded her sternly, hiding his exasperation, and handed her into the carriage. Then he spoke to her through the open window, feeling obliged to give some counsel. 'At the moment I can only think of one way in which you could reside elsewhere with a clear conscience.'

She leaned towards him. 'What is that?'

'Through a suitable marriage, Mademoiselle Eastwood. It is a wife's duty to follow her husband. Your grandfather would not have had it otherwise.'

She drew back in disappointment and regarded him coldly through her veil. 'I trust you will have a better solution than that to offer by the time we meet again, sir. I have no intention of tying myself for life to the first man who comes along. There must be other avenues of escape. I am relying on you to find one. Farewell, Monsieur Bataillard!'

With a clip-clop of hooves and a creaking of harness the carriage bore her away. Her journey to the Château de Louismont had begun. With despair she thought that heaven alone knew what awaited her there.

CHAPTER THREE

The long and tiring journey with its overnight halts at wayside hotels was nearing its end. Rosella had never felt more alone. Or more lonely. She found herself unable to appreciate the magnificence of the landscape through which the Loire flowed at a quiet, leisurely pace, for every mile brought her one stage closer to her dreaded destination. Inevitably she contrasted her present mood with the gaiety and excited anticipation that had marked every milestone of her route from Calais to Paris, when even grey skies had been unable to dampen her spirits. Those dark, low-slung clouds had been yet another omen that all was not to go well for her. She realized now as she gazed listlessly at the sun-drenched spread of green-brown vineyards, lush meadows, and abundant orchards. In many places tall and slender poplars bordered the long, straight roads which the carriage followed at an easy speed, a white cloud of dust billowing perpetually in its wake.

She saw a number of châteaux, perched on slopes and hilltops, pepper-pot turrets gleaming, windows flashing back the sun, looking rather like stage sets for the finale of a pantomime, but she gave them no more attention than a casual glance. Normally the sight of these mediaeval fortresses and the grand mansions of a previous century and earlier would have captured her interest and joy.

Occasionally the carriage rolled across a bridge when the river curved like a looped ribbon, giving her glimpses of willow-shaded islands, greyish-gold and mysterious, which lay in mid-stream, splitting the rippled surface into separate ways. On they went through villages, past farms, and in and out of ancient townships where the old buildings seemed to be propping each other up along the cobbled streets, and all were dominated by the splendour of some old church or cathedral. By night the hotel windows showed her velvet rectangles studded with stars, and by day the air held a diffused brilliance which gave a rich depth to the ever-changing pattern of surfaces, colours, and textures of a countryside that she had thought never to visit again. Now the Loire valley was to be her home.

She recognized the market town as soon as they drove into it. Once she had walked there on her own to post a letter to André Cadel, wanting to get away from the château and everybody in it, but a hue and cry had been raised when it was discovered she was missing, and she had been forbidden to go anywhere unaccompanied again. There was the very post-box on the corner by the *pâtisserie*, and the café where she had sat at a table under the awning and ordered hot chocolate after sending the letter on its way. She had not mentioned the misery and torment she was suffering under the château roof, but she did express her pent-up longing to see her benefactor again, for his return meant an end to the purgatory that had started out as a holiday. Only Sébastien remained a beautiful memory.

She leaned back in her seat, trying to conjure up Sébastien's features in her mind, remembering how she had hero-worshipped him. But no, it was more than that. She had loved him. He alone had stood between her and the terrors of the château itself.

The outskirts of the market town were left behind. The banks on either side of the road rose up into thick forest, and deliberately she turned her head to avoid catching

30

sight of the château above the tree-tops. Time enough to view it when she had to. Nervously she delved into her purse and took out a small hand-glass.

She had no colour in her face, but she could remedy that in a way that had been forbidden at the seminary. A powdery fragrance rose about her as she opened a tiny pot of rouge and carefully blended a touch of it into each cheek. She studied the result. That was better. Her eyes looked wide and wary, but there was nothing she could do about that, except try to compose herself in the last minutes that were left. She moistened her lips, put away the hand-glass, and sat clasping her purse with both white-gloved hands. The road was curving towards the great iron gates. Already they were being opened by the lodge-keeper. She had arrived!

The lodge-keeper looked at her incuriously when the carriage swept past him, although his attitude was deferential, a hand resting on one of the gates, ready to close it again. She did not know him. Old Marcel must have retired.

The wheels spat aside the gravel of the mile-long drive. She had forgotten how beautiful the parkland was that surrounded the château. Trees and lawns and the gleam of a lake shadowed by willows, which dipped lacy branches into the water where a pair of swans drifted. But she felt no pride in her new possessions. Her heart began to palpitate painfully, and her sick dread of the place had increased beyond all measure.

The rustling beech-trees bordering the drive drew back, and the petit-point perfection of the formal gardens spread out on either side like a tapestry laid down before the château itself, which rose against the sky in gothic splendour. The age-worn stone was hung with creeper which framed a magnificent entrance flanked by boxed orange-trees brought from some greenhouse to stand

31

sentinel. Tall cylindrical towers, topped with pepper-pot roofs of sienna-coloured slates, had windows narrow as the iris in a cat's eye, dark slits facing in all directions over the surrounding undulating countryside. The château showed every sign of being a well-tended residence, obviously cherished by those who lived in it, but its beautiful façade was deceptive. She knew it to have a black and evil heart.

The carriage slowed to a halt. One of the grooms leapt down to help her alight while the other hurried up the flight of stone steps to the oaken door and pulled on the bell. It was opened almost at once by a manservant who was another stranger to her.

'I wish to see Madame de Louismont,' she said, sweeping over the threshold. 'Tell her that Mademoiselle Rosella Eastwood is here.'

'I'll see if Madame is at home.' he replied, looking askance at the massive amount of luggage being unloaded, for her recent purchases had necessitated the hasty buying of three more trunks and several travelling hat-boxes.

She was shown into an ante-room to wait, but she was too tense to sit down. Instead she paced across to the window and back again, taking a few deep breaths in an attempt to calm her hammering heart. The minutes ticked by. She went again to the window and stood looking out over the gardens, tapping her foot nervously, wanting to get the terrible ordeal over with, feeling slightly sick.

The manservant returned at last. 'Madame de Louismont will receive you in the garden-room, mademoiselle. This way, if you please.' She knew the way, but thought it better to say nothing. The manservant led her across the palatial hall where marble statues stood in niches inlaid with lapis-lazuli and tall columns supported a gallery that was approached by a grand staircase of immense proportions. A chandelier, shaped like a fountain of crystal, hung suspended from a blue ceiling high above where painted

32

nymphs and satyrs cavorted with a freedom that had been beyond her understanding in those earlier days.

As she walked through one corridor and then another, she noticed where chairs and sofas had been rearranged, and was amazed to find she remembered such small and unimportant details. Then the manservant swung open a door and announced her.

She went from the gloom of the corridor into the eye-dazzling brilliance of the garden-room where the sun poured through the glass sections in the ceiling, making a mottled pattern on the chequered floor. Her scarlet outfit made her blaze like a vivid rose against the pale green walls and white wrought-iron furniture, the plume of her hat rippling as though with a life of its own.

Facing her, among the potted palms and ferns, the clusters of heavily-scented and exotic blooms, were the three de Louismont women, grouped together in an unconsciously beautiful tableau formed by a flow of frilled and bustled gowns in muted shades of grey, violet, and purple. Rosella saw at once that Louise and Sophie, standing by their mother's chair, showed undisguised hostility in their faces. But Madame Marguerite de Louismont seemed more detached and withdrawn than unwelcoming.

'Rosella! Is it really you?' she enquired in a voice full of melodious cadences, one slim hand upraised. The sun threw rainbow sparkles from her rings.

'Indeed it is, Madame de Louismont.' Rosella dipped politely to her, but remained where she was. 'I sent no word of my coming, but there is good reason for that, which I shall explain.'

'After all these years.' Marguerite spoke on a reminiscent note, lost in her own reflections, almost as though she had not heard what Rosella had said. She rose to her feet in a rustle of silk and stepped towards Rosella with a glint of tiny, buckled shoes. 'How you have grown, child. And yet a child no longer. A pretty damosel instead. *Hélas!* How time flies.'

But time, although it had softened Marguerite's skin and etched lines across her forehead and about her mouth, had dealt kindly with her. She was still a very lovely woman, although her features were drawn taut as if her nerves were too near the surface; her eyes were pale blue and gentle, and her mane of luxuriant brown hair, which was only lightly threaded with grey, was drawn back into a thickly-plaited coil at the nape of her slender neck. She had the small, fragile bones of the aristocratic French-woman, and every gesture was fluid and full of grace. With a flowing sweep of her hand she indicated her daughters, who had remained motionless, their expressions rigid.

'You remember Louise and Sophie, of course. What friends you were as children! That summer you stayed here it was as though I had three dear daughters instead of two.'

Her remark left Rosella speechless. It was incredible that any mother should have been so completely ignorant of the true state of affairs, but then Marguerite's social whirl had left her little opportunity to discover how her family was passing its time.

Rosella's lack of response went unnoticed. Marguerite half-turned to look towards another part of the room, giving one of her vague, sweet smiles, making Rosella realize for the first time that someone else was present. So she and the de Louismont women were not alone together after all.

'Come and meet Rosella,' Marguerite invited with her odd, preoccupied air.

Rosella slowly turned her head to follow the direction of Marguerite's doe-like gaze. A man had been standing out of her line of vision, half-concealed by the potted palms, but he had been watching her since she had entered the room. All the time. With recognition. When he came towards her she saw that he was not Sébastien. Or Jules, whom she might have expected. But the stranger who had eyed her with such impudent boldness in the Hôtel du Louvre and again from the seat of his landau. Rosella felt the colour flood to her cheeks with astonishment, but her amazement increased when the introductions were made.

'This gentleman became our neighbour last summer,' Marguerite said to her by way of explanation for his presence, 'and now he has returned again — like the swallows. Allow me to present Monsieur Philippe Aubert. Philippe — Mademoiselle Rosella Eastwood.'

'*Enchanté*, mademoiselle.' His voice was deep and his mood serious, although the same keen interest showed in the narrowed eyes that he fixed on her.

Philippe Aubert! This was the man who had left the note for her grandfather. The man whose address she had hoped to discover.

'Monsieur Aubert!' she stammered. 'Your letter to André Cadel. I read it. I had become desperately anxious as the days passed without a word from him. I thought you might be able to help me decide what to do. But you had left Paris already.'

'I was impatient to take up residence in my villa here,' he said gravely, 'and saw no real need to wait any longer. You will remember that I was expecting to entertain you and André some time in the near future when all business matters could have been discussed at leisure. Now I deeply regret not postponing my departure from Paris. At least I might have been of some assistance when it became known that you and I had been waiting for him in vain.'

He saw how she had started at his words, and his glance flicked at her scarlet coat and elaborate hat before he lowered his head to peer more closely into her face, his expression one of extreme concern. 'You do know what happened to him, don't you?'

She realized that he took her lack of mourning as a sign that she might still be in ignorance of André Cadel's death, but she was bewildered that he should already know of her bereavement. 'The news was broken to me at the hotel by his lawyer,' she explained, 'but how did you find out?'

Louise spoke for the first time, her voice cutting across the room. 'We told him! We heard yesterday that Cousin André had died at sea. Jules read about it in a week-old Marseilles newspaper. Have you not noticed that *Maman* and Sophie and I are wearing shades of mourning? I must say that I find your brazen finery in poor taste.'

Rosella did not quail. 'It was André Cadel's wish that no mourning clothes should be worn.'

'Is that so?' Louise's large dark eyes, deeply set under black winged brows, had hardened into a glare of intense rancour. Although she resembled her mother in features and build, hers was a passionate face, reflecting her tempestuous nature, the cheek-bones wide, the delicate almond-shaped nostrils of her fine-shaped nose quick to quiver and flare, and her mouth was full-lipped, red, and curved. 'Then you should have stayed away from those who cannot let the passing of a relative go unmarked by some show of respect.' Her tone became aggressive. 'Why *have* you come anyway? You may have been the old man's ward, but there are no pickings for you here!'

'Hush!' Marguerite turned agitatedly towards her elder daughter. 'That is no way to speak to Rosella!'

'I disagree, *Maman*!' Louise retorted. 'She has arrived uninvited and unwanted! A little plain speaking will not go amiss.'

Philippe frowned uncomfortably and spread his hands. 'I am intruding. I should not be present —'

He made a move towards the door that led out into the

36

garden, but Louise stepped into his path and gripped him by both arms. 'Don't go!' she cried. 'I want you to stay. Your father and mother were Cousin André's close friends in Martinique. You have known him all your life. Have you not enjoyed his trust as his business representative in Paris for the past few years?' She let her hands fall from his arms, and stole an angry look at Rosella, although she continued to address him. 'Tell me, Philippe, do they have scavenger birds in the Caribbean that descend in scarlet plumage to plunder and rake over the spoils?'

Her meaning was unmistakable, bitter and barbed. Philippe kept his eyes on her and answered with slow deliberation. 'No, Louise. There are none that I know of. But there are plenty of parakeets that screech their heads off, often without cause.'

She flushed, meeting his eyes and looking away again. 'That was unfair of you!' she declared sulkily.

'You can't blame Louise for being upset, Philippe.' It was Sophie who intervened on her sister's behalf. She had watched everything with interest from beside the chair that her mother had vacated, and she moved to rest an arm along the back of it.

Unlike Louise, who was exceptionally slim with small, high, shapely breasts, Sophie was softer and rounder, heavier in her movements, her figure fashionably full. Her hair curled naturally, not as dark as her sister's in colour, but a fine chestnut shade, framing a well-moulded face with green-hazel eyes that was marred by the petulance in the small, thin-lipped mouth and in the disdainful tilt of the uppish nose.

'You must realize that Rosella had only visited the château once before in her whole life,' she continued. 'Why should she turn up out of the blue now except to demand this or that as a keepsake from the various things that Cousin André left around here from time to time? It always happens when someone dies. Distant relatives come flocking in like vultures – and Rosella wasn't even related to Cousin André!'

Philippe shrugged and put his hands into the pockets of the belted jacket he was wearing. 'May I suggest that you ask Mademoiselle Rosella why she has come.'

Louise stiffened slightly. She seemed to have regretted her outburst in his presence, and made a show of trying to put matters right. 'Well, Rosella,' she enquired cynically, 'what has brought you back to France? Perhaps I have been wrong in jumping to conclusions. Let us hear the reason you promised us for this unexpected visit.'

Rosella drew a deep breath. The moment had arrived and unpleasant though it was, she must not show any sign of timidity or weakness. 'What I have to tell you will not be to your liking. In fact, it will come as a great shock. André Cadel has bequeathed the Château de Louismont and all its lands and properties to me.'

They all stared at her. In silence. The three women in complete disbelief, too stupefied to speak. Then gradually an expression of utter dismay dragged at their faces. Marguerite de Louismont gave a sudden, strangled sob. She swayed and would have collapsed on to the floor if Philippe had not darted forward in time to catch her in his arms and lower her into a chair. Both daughters sprang to attend her, Sophie rubbing her wrists while Louise whipped a bottle of smelling-salts from a brocade drawstring bag that lay on a table nearby, and waved it to and fro under her mother's nose.

When Marguerite stirred, rolling her head away from the acrid aroma, Louise spoke reassuring words, showing that she was not unused to her mother's attacks of refined suffering and knew them to be geniune. Philippe bent to raise Marguerite's feet carefully on to a footstool, and Sophie patted into place the cushion she had put under her

38

mother's lolling head. Rosella noticed with deep distress that the wide and gentle eyes were glazed and vacant with shock, all power of concentration lost for a while.

Louise, still bending over her mother and holding one limp hand, looked savagely over her shoulder at Rosella. 'It can't be!' she declared wrathfully, commenting on Rosella's traumatic statement as though there had been no intervening diversion. 'Sébastien was André Cadel's heir! He was to have the château and all pertaining to it. You're not even family! You can have no claim.'

Rosella was very pale. 'André Cadel was my grand-father,' she declared as calmly as she could.

'Your grandfather?' Louise echoed incredulously. 'But he couldn't be! You're lying! He only had one daughter and she never married. She died young.' Her eyes narrowed. 'Unless —?'

'My mother ran away from Martinique with an English-man of whom my grandfather did not approve. There was no marriage and I was left an orphan. In order to keep the scandal from me he let me grow up in Kent. Perhaps it was his intention that I should never learn the truth of my relationship with him. Had I married, I don't doubt that the château would have passed to Sébastien, for I should have been established with no need of property to give me security. Thus I would never have known that I was anything more than André Cadel's ward.'

'Then what has Cousin André left to the rest of us?' Sophie demanded, crimson spots of anger in her cheeks.

Rosella answered with reluctance. 'His lawyer, Monsieur Bataillard, read the will to me. There were other bequests, but your names were not mentioned.'

'None of us? Not even *Maman*?' Sophie cried. 'Nothing at all to Sébastien?'

Rosella shook her head, and Sophie gave a long moan, pressing folded arms across her chest as though the blow

39

were physical. 'The devil! The tight-fisted old devil!'

Louise had sprung up and she moved restlessly, seeking to assuage the turmoil of her emotions, the fingers of her hands stretched tight. 'It's unbelievable! To think of being turned out of our home by an outsider! I won't have it! I can't endure it!'

Rosella took a step towards her. 'I have no intention of asking you to leave your home. I'll have my own apartments and we can live under the same roof. Suitable arrangements can be made, and my grandfather's lawyer, Monsieur Bataillard, will be arriving in a week or two to adjudicate over any difficulties that might arise.'

'That sounds reasonable,' Philippe commented.

'Reasonable?' Sophie flashed out on a shrill note of outrage. 'What happens when Rosella marries? What of my family then? I have my own residence in the town, but are they to be evicted like paupers?'

'I assure you that I've no thought of marriage for a long time to come,' Rosella said patiently, 'but should I marry at some future date it would naturally release me from any obligation to go on residing at the château.'

Sophie's expression did not change. 'But suppose your husband-to-be should have other ideas and decide to make the château his home and yours? Nobody in his right mind would surrender such a palace for anywhere else.'

'It depends on the husband that Rosella chooses, of course,' said an amiable male voice from the garden doorway.

It was Jules who stood there, lolling one shoulder against the jamb. He had grown tall and lean, his features stamped with the family handsomeness they all had inherited from their mother, but evident in each of the de Louismont offspring there was also that steeliness of character that stemmed from the father, who had been a ruthless, autocratic man of terrible pride and no mercy, quite unapproachable. Now, searching Jules's face, Rosella found it difficult to assess how much or how little the years had mellowed his nature since she had last set eyes on him. Perhaps he saw the wary uncertainty in her eyes, for he swung himself away from the support of the doorway and came across to her, his smile very wide as though he would charm her into trusting him as she had been unable to do before.

'Have you forgiven me for all my youthful crimes?' he asked contritely, taking her hand and putting it to his lips. 'I was a wretched monster. What was it? A dead cat in your bed or a spider down your back?'

'Both!' she said with distaste. She had cried over the cat. Bitterly. It had been one of the kitchen cats that she had befriended. No doubt it had been chosen for that very reason. There had been an insane and vindictive campaign by Jules and his two sisters to keep her isolated from any friendly contacts. They had been jealous of her as they were jealous of each other, but it had amused them that summer to find a joint target on whom to vent their spitefulness.

'I don't doubt that my crimes were many,' Jules said with an unrepentant chuckle. Then he suddenly thumped his forehead with the heel of his hand. '*Mon Dieu!* It all comes back to me! I recall the time we all jumped out of the darkness at you and you nearly went mad with fright. And then there was the night I put the skull from the library on your pillow.' He gave a robust shout of laughter. 'But that turned me into the frightened one. My father gave me a thrashing that I never forgot – as much for touching his possessions in the library as for teasing you.'

'Did he? I never knew about that. I only know I went in terror of your practical jokes all the time I stayed here.'

'I'm not surprised. I remember my father went off on his long business trips somewhere after that skull

41

incident — it left me free to go on baiting you without the danger of further punishment. *Maman* always let us go our own ways even in those days.'

Rosella silently agreed with the truth of that statement. Marguerite de Louismont had spared time only for Sébastien, her favourite child, and many people might have believed him to be her only child, for the other three scarcely saw her. Perhaps their ungovernable behaviour, which had made tutors and governesses come and go with monotonous regularity, had been a desperate bid for attention and affection. There was even the smack of rivalry in the way the two sisters had fussed over their mother in her faint, although Louise had left her to Sophie at that moment and had swung about to burst out in mounting scorn at their brother.

'Jules! How can you stand there chatting in that absurd manner about the past as if Rosella had merely come on a social call? You do realize what has happened, don't you? It has sunk into your selfish, egotistical head, I suppose? Cousin André has left us nothing! Not a franc! That won't help your gambling debts, will it? Or settle your bills!'

Jules regarded her with a tolerant impatience, unmoved by the taunts she had shrieked at him. 'Unlike you, my dear sister, I have never counted my chickens before they were hatched. Old Cadel never liked me. Why should he leave me anything? Sébastien is a different case. He was the golden boy, I thought. Where is he, by the way? Does he know yet?'

'Not yet. He's out somewhere. Maybe he'll be able to think of what to do. Perhaps we could contest the will or something.'

Sophie groaned elaborately and threw up her hands. 'You would make an idiotic suggestion like that! We wouldn't have a leg to stand on. Even I know that. There was never anything written down to protect us from such a turn of events. How could we compete with the blood tie of the old man's granddaughter, whether she was born the wrong side of the blanket or not!'

'What an indelicate turn of phrase!' Jules rebuked wryly. 'Your bourgeois husband would have been quite shattered by it, had he been here. Or has he discovered just how vindictive you can be when thwarted?'

Rosella was struck by the familiarity of it all. The constant squabbling, the continuous disharmony. None of them had ever agreed. Nothing had changed. Then Marguerite de Louismont appeared to collect herself with a great effort of will, and rose to her feet, making a little deterring gesture of protest when her daughters would have assisted her.

'Enough. Please. All the noise confuses my head.' She stood alone, slightly unsteady, but with immense dignity, to address Rosella. 'You are the new mistress here. It is an amazing change of circumstances, but you must learn to hold the reins of authority in your hands as I did when I was your age and came to the château as a bride.' She looked about vaguely. 'What else should I say? Oh, yes. Which rooms would you like? There are so many.' She touched her temples with a stroking movement of her fingertips and added helplessly: 'Silly – isn't it? – but I can't remember how many.'

Louise and Sophie exchanged glances and closed in again on each side of her. 'Don't worry, *Maman,*' Louise said soothingly. 'Go and rest now. Sophie will take you to lie down for a little while. I'll see that Rosella is accommodated.'

But shock seemed to have deprived Marguerite of her ability to walk, and once again Philippe went quickly forward to give her his supporting arm.

'Allow me to assist you, Madame de Louismont. Take a step at a time. That's right. Slowly. Fine!'

43

Sophie sprang ahead to open the coloured glass door, and together the three of them went through into the corridor and out of sight. Louise gave a long drawn-out sigh before turning again to face Rosella. 'Well? You heard what *Maman* said. Which rooms do you want?'

Rosella answered without hesitation. 'Those of the west tower wing. You may remember that I slept in the tower itself when I was here before. I want that to be my bedroom again.' She had made up her mind to do everything she could to conquer her fear of the château, and the best place to do that was in the very room in which all her childhood terrors had started.

Louise raised surprised brows and behind her Jules gave a snort of amusement. 'Suppose I put the skull on your pillow again?' he teased, but not unkindly.

'It would take more than a foolish prank to frighten me now,' Rosella retorted calmly.

'You must realize that the wing has been closed up for some time,' Louise said, as if wanting to dissuade Rosella from her choice. 'It's difficult to keep all the apartments in the château in full use.'

'I want no other rooms,' Rosella said determinedly. Then she used her new authority for the first time. 'Let the wing be opened up for me.'

Louise shrugged her shoulders scornfully. 'As you wish.' She crossed to a bell in the wall and gave it a sharp stab with her finger.

The housekeeper, a capable-looking woman with stern features and black, shining hair was too well trained to show her surprise when informed by Louise that Mademoiselle Rosella was the new mistress of the château, but her eyes gleamed with curiosity. She showed obeisance in her respectful curtsy and her use of the courtesy title of *madame* when addressing Rosella as she led the way to the west tower wing, the bunch of keys that swung on a chain

44

from her waist jingling at every step.

Menservants were summoned to carry Rosella's luggage from the hall. Although she glanced at each one in turn before proceeding up the grand staircase in the wake of the housekeeper she did not see a single familiar face among them. In the past several of the house staff had been friendly to her, taking pity on her plight, and once the chef had hidden her among the vegetable baskets when the two sisters and Jules had come after her in hot pursuit, each swinging a dead rat by its tail. She wondered if there had been a complete turn-over of staff since those days. It certainly seemed like it, but what would be the reason for that? It had been a matter of pride with the staff that they had been in the service of Pierre de Louismont for years, and their fathers had served his father and his grandfather before them.

When the double doors to the west tower wing were reached the housekeeper selected a key and turned it in the lock. 'Everything is covered with dust-sheets, madame,' she warned before leading the way into its shuttered darkness, 'but that does not mean that this section of the château is left untouched. There are too many fine pieces of furniture and rare carpets to risk woodworm and moth through neglect. It is less than a month since the wing was completely spring-cleaned.'

Nevertheless the wing smelt stale and airless. The long corridor that led to the tower itself was faced on one side by the closed doors of unused rooms and on the other by many tall windows where all light was excluded by shutters which fastened on the inside. A maid darted ahead of the little procession to fold back a shutter at intervals, letting in some sunshine to show the way. It resulted in a walk of light and shadow, the draped cream silk curtains wafting ghost-like in the draught that cast dust-motes into the sun's rays.

45

'There are two bedrooms in this wing,' the housekeeper said, unaware that Rosella was familiar with it. 'Which would you prefer, madame? The Rose Room, which is the larger and looks out over the inner courtyard, or the Blue Room, which opens out of the largest salon?'

'Neither,' Rosella said with a faint smile. 'You have forgotten to mention the tower room. That will suit me very well.'

The housekeeper gave her a sidelong glance of suppressed inquisitiveness. 'As you wish, madame.'

The curved steps rose steeply in a spiral all the way up the tower, and the menservants, grunting and puffing, had difficulty in keeping the sharp brass-bound corners of the heavy trunks away from the fine walnut panelling which had concealed the mediaeval stones beneath for two centuries or more. At the top of the flight the housekeeper paused to get her breath, but Rosella swept swiftly past her into the circular tower room. Cracks of light showed between the shutters. She ran to draw them back and they folded with a bouncing clatter on either side of her. Then she opened the window and flung it wide, letting the clean, sweet country air fill the room.

There was the view she remembered so well. The gardens and lawns lay all around, the thick woods hiding the far distant walls that bordered the château's parkland. Beyond, rising amid foliage, was the grey-slated roof of the villa that was the only neighbouring habitation in the area and must be the residence of Philippe Aubert, while stretching away to a backcloth of hills under a clear blue sky were rich vineyards and green slopes and dense forests. The market town lay several kilometres away in the opposite direction and could not be seen from the west tower. Had she dared to risk her life by leaning out she could have caught the sparkle of the great Loire itself, but this she did not dare to do, for the sheer drop to the ground below was head-spinning.

Turning about, she watched the housekeeper whisk away dust-sheets while the menservants set down her luggage and departed. Later, when the room had been set to rights, the trunks would be unpacked for her. She must think about getting a lady's maid, and she realized that she should have brought one with her from Paris, but there had been no time.

The tower room was smaller than she had remembered, its rococo splendour somewhat faded and shabby, but the gilt still shone and she was reminded of a circular birdcage. In the plaster mouldings around the ceiling fat-bellied little cherubs held garlands of flowers, which cascaded down to frame the panels of rose damask silk that covered the walls. Elaborate sconces held candles that had not been lit for a long time, and she wondered if they had last flickered for her a full seven years ago. When she had first seen the room with a child's eyes she had been enchanted, feeling like a princess in a fairy-tale tower, but that impression had not lasted long. Soon it had seemed to enclose her like a prison.

She removed her coat, revealing the matching dress of scarlet taffeta under it, and moved across to the toilet-table which was prettily draped in sprigged ivory silk. Sitting down before the hinged looking-glass, she took off her bonnet. 'Why has this west wing been closed up?' she enquired carefully, touching her hair into place. 'Every room was open the last time I was here.'

The housekeeper paused in folding a dust-sheet and gave her a quick glance. 'That must have been several years ago when the late Monsieur de Louismont was alive. I have been told he had every room open and ready at all times. Apparently he and Madame de Louismont entertained on a grand scale in those days. Monsieur Sébastien is of a more practical turn of mind. He had the west wing closed to save expense and labour.'

She gathered up the dust-sheets into a pile and stood ready to leave. 'There was also a lot of foolishness about the legend concerning this wing, and it was difficult to get local maids to clean it properly without skipping their work and bolting away again. That's why no village labour is employed here nowadays. I wanted none of that nonsense and I engage respectable girls from farther afield.' Failing to get the reaction she had obviously expected from Rosella, she prompted it with a question of her own: 'As you've stayed in the château before, I suppose you are familiar with the legend?'

'I am indeed,' Rosella replied crisply in a detached voice that put an end to any further discourse on the subject. She deliberately turned the conversation to the more mundane matter of arranging that after she had washed and tidied herself from the journey, she would vacate the room for an hour to allow the maids to make up the bed, unpack, and leave everything spick and span for her.

The housekeeper left the room, and her heels tapped briskly away down the stone stairs and out of earshot. The ensuing silence was broken only by the twitter of birds through the open window. Somewhere a dog barked and there was the distant rattle of farm machinery. Rosella leaned her arms on the toilet-table and looked unseeingly at her own reflection, lost in thought.

She had good reason to remember the legend of the tower, but she thrust that side of it from her, recalling only the tale of the beautiful wife of a great nobleman who had lived in the château early in the fifteenth century. He had ridden away to the wars, but in his absence the château was captured in a surprise raid. There had been looting, rape, and murder. The lady had hidden herself in the west tower where she had remained undiscovered by the marauders plundering the château. But when the enemy soldiers had ridden off, leaving only death and destruction in their wake, the lady had not been able to find her way out of the tower again. Her cries for help went unheard. There was no one left alive to hear, and the villagers had fled into the forest from their burning hovels. Like a lovely bird the lady had beaten herself against the walls in a desperate attempt to escape. In vain. When at last the sunlight danced on the armour and lances of the returning nobleman and his men-at-arms, his lady lay dead on the floor of her high and terrible cage.

A shiver ran down Rosella's spine. She swung round on the stool to let her gaze wander about the room, wondering which past owner had sought to erase the mediaeval horror of that legend with the ornate décor of a later age. Nevertheless the illusion of a room without doors remained, for the handle was cleverly concealed in the moulding in order not to spoil its symmetry. But where was it?

Rosella rose and moved into the centre of the room, looking about her, and aware of an absurd sense of panic rising within her, which she tried with cool reason to suppress. When she had stayed in the room before she had tied a hair-ribbon to the handle in order to see it at a glance, for once – very much like the lady in the legend – she had beaten hysterically on the walls, unable to find her way out.

Ah! The door was there! It came back to her now. Purposefully she swept across to one of the panels, found the handle, and flung the door open. But it was a clothes closet. She shut it quickly and leaned her forehead against the panel. Take it easy, she told herself. Calm down. Get your bearings. Surely next to the clothes closet was the mediaeval *garde-robe* that had been turned into an elegant bathroom?

She was annoyed to see that her hand was trembling slightly as she sought out the concealed handle and turned it. Yes. She was right. The rose-patterned porcelain of basin, ewer, and hip-bath shone in the light from the narrow window.

Slowly she continued her progress around the room, her fingertips searching sensitively among the curved garlands. When the tap came on the door from somewhere outside she was unable to locate its exact direction, aware for the first time of the strange acoustics, and she stood back by the foot of the bed, watching keenly to see which panel would open.

'Come in,' she called with bated breath.

A panel that she had not been expecting to open swung wide and a young maid entered with a jug of hot water, soap, and clean towels. 'The housekeeper sent me, madame,' the girl said in the soft accents of the distant Roanne district.

Rosella nodded her head, giving permission for the water to be carried through to the bathroom, which the maid did with enormous care, obviously afraid of spilling it. When she was left alone again Rosella took up the scarlet hat she had worn from Paris and tugged at the ruched ribbon bow, snapping the fine thread. As soon as she had stretched out the shining length she tied it with a knot to the door-handle. A sense of relief flowed over her at the sight of the rippled streamers hanging bright against the pale damask. Never again would she be at a loss to find a speedy way out of the tower room should the need arise.

With a smile in her new sense of security she stood back and inwardly mocked the small precaution. That must be the only concession to her old terrors, and even that must be removed when she had gained her bearings. She was no longer a child staying on sufferance, she was the mistress of the Château de Louismont. No matter that the position had been forced on her. She must bear it with dignity — and with courage!

50

CHAPTER FOUR

When Rosella came down from the tower room a quarter of an hour later she found a contingent of servants already hard at work throughout the wing. Dust-sheets were being whisked away, and everywhere housemaids were busy with dusters, upholstery brushes and polishing cloths.

Leaving behind the bustle of activity she made her way through a labyrinth of corridors to the open landing at the head of the main staircase, which was wide enough to hold a ball. Set in the walls and continuing along the circular gallery were pillared alcoves, which contained velvet seats in a shadowed intimacy more suited to lovers seeking privacy than for art-lovers to sit and view the exquisite pieces of furniture which had been placed in each one.

Rosella cast an unconsciously wary eye towards the alcoves, remembering how often in the past Jules had chosen to jump out at her with a yell from the darkness, making her shriek with fright. No wonder her nerves had played tricks with her, bringing her to a state of hysteria in which she heard sounds that nobody else could hear. Eerie cries that had been conjured up by her own unbalanced imagination. She had imagined them of course. She was convinced of that, which was a sensible and comforting step towards conquering her feeling of aversion to the château and everything to do with it.

She moved towards the stairs, settling a lacy shawl about her shoulders, for she had decided to take a stroll in the grounds while the tower room was being put in order.

She badly needed some exercise after being cooped up so long in the carriage, and the breeze might be cool enough to cut through the gauzy taffeta of her scarlet gown without some protection. Holding up her rustling skirt with one hand and resting her other fingers on the mahogany banister she descended the curving flight of stairs. The hall was deserted, and she was able to take her time, looking about her at the splendour on all sides.

She had reached the bottom stair when suddenly one of the huge entrance doors swung open and a man entered, his shadow long in the square of sunlight thrown across the floor before he closed the door after him. Not noticing her, he stood taking off his gloves, and when his hands were free he removed his hat, tossed the gloves inside, and placed it on a chair.

She stood very still. She had recognized her dear Sébastien instantly. He had grown taller, and broader, but she would have known him anywhere. That black tousled hair, which was full of indigo lights. That handsome face, which took its marvellous shape from the clear-cut bones beneath the smooth olive skin. Those thick-lashed Gallic eyes, dark and warm and melting, which at any second would turn towards her. She could not wait!

'Sébastien!' she exclaimed breathlessly.

He spun about in some surprise at hearing his name spoken unexpectedly. She saw his expression of blank bewilderment and knew he did not recognize her.

'Have I changed so much?' she asked with a gurgle of happy laughter, stepping down from the stair to advance towards him.

Then incredulous recognition dawned in his eyes and his whole face became suffused with pleasure. 'Rosella! Can it be you? The charming little duckling has turned into a beautiful swan!'

She wanted to throw herself into his arms as she had

52

done on the night she had flown in terror from the tower room, but not for protection, but to have his quiet voice soothing away her fears; now she felt no fear, only exultation. There was no denying the wild rush of re-awakened love that surged through her at the sight of him.

'It's wonderful to see you again!' she cried joyously.

'I echo that!' He caught her hands in his and bent to kiss her on both cheeks, causing her to close her eyes in the bliss of their reunion. But she fixed her delighted gaze on him again when he raised his head, still retaining his hold on her fingers, and she forgot all else in her excitement, except that they were meeting for the very first time on equal terms. She was no longer a child to his lanky youthfulness, but a woman to his manhood, able to attract and bewitch and enslave. Beneath the admiration naked in his eyes she saw a deeper look, which set her high on a pinnacle of hope and happiness. It was as heady as champagne.

'What on earth are you doing here?' he demanded, his smile dazzling her. 'Nobody told me you were coming. I suppose Cousin André's lawyers sent for you. It was a bad business, his dying at sea, but I'm certain that, when the will is read, we shall hear that you've been well provided for.' He frowned, seeing the distress in her eyes, feeling her fingers tremble in his before she snatched them away and withdrew a step. 'Poor little Rosella,' he said gently. 'You were very fond of him, weren't you? Forgive me. I spoke too abruptly of his passing.'

She shook her head helplessly, trying to find the words that she must say to him. 'It's not that. There's something else.'

She wanted to soften the blow she had to deal him, but was at a loss to know how it could be done. As she hesitated there came a snort of derision from the head of the stairs, and they both looked up. Louise stood there, her face sour, a sneer on her lips.

'Well, Rosella? Why do you hold your tongue?' she taunted. 'Take a good look at her, Sébastien! Don't be deceived by her show of friendship. She is your enemy. A viper in our midst. The bearer of evil tidings.'

'What is this?' Sébastien exclaimed, exasperated with his sister and disturbed by Rosella's stricken state. 'Tell me –'

But Rosella was given no chance to tell him. Louise came down the stairs at a rush, shouting as she came. 'You're landless – that's what she has to tell you. And you are virtually penniless too. There'll be no reading of André Cadel's will in this home. Rosella is his heiress. He was her grandfather! Her grandfather, do you hear? And he's left us nothing. Standing before you is the new owner of Château de Louismont and all its lands.'

His reaction to his sister's brutal announcement tore at Rosella's heart. He went absolutely white, so white that there was almost a greenish tinge to the shadows beneath the high cheekbones. Slowly his eyes narrowed to a cold and deadly stare, and a nerve twitched violently in his temple.

In an awful silence, more terrible than anything he could have said, he backed away from her. In mute appeal she half-raised her hands, but blinded by temper he swung about, and in charging for the door through which he had recently entered he blundered against a table, catching himself a blow on the hip. The vibration sent tottering a tall Chinese vase that stood on it, and with a deliberate flailing blow of his fist he sent it smashing to the floor. Red, emerald, and turquoise fragments of porcelain went skimming in every direction. Without even a glance at the damage done he reached the door, wrenched it open, and flung himself out, coat-tails flying.

Rosella stood stunned, rooted to the floor. Louise gave

an angry exclamation. '*Mon Dieu*! What has he done? *Maman* adored that vase. Oh, that crazy temper of his. Can it be mended?' She scrabbled about, picking up one piece and then another, scrunching others underfoot, and she wailed her dismay. 'Look! Look! Smashed beyond repair!'

Rosella scarcely heard Louise's tirade. She moved like an automaton to the open door and saw Sébastien striding away across the forecourt, his head down, hands thrust into his pockets, as if rushing away from the unbearable. Rosella ached for him. His agony was hers.

As if impelled by an unknown force, she drifted out of the door, down the stone steps, going from the coolness of the shadowed archway into the sun. Shading her eyes with her arm, she watched him go through the rose garden, making for the spread of wooded parkland. She could not let him go alone to brood over the disaster that had befallen him. She must go to him!

He moved swiftly, disappearing into the woods, unaware that she was striving to catch up with him. She had broken into a run, but was hampered by the fullness of her draped gown.

In among the trees she plunged, hoping desperately that she would not lose sight of him. She wanted to call out to him to stop, but did not dare. Twigs and brambles caught at her, snagging fine threads from her taffeta gown, tearing at her hair. Her shawl slipped from her shoulders, but she left it where it fell. At every step her high-laced white boots sank deep into the mould of last year's leaves, which lay like a damp, dun-coloured carpet under the trees. Twice she stumbled and fell to her knees, and once she pitched forward on her face, but each time she scrambled up and ran on again.

He had come to a halt on the bank of the crystal-clear tributary that skirted a curve of the château's parkland before swirling on to join the Loire itself. Hearing the rustling of twigs and leaves he turned and saw her approaching through the trees like a little bird of vivid plumage. Stepping to one side he stood concealed by a chestnut tree and waited for her. Rosella believed she had lost her quarry, but breathless though she was, she kept up her pace and lowered her head to dive under yet another low-hanging branch.

It was jerked aside abruptly and she gasped, startled. He allowed the branch to fall back into place again behind her and they were enclosed together in a green and gold cave of sun-shot foliage. Wretchedly she saw how his eyes glittered at her, how his quivering mouth compressed into a razor-thin line from the burning, cursing wrath that possessed him.

'Why do you follow me?' he demanded harshly. 'No one else would have dared!'

'I – I wanted to be with you,' she confessed breathlessly.

'You were foolhardy!' He thrust his head towards her. 'Suppose I decide to murder you in this quiet place?' He gave a dramatic emphasis to his words by slicing his hand menacingly through the air within an inch of her face.

She bit her trembling lip, chilled by what he had said, although she could not believe that he would carry out such a threat. She recognized that now was the time for speaking the truth with a raw frankness and candour that could never have been possible in the château within earshot of family and servants. She did not quail before him and kept her chin high, unaware that she had moved her hand nervously up to encircle the base of her throat protectively.

'If it were possible,' she said, 'I'd sign away the château to you this instant. I don't want it. I loathe it. I told you once that I never wanted to see it again and time has not changed my mind one iota. It should be yours!'

'It *is* mine! Mine!' He thumped his thumb against his waistcoat. 'No matter whose name Cadel penned in the will. I was born here. The land is in my blood. When I was a young boy I'd slip away from the château to take off my coat and dig the soil and tend the vineyards with the peasant labourers. Later I studied and learned all I could in order to get the best yield, the finest crops, the most superb wine. No estate in all France is better husbanded. And as for the château — it is my home! How could you imagine I would allow you to take all this from me?'

She stared at him dumbly, but still she did not shrink at his rage.

'Why aren't you afraid of me?' he stormed. 'Think how easily I could throw you down on the bank and hold your head under the water. I could swear that you fell into the river while looking for me and it was an accident. Nobody would ever doubt my word. I am the local *magistrat*. Your time as the new owner of the château would be pathetically short. I need not remind you that I am the next in line.'

Goaded at last, she gave a wild laugh. 'Better to marry me than murder me!' she cried in a fierce challenge. 'Take your choice! Either way would make the château yours.'

His eyes cracked on an odd look blended of anguish, frustration, and abject misery. The fingers of his shaking hands were jerking spasmodically, and abruptly he clenched them into tight fists and whirled about to smash them against a tree-trunk, seeking to assuage the torment of mind and heart with a more basic, physical pain, and the blood spurted from his gashed knuckles.

She flew to his side and would have taken his torn and bloody hands into hers, but he seized her by the shoulders and hurled her back against the tree, his mouth devouring hers in a kiss of such savagery that she was only conscious of the violation of it and the all-enveloping darkness of his face over hers, shutting out the sun. Her breasts were crushed painfully against his chest and the violent strength of his limbs trapping hers made the layers of their clothing seem non-existent between them, so hard did he thrust himself into her.

She was a prisoner in the cyclone of his passion, utterly powerless, gouged by his possessive tongue and half-smothered, her eyes wide and dilated and frantic. There was the rip of taffeta and the lace beneath, exposing her shoulder. He sought to bear her to the ground, but she managed to wrench her mouth free.

'Sébastien!' she gasped. 'Sébastien!'

The tense but quietly spoken use of his name in a distraught plea was instantly effective. He released his cruel hold on her. He became conscious of how he had sought to abuse the girl, her hair disarranged and falling from its pins, her mouth bruised, who was ineffectually trying to hold together her torn bodice while she met his hard stare of stoically checked passion without any foolish display of hysterics or reproachful tears, such as he might have expected from her sheltered upbringing. But she was breathing as deeply as he, and he sensed her arousal and the fathomless depths of the true woman within her.

'You must get your hands bathed and bandaged without delay,' she urged, her concern only for him.

'There's something I must tell you first.'

'Later!' she said hastily, thinking he intended to apologize.

'No. Now!' he insisted. His eyes shifted away from her, but not in remorse at the brutal way he had handled her, for he knew that, when she had heard what he had to say, she would understand fully the volcano of emotion that had erupted with such disastrous results, bringing him to the brink of rape for the first and the last time in his life.

His air of trapped helplessness made Rosella long to

comfort him, to hold him gently in her arms.

He looked across the river with a blind, unfocused gaze, his face haggard. 'Cousin André did not even die soon enough to save the situation,' he said bitterly, speaking more to himself than to her. 'He would have been the first to sacrifice willingly that last short span of his life had he known, and it would have brought you back to the château while there was still time. Merciful heaven! He must be turning in that sad watery grave of his.'

'What do you mean?' she cried. 'I don't understand.'

His words came clipped and caustic. 'You have returned to the Loire valley in time for a wedding. I am to marry Claudine de Vailly, only child of the Comte de Vailly, whose lands border those of the château and whose vineyards run side by side with mine – or those I had thought belonged to me, for Cousin André never gave me cause to believe otherwise. The betrothal has been short, a matter of three months. I intended some time ago to write and tell Cousin André my intentions towards Claudine, and then we heard he was returning to France.'

The shock of his announcement drained all strength from her, and she grasped a dipping bough as though she might fall without its support. 'What difference would a letter have made?' she managed to say.

'All the difference! There would have been no betrothal to Claudine. Cousin André would have forbidden it.' One corner of his mouth quirked into a wry, unhappy smile. 'Surely it must be obvious to you whom he intended I should marry. Cousin André had laid his plans well. His roots went deep into old France, in spite of his years abroad. Lineage, family, the rightful inheritance of property held in trust for the generations that are to come – these were the things he believed in. The château was to have been your dowry, Rosella. Your dowry as my bride!'

Her eyes widened. Sébastien's bride. So her grandfather had planned a marriage for her, but not in the way she had feared. He had decided on the one man in all the world whose ring she longed to have on her finger! If that betrothal to Claudine had never taken place Sébastien would have married her. He whom she had loved for so long! The château would have been theirs to share, and he would have come between her and its terrors as he had done in the past, leaving no cloud to darken their horizon. Through him she might even have come to feel a fondness for that graceful edifice of stone, simply because it meant so much to him.

As each aspect of what might have been crashed home to her, she clutched tighter at the bough to steady herself, but although she had become bereft of speech the yearning, unspoken question must have showed in her dilated eyes.

His expression hardened as though he had succeeded in crushing all his feelings on the matter, but something seemed to have died inside him. 'I regret that nothing can be changed at this late hour,' he said. 'Nothing! The marriage with Claudine must take place.'

The finality of his statement was like a dash of cold water in her face, forcing her to accept the situation with as much dignity as she could muster. 'Then you must forget what I said to you,' she said quietly. 'It was ironical that I should have voiced the suggestion that we might wed as an alternative to my demise!' Reaction to the tempestuous interlude was setting in. Her whole body was shaking and her legs were as weak as if she had risen from a sick-bed. She would never have thought it possible for conventions and proprieties to be swept away as they had been in that leafy glade.

'It is I who should ask you to forget my inexcusable behaviour a few minutes ago,' he said with a sudden rush of contrition. 'I frightened you. I hurt you. Forgive me.'

She wanted no discussion about it and inclined her head in a quick little nod to show her acceptance of his apology. At all costs she must direct the conversation towards the most important issue at stake. 'When is your wedding day to be?' she enquired, struggling to keep her voice level and under control.

He answered her on a heavy, long drawn-out sigh. 'Within the month. My plans were to take a short honeymoon with Claudine and bring her back as the new mistress of the château. Now that is impossible. I'm at a loss to know what to do.'

'There's no need to change your plans,' she said tautly. 'I have chosen to occupy the west tower wing and the rest of the château can be yours. It is the de Louismont home more than it can ever be mine. I have no wish to impose my presence.'

He was astonished and showed it. 'Do you mean what you say?'

'With all my heart.'

His eyes narrowed on a flare of fiercely injured pride, the skin drawing tight over the bones in his face. 'Don't expect me to praise your magnanimity! You are only releasing that to which I have the true claim.'

She flinched at his biting tone, thinking that they each had an extraordinary power to wound the other. 'The opportunity to leave the château will come to me one day,' she said, lifting her head. 'Then it will be yours in all but the shadow of my distant ownership, which shall never interfere in the running of the château and the estate in any way.'

He gave a derisive little bow. 'I'm overwhelmed.' Then he saw her eyes flood with tears for the first time and reminded himself that she had suffered enough, and he had no right to add to her unhappiness. 'Rosella, my dear,' he said gently, 'I'm behaving like a boor. The situation is as abhorrent to you as it is to me. We must learn to live with it, I know. But I cannot promise that I'll ever be able to make the best of it. I can only ask you to be patient with me.'

'I'll be patient.' She was fighting back the tears, determined not to give way before him. She attempted a smile. 'After all, we are old friends.'

Somehow her attempt to put the two of them on a surer footing misfired, and she seemed only to give emphasis to the fact that they could have been so much more. Sweethearts in courtship. Lovers in wedlock. His eyes held hers. A poignant silence grew between them. It was she who broke it, seizing on the state of his raw and swollen hands to break a renewal of tension.

'You must get your hands dressed, Sébastien. Go back to the château and find someone to attend to them.' She answered the question on his lips before he had time to ask it. 'I'll stay here for a while. We must not be seen together – you with your injuries and myself like this. I must tidy myself before I venture out of the woods.'

'But how will you do that? Your gown –'

'I dropped a shawl somewhere along the path. I'll find it and wrap that around me.' She was making an ineffectual attempt to tuck in some of her fallen hair with her free hand, the other still clutching her bodice together.

'I have a comb in one of my pockets,' he said, trying to be helpful. He located it, but his attempt to reach it was defeated by the puffed condition of his fingers.

'Shall I?' she offered.

She had to come close to him, for the comb was in an inside pocket, the silk lining warm from his body. 'I'll see that it is returned to you soon,' she said, wanting to avoid another disturbing silence.

He shrugged to show that its return was of no

importance, but as she stood holding the comb he reached out to stroke her cheek with the inside of his wrist, keeping his injured hand curved back in order not to let any blood touch her skin. It was a tender gesture.

'My poor little swan,' he said sympathetically. 'Life is not going to be any easier for you now at the Château de Louismont than it was in the past. But this time I can do nothing for you. This time I am, through circumstances beyond our control, the last one to whom you can turn.'

Turning from her, he pushed aside the foliage and left the glade, taking a short cut to the château through the woodland that he knew so well. She remained motionless, listening to the whispering of leaves brushed by his shoulders and the crackling of twigs underfoot that marked his passage until finally he was out of hearing. Then her self-control snapped and she gave way to the tears which had been threatening and sobbed as if her heart would break.

There could be no love in Sébastien's relationship with Claudine de Vailly, of that she was certain, for the tone of his voice had admitted it. But he was trapped by a contract of marriage drawn up when he had been secure in the expectation of his inheritance, able to command a sizeable dowry from the future bride's father. It would make no difference that the circumstances had changed. The bond could not be broken without scandal on either side. It was from such a marriage of convenience that she herself had hoped to escape when it had occurred to her that André Cadel might have that plan in view. Never dreaming that Sébastien was his choice for her!

Now Sébastien had gone from her almost before they had come together again, her love over before it had had the chance to flower to its full richness. Over, that is, in the sense that she and Sébastien must go on with their separate lives, never allowing themselves a backward glance at what might have been. But their particular tragedy was that they lived under the same roof. No matter that the château had a hundred rooms or more, they could not avoid meeting sometimes, even though she would try to avoid that, and was certain that he would do the same. It would give her devotion to him no chance to ease, to lessen, and even to abate with the passing of time — if such a thing were possible. And the sight of her would be a constant reminder to him of his lost birthright. How was he to endure it? How was she?

The sun was thrusting long red-gold rays through the trees when she stirred at last.

It was a simple matter to coil her hair into place. But her gown was completely ruined. At all costs she must recover her shawl before returning to the château.

She returned the way she had come, and found her own footprints in places along the muddy path, but the white shawl, which should have been easy to spot, was nowhere to be seen. She searched until she feared to lose her sense of direction, but there was no sign of her shawl.

She ran across a stretch of lawn to take a roundabout route through the formal gardens, which would offer more opportunities to keep hidden from the gaze of anyone looking out over the grounds from the château. She kept close to the box-hedges and the topiarian bushes, which stood black against the rosy sky. Pausing by a skilfully clipped peacock, she looked towards the château, knowing she must avoid the main entrance and wondering which other door would give her the most secluded route to the west tower wing. Her gaze turned towards her apartments there. Like the rest of the château, it was bathed in a pink light, the windows glinting amber, gold, and topaz, the pepper-pot roof of the tower itself holding the sheen of hammered metal.

Suddenly she caught a pale flicker against one of the

windows of the long corridor. For a second, no longer, she had the impression that a hollow-eyed face had come to the glass and gone again. She froze, feeling an eerie stab of fear, straining her eyes in the gloom to confirm that trick of light, for it could have been nothing else – unless a servant had paused there briefly. Reason backed this thought, but instinct fought with it. Unbidden, the hateful legend sprang into her mind, and her old fears crowded in on her again.

Angrily she jerked her shoulder, resolutely shaking off that legacy from the past. It must have been the housekeeper whom she had seen. The woman was probably wondering where she was and what was keeping her. No doubt the servants were waiting to serve dinner to her in the small dining-room, for she would not be invited to dine at the de Louismont table and she had no wish anyway to sit down with the family. Heavens! That meant she would have to run the gauntlet of the footmen's stares at her dishevelment unless she could find something to cover her shoulders before she arrived there.

Deciding that the garden room was the least likely to be occupied at this hour when the de Louismonts would be dressing for dinner, she darted along under the château walls and reached the glass doors that led into it. Cautiously she peered through to make sure nobody was there. The last tinge of the sunset had left the sky, letting the deepening darkness take over, but a single lamp in a fluted shade suspended from the ceiling had been lit and its soft glow threw a circular patch down on the black and white tiles and touched to a glossy green the leaves of the neatly arranged jungle that came within its range.

Turning the handle, she entered the garden room soundlessly and closed the door behind her. The scent of the flowers was even stronger in the stored-up heat of the day, giving a languorous, sensuous atmosphere. She took one step and then another. A trail of dried blood spots on a white tile showed that Sébastien had come into the château by the same route. The sight of them wrenched at her heart, and she clenched her hands, identifying herself with the pain he must have suffered.

Moving on, she passed out of the aura of the lamp into the shadows, making for the door at the far end of the room, which she had entered only a few hours before to find the three de Louismont women awaiting her. And then she saw her shawl, its snowy softness folded over the arm of the chair where Marguerite had been sitting. With a little exclamation of relief she flew to snatch it up.

'It is yours, is it?' said Philippe Aubert's voice.

Spinning round, she saw him standing with feet apart, a dark silhouette with his back to one of the windows amid the fronded palms, his stiff white shirt-front gleaming, the three diamond studs in it a-glitter. As he struck a match she threw the shawl quickly about her shoulders and clamped it across her waist with her forearm.

'Did you find my shawl?' she asked a trifle breathlessly.

He was lighting a cigar. As he had been the first time she had seen him in the lobby of the Hôtel du Louvre. In the dancing light of the match-flame he studied her intently, making her wonder how much he had seen of her torn gown.

'I found it in the woods,' he replied lazily. 'It was lying at the side of one of the paths. How did you come to lose it?'

'I dropped it. I walked as far as the river.' There was no need for lengthy explanations. It was her land. She had a perfect right to be on it without his questioning her. Why had he been in the woods? That was more to the point. And then the thought occurred to her that he might have overheard her conversation with Sébastien. 'Why were you there?' she enquired warily.

66

The match had gone out. The cigar-tip glowed brightly for a moment before he replied, and the aromatic smoke lifted to blend its fragrance with that of the flowers. 'There are some handy stepping stones in the river near that path. I can come from the garden of my villa into the château's grounds without going round by the road whenever I visit the de Louismonts – as I am this evening. I have been invited to dine. Did you know?'

So he could only have picked up the shawl a matter of ten or fifteen minutes ago. She gave an inward sigh of relief. 'No, I didn't know. Why should you imagine I would know? The de Louismonts' social affairs are not going to include me. Well, thank you for returning my shawl, Monsieur Aubert.'

She turned to leave, but his next words halted her. 'The dinner this evening is to be in your honour.'

'In my honour?' she echoed. 'But that's impossible!'

He strolled leisurely towards her. 'Don't misunderstand me. The dinner itself is not a last-minute arrangement. Indeed, I was invited a week ago. But Sébastien is entertaining a number of prominent local people – not that I am among those particular guests – and Louise has decided it would look odd, to say the least, if the new owner of the château who only arrived today, is not at the host's right hand.'

She was flustered by this unexpected development. 'No! That's not what I intended at all! I must find Louise and speak to her.'

'Wait!' He reached the door before her and rested his hand on its polished knob, politely barring her way. 'I understand how you feel. You have already made enormous concessions towards the de Louismonts, but this is one step more you should take, or else the rest will be worthless. By appearing to be on sociable terms with the family you will save them from endless embarrassment and humiliation. Think what it would mean to them, proud people that they are, to have the whole district whispering about the situation and saying that they were being allowed to remain in the château on sufferance. On charity. The de Louismont family lost its fortune and its own lands in the Revolution, which is the reason why the Cadels allowed them to move into the château three generations ago. That is common knowledge, but the years have overlain the fact, giving the de Louismonts the prestige and position enjoyed by the other great land-owners in the Loire valley, and the income from the estate has been shared with the absent Cadels, a fact which Louise revealed to me and which you must surely know from your lawyers.'

'Did Louise ask you to put all this to me?' she asked with a direct look.

He nodded. 'That is why I came earlier than the other guests to talk to you. She felt that someone outside the family should explain it to you, and as I had been present when you arrived and was in possession of most of the facts it was natural that her choice fell on me.'

She was forced to admire Louise's astuteness. The de Louismont arrogance had made it impossible for Louise to request anything from someone whom she had always despised, and there had been the added threat of the fiery de Louismont temper, which would have exploded in the face of a refusal, even if Louise had merely voiced the dinner invitation without humbling herself by giving the reasons for it. Rosella was thankful that Philippe had agreed to act as an intermediary. It had saved more trouble all round. And the last thing she wanted was for Sébastien to suffer anything more on her behalf.

'I'll attend the dinner party,' she said quietly.

Philippe gave her a slow, approving smile. 'You have courage, Rosella. I'll do what I can to help you through the ordeal.'

She managed a smile in thanks for his kindly thought, unaware how wan it appeared. She passed through the door he opened for her and hurried along to reach the grand staircase. Louise was coming down, dressed for the dinner party in a satin gown that swished with every step.

'Well, Rosella?' she demanded fiercely, cutting past any preliminaries.

'What time are your other guests arriving?' Rosella asked.

'At eight o'clock.'

'I'll be ready.'

Relief showed in Louise's eyes, but it did not soften the sharpness of her tongue. 'I trust you will! Did you have to go traipsing off for hours in the grounds? Why didn't you stay with Sébastien when you went out after him? If you had talked to him and explained that you were only intending to occupy the west tower wing, leaving the rest of the château to us, it might have helped to calm him down a little, and then the accident would not have happened. Instead I had to do all the explaining when he returned, no longer in a rage, but in an equally unbearable mood —'

'Accident!' Rosella interrupted, her face showing her anxiety. 'What happened?'

Louise gave an impatient flick with her folded fan. 'Oh, nothing serious. That foolish brother of mine went dashing off to the stable intent on riding out his fury on that mad-brained black stallion of his. I suppose he handled the beast with unusual roughness in his distraught frame of mind, and it reared when he backed it out of the stall. I'd have the wretched creature shot! You should see Sébastien's knuckles! Ugh!' She shuddered delicately. 'I couldn't touch them. He took a carriage to the doctor's in town and was then going on to call on Claudine —' here her eyes flashed her malevolent hatred at Rosella – 'and break the news to her of your untimely intrusion into our home.'

Rosella was relieved to hear that Sébastien had found some sort of explanation for his injured hands, which should put a stop to any awkward questions. How would Claudine react to the ill tidings brought to her? It was impossible not to cherish a small faint hope. 'Will Claudine have second thoughts about the marriage, do you think?' she enquired cautiously.

Louise lifted her eyebrows. 'La, what a bourgeois idea! You have lived too long in that land of shopkeepers for your own good, Rosella. This is France. Even if Claudine were not besotted over Sébastien, she would go through with it to avoid the gossip and scandal that neither her family nor ours could hope to live down for decades. In any case,' she added, continuing on down the stairs and passing Rosella, 'Claudine is heiress to her father's fortune and she'll have money enough for Sébastien to squander however he wishes when the time comes.'

'I would not call Sébastien the squandering type,' Rosella remarked indignantly, quick to fly to his defence.

Louise's animosity flared, flooding her face with crimson, and she twisted round to look up at Rosella. 'Would you not? Well, *I* call it squandering to have ploughed back into the estate almost every sou he gained from it – to say nothing of endless repairs to the château, which were long overdue. And there have been *Maman's* endless whims. One season she wants her boudoir lilac, and another it must be white with specially woven curtains and bed-drapes of gold thread. Then there are her carriages, her hats, and her Parisian gowns. And he always panders to her. No wonder she worships him with no eye for the rest of us!' She drew breath. 'That's why he's practically a pauper now that you have taken the château and its lands

70

from him!'

She flounced off, leaving Rosella to mount the staircase slowly, her heart even heavier than before. It sounded as if Sébastien had debts to add to his troubles. She must consult Monsieur Bataillard when he came. There must be some loophole that would enable her to see that Sébastien was recompensed without offending that touchy pride of his.

Lamps were alight in the west tower wing, but there was not a servant to be seen. Louise must have been completely confident that Philippe would succeed in persuading her that she should attend the dinner party, for the table in the small dining-room was not set for a solitary meal.

In the tower room a great weariness descended on her. She took off the torn gown and threw it aside. Without interest she went to the clothes closet, wondering what to wear. When the door opened behind her without a preliminary knock she glanced back listlessly, guessing that it was a servant coming to turn down the bed. It was the same little maid who had brought the hot water soon after her arrival. Seeing Rosella, her small, round face showed confusion.

'I beg your pardon, madame!' she exclaimed apologetically, giving a quick bob, which set her cap-ribbons a-flutter. 'I thought you had gone down to dinner.'

'You should always knock on a door,' Rosella said in gentle reproof. 'Never assume a room is empty.'

'Yes, madame. I will not forget again.'

'The housekeeper had instructed you then?'

'Yes, madame. But there is so much to remember. I have never been in service before.'

'How long have you been at the château?'

'Only two weeks. It's my first time away from home.' Shyness was overcoming her, reducing her voice to a

71

paralysed whisper. To cover up, she snatched up the discarded gown, feeling that she must do something with her hands, intending to drape it over a chair, but her mouth dropped open in surprise at the state of it. 'Whatever's happened to this?'

'That is another lesson you must learn,' Rosella rebuked, sitting down on the edge of the bed. 'Never to ask questions that might not be welcome.'

'Forgive me, madame! That was another thing I was told. Oh, dear!' In spite of herself, the maid's attention was drawn back to the garment in her hands, for it had been distress at the ill-use of it and not curiosity that had prompted her question. 'Would you like me to repair it for you, madame?'

Rosella waved the suggestion away. 'I never want to see it again!' she declared vehemently.

'But I am skilled with a needle. My mother was a seamstress and taught me how to sew. I could mend it in tiny seams under the ruchings where the stitches would be completely hidden.' The girl reddened at her own persistence, but such waste dismayed her — it was completely against the grain of her peasant upbringing when nothing was ever thrown out until it had been turned and mended and made into something else.

Rosella, about to dismiss the offer for the second time, hesitated and gave some thought to an idea that had come to her. 'What is your name?' she asked.

'Marie Leroy.'

'I need a personal maid, Marie. I think you would suit me very well. I'll inform the housekeeper of my decision without delay.'

The look of joy in the maid's face was overshadowed almost immediately by the realization of the responsibilities that such a position would entail. Her forthright nature compelled her to point out her own failings in no uncertain terms.

'I cannot dress hair! I have had no training, except what I learned from my mother, who showed me the right ways to steam velvet and goffer frills and starch linen – but I know nothing of matching up boots and shoes with riding habits and tea-gowns and evening wear and all that. And I am often forgetful, as you know.'

'How old are you, Marie?'

'Seventeen, madame.'

'The right age to start off on a new career as a lady's maid,' Rosella said firmly, not to be swayed by nervous argument. She had noticed that Marie's movements were quick and neat, her hands squarely capable. 'I can be patient. I'm prepared to train you. Until now I've always dressed my own hair, but there's no reason why together we shouldn't copy all the latest coiffures from the ladies' magazines that I'll order from Paris.'

Excitedly Marie flung the taffeta gown across a chair and clasped her hands together fervently. 'I'll try! I'll learn! I'll serve you faithfully, madame!'

A smile touched Rosella's lips. 'I'm sure you will, Marie,' she said warmly. 'You may start by ordering bath water to be brought up to me – order it, remember, and do not bring as much as a jug of it yourself. Your status in this household has changed and your duties lie in other directions. Make sure the water is brought quickly – I have no more than twenty minutes left to me before I must appear in the drawing-room downstairs. While I'm bathing you can get out my apricot silk gown with the lace ruffles and the shoes to match.'

The bath and the dressing took place in record time. While Marie was hooking up the back of her gown with lightning fingers Rosella, having done her hair, put on the pearl-drop earrings, which had been a birthday gift once from her grandfather. She felt she had made a wise choice

73

in looking no further for a lady's maid than Marie Leroy, whose open looks had revealed a lack of guile even as her crisp appearance had denoted a personal fastidiousness. It had also been satisfying to Rosella to have her first impression of an honest country nature quickly confirmed by that impulsive confession of talents lacked, which a less truthful person would have tried to conceal in the face of such an opportunity; moreover, Marie had not been long enough at the château in her simple position as housemaid to form any conflicting loyalties towards the de Louismonts, and Rosella was convinced that in the future she would find herself needing someone around her whom she could trust implicitly.

'There!' Marie stood back admiringly. 'You look lovely, madame.'

'Thank you, Marie. Now the wrist-length white gloves and my fan.'

She was ready, but the whole operation had taken seven minutes longer than she had planned. It meant she would be a little late arriving in the drawing-room, but perhaps it would not go amiss to make an entrance when the others had already gathered. As she turned to leave, she noticed the taffeta gown still lying across the chair and looked from it to Marie, who was very much the same height and build as herself. If anything, the maid's waist could be even smaller than her own narrow span.

'If you care to repair that red taffeta, Marie,' she said, 'you may have it, but on one condition – that you never wear it in my sight.'

Marie was too stupefied to say anything until Rosella had gone out of the door. Then she rushed out to the head of the tower stairs and called down after her. 'Thank you a thousand times, madame! Thank you! Oh, thank you!'

The buzz of conversation reached Rosella before she paused on the threshold of the Gold Salon. Against a background of yellow silk panelled walls and in the light of unnumerable candles in the gilded chandeliers about twenty people were split up into small groups, the gentlemen in their black evening attire all standing and most of the ladies seated. She looked immediately for Sébastien, but he was not there and her heart lurched with mingled relief and disappointment. Sophie was present, but had not seen her yet, and Marguerite de Louismont, exquisite as some rare fading rose, was holding court from a high-backed chair near the huge marble fireplace where dancing flames kept the evening chill at bay. Louise was talking to two gentlemen, one of whom was Philippe. He must have been watching the door out of the corner of his eye, for with a word to Louise he broke away and came smiling towards Rosella, one white-gloved hand out-stretched to take hers.

'You see!' he said in a low voice for her ears alone. 'It is not going to be so bad after all, now that you have taken the plunge. There are some extremely civilized people here. You will find the evening interesting. Louise wants me to introduce you to everyone.'

He did it well. With tact, with the right words, and with a perfectly relaxed air, which had its effect on her, he presented her as the new mistress of the château in such a way that the impression was left that it was a joint inheritance shared with Sébastien, for which she was overwhelmingly grateful, never imagining it would have been possible to have pulled off such a feat with only the truth spoken. Louise, keeping an ear cocked in their direction while appearing to hang on every sentence uttered by the gentleman still in her company, relaxed visibly. She showed a vivacious gaiety that Rosella had never seen before when she came to tuck her fingers into the crook of Philippe's arm to draw him to her once again. Rosella found herself left with the one person in the room to whom she had taken an instant dislike: Sophie's husband, Armand Montargis.

'The others may be fooled, but I'm not, you know,' he said patronizingly in his grating, gravelly voice, his eyes curiously alive and alert between their fat lids in an otherwise immobile face with its rather formless features, its thick jowls, and the fleshy lips showing pink and moist beneath the black moustache that linked bushily with his abundant side-whiskers. He was twice Sophie's age, a broad, heavily-built man with fast-receding hair.

'There are some matters best kept to the family,' Rosella answered. 'It was not intended that anyone should be deliberately fooled, as you suggest.'

'Hmm.' He regarded her with a sinister lack of goodwill. 'Aubert is not family − not yet anyway, although things seem to be going in that direction with Louise − but he seems to know a great deal more than I do about what's going on.'

Louise and Philippe. Of course! Rosella's mind flashed back to that letter written to André Cadel in which he had expressed his eagerness to return to the villa. Louise was the attraction. No wonder she turned to him in this emergency.

'When Sophie came home this afternoon in a high state of nerves I knew something was wrong,' Armand continued unpleasantly in a self-congratulatory tone at his own shrewdness. 'She said her mother had suffered a swooning turn, but there is nothing unusual in that. You may not know it, being a stranger to the château, but Madame de Louismont is a sickly woman and never ventures a step without someone in attendance.' He gave an irritated nod in the direction of his wife. 'Look at Sophie now. One eye on her mother instead of giving her mind to enjoying herself. It's always the same − *Maman* this, *Maman* that, all the time. So much fussing sticks in my gullet. Madame de Louismont is a spoilt woman. I understand that Pierre de Louismont doted on her, and her children are no better — all except Jules, who goes his own damned way.'

Armand's lack of liking for his in-laws was an embarrassing topic that Rosella wished he would drop, wanting no part of it. It was obvious that Sophie's concern over her mother's failing health was a constant bone of contention between husband and wife. But seeing that he believed Sophie's account of Marguerite's faint to have been exaggerated — perhaps even fabricated — she felt bound to confirm that it had taken place.

'Madame de Louismont was overcome by faintness in the garden room,' she said. 'Soon after my arrival. In my opinion she still looks far from well this evening. It must have been a tremendous effort on her part to come downstairs for this affair.'

'Taken ill soon after you arrived, eh?' Armand's eyes pierced her. 'What brought it on? Shock perhaps? Sophie was shocked too. I know it, although she tried to cover it up. What does it mean, eh? Has Sébastien been left less than a half-share in the château? Is that it?'

'You must ask Sophie. Or Sébastien,' Rosella said, making a move to escape from the man, but he was beside her.

'Sébastien isn't here this evening, and Sophie let it go this far without even telling me of your turning up at the château this afternoon. I want to hear the facts from you.' He was stubbornly insistent, keeping her close to the wall and away from the rest of the company. 'Is there more to it than Sébastien being disappointed with old Cadel's will? Have there been cuts in the bequests to the rest of the de Louismonts? Is that what Sophie was afraid to tell me?'

'Monsieur Montargis,' she began, determined to put an end to his questioning, which she was finding increasingly offensive, 'this is no time —'

She had no need to say any more. A diversion was created by the sudden appearance of Sébastien in the doorway. He had changed into evening clothes but white bandages swathed his hands and there was pallor and strain in his lean, sensitive face, which Rosella knew must be more from the distressing interview he must have had with Claudine than from the pain of his injuries.

'My apologies, ladies and gentlemen,' he said, looking round the room. 'I had hoped to return to the château before you arrived, but I was unavoidably delayed.' He lifted his hands expressively to display the bandages as though the doctor's house had been his only port of call.

'Louise told us about the accident,' one lady remarked with sympathy. 'How unfortunate.'

'When are you going to learn how to handle a horse, de Louismont?' joked her husband. Everybody, except Rosella, joined in the laughter, sharing her knowledge that he was a superb horseman, and he gave a smile at the remark, but it was an automatic acknowledgment of the joke and his thoughts were obviously elsewhere. His arrival proved to be the signal for the announcement that dinner was served. He turned at once to Rosella, showing her that he had located her in that first swift survey of the room, although he had not allowed his attention to linger on her.

'Allow me to take you in to dinner, Rosella,' he said with a bow.

There was a rustle of movement as the ladies rose to take the arms of their partners for the procession across the hall to the dining-room. At the head of it Rosella walked at Sébastien's side, and only she was aware that he had exerted a slight pressure in the crook of his arm to hold captive her trembling fingertips. The dining-table appeared before them beyond doors flung wide, a stretch of white damask glittering with silver and crystal and candelabra, flanked by footmen in dark blue livery.

She sat at his right hand. Philippe Aubert, who had brought Louise to the table, sat on the opposite side a few seats away, but whenever Rosella happened to turn her head in his direction she found his eyes waiting for her, sometimes surprising a look that was oddly speculative and probing, although otherwise he merely smiled and once raised his glass to her. On the whole, she gave little thought to him, concentrating on the conversation at the head of the table, which was innocuous enough, but made lively by the lady sitting at Sébastien's left hand, whose witty tongue was appreciated by those within earshot. Rosella noticed that Sébastien barely touched any of the courses served, and she guessed it was more through lack of appetite than from the difficulty he had in holding a knife, fork, or spoon.

When the ladies withdrew to the Gold Salon afterwards Marguerite sat down on one of the sofas and beckoned to Rosella, patting the space beside her in invitation.

'Sit down and talk to me,' she said with one of her vague, exquisite smiles. 'How long have you been at the château now?'

Rosella felt remorse at the shock she had given the poor woman, seeing that the beautiful eyes still held that slightly blank look. 'I came this afternoon. Only today.'

'Of course! Of course!' Marguerite fluttered her fingers in a confused attempt to cover up her lapse of memory. 'How foolish of me. You were wearing such an elegant outfit. You looked like a peony in that magnificent colour. No. Not a peony – a poppy. That's it! A poppy.' She gave her throaty little laugh at her success in finding the perfect simile, and Rosella smiled at her pleasure, which was almost childlike in its open simplicity.

Louise came forward and rested her hands on the back of the sofa. 'You are not getting tired, are you, *Maman*?'

Marguerite frowned and seemed to have rallied her powers of concentration. 'No, I am not. Leave us.' She snapped open her fan and held the lacy spread like a shield between herself and Louise in a contemptuous gesture of dismissal, which made her daughter draw quickly away. 'I think we should hold a ball for you, Rosella,' she said, continuing the conversation as if there had been no interruption. 'You must be presented to society. No doubt invitations will come within the next few days from those whom Sébastien is entertaining this evening, but you must be properly launched. Some of the local families are in residence all the year round, but others come and go, dividing their time between their mansions in this district and those elsewhere. The Comte de Vailly, for example, only comes to inspect his property about once in every two or three years, and the rest of the time he's travelling here, there, and everywhere. But he is an extreme example.'

'Have Sébastien and Claudine always known each other?' Rosella asked quietly.

'Oh, no. The Comte and Comtesse had separate establishments for many years – Claudine lived with her mother until the poor lady died. After that she travelled with her father and he brought her with him to the Loire valley for the first time last year.' Marguerite, who was waving her fan with a languid grace, gave her attractive, husky gurgle again. 'She became enchanted with the district – and with Sébastien. She refused to leave with her father again and stayed on for the winter.'

The movement of the fan became slower, almost like the swoop of a bird's wing losing strength. 'There is to be a wedding soon. Next month? This month? I forget.' She gave a weary sigh. 'I should remember. I can remember when I came to the château as a bride.' Her voice became dreamy and reflective. 'I wore a crinoline of white

Chantilly lace. Pierre knew I loved gardenias and there were garlands of them everywhere – in the ballroom, in the drawing-rooms, on the balustrades. In my boudoir I found a silken spread of gardenias and lovers' knots covering the bed.'

Her long lashes drooped sensually and her lips parted slightly. 'A de Louismont will do everything in his power to please the woman he loves. Such men are rare. They have liquid fire in their veins where other men have blood. But although they give, they demand. They adore, but they ravish. They idolize, but in the end they master.' Unexpectedly she turned her huge luminous eyes on Rosella with that oddly sweet Mona Lisa smile that hid away all her secret thoughts, and closed her fan with a little snap. 'When did you say you arrived at the château? Last week, was it?'

Rosella was saved from answering all over again by the doors opening to admit the gentlemen coming to rejoin the ladies, and Marguerite's attention was distracted. One of them crossed over to chat to her, leaving Rosella to turn elsewhere for conversation. She found Philippe drawing up a chair to drink coffee with her, which was being served.

'Are you going to survive?' he enquired with a grin when they had both been handed porcelain cups and the cream had been added.

The corners of her lips curled in response and she sipped her coffee. 'I think I'll get through now,' she replied. 'Thanks to you. You explained my presence so splendidly that everybody's feelings were spared, including mine. I feel you've missed your vocation in life.'

He raised surprised eyebrows. 'How?'

'You should have been a diplomat. You handled a delicate situation so famously. You're not, are you?' she asked, not seriously.

'A diplomat?' He flung back his head with a laugh.

'Good heavens, no! I'm in honest-to-goodness trade. Shipping in spices and rum and sugar from Martinique and some of the other islands. I was in business with your grandfather as my father was before me. I took all the sugar that André Cadel's plantation could produce. That's why he wanted to see me when he returned to France, quite apart from the fact that my parents were his friends and I have been able to treat his house as a second home. I had made an offer for his plantation, knowing that he had talked of selling when the time came for him to leave Martinique, but he was in no hurry to dispose of it and wrote that we should discuss the matter during the coming months. I was keener to get it than he realized, and that was why I'd hoped to make some progress towards a business settlement before leaving Paris. But when he failed to arrive I decided it would be foolish to hang about indefinitely. He could have changed his sailing date at the last minute for all I knew.'

She gave a nod, looking down at her half-emptied cup, stabbed by her still-raw grief. It was strange how dreadfully she missed somebody whom she had seen so rarely. 'That is what I had hoped at first. I mean, I kept hoping there would be some perfectly simple explanation for his non-appearance.' Her voice quavered unexpectedly, making her jerk her head with widened eyes in alarm that she might show too much emotion in this sophisticated company.

Philippe Aubert reached out and touched her hand very lightly. 'We'll talk about André Cadel another day. Not now. Not here. But another day.'

'Please,' she said fervently. 'There are so many gaps. So much I want to know.'

As it happened there was no more chance to talk then anyway, for one of the gentlemen was preparing to sing, and Louise, who was to accompany him on the piano, asked Philippe to turn the pages for her. During the singing of several love-songs, and throughout the duets that followed, Rosella noticed how often Louise flashed a glance and a smile at Philippe. She was violently attracted to him, no doubt of that. Perhaps even in love. But what of his feelings? He had that way of looking at a woman as though she alone existed for him, which came naturally to the experienced, sensual Frenchman, but what other signs were there of an ardent passion that had made it impossible for him to wait any longer in Paris and come hot-foot to his villa in order to be near Louise again? Perhaps it was there in an invisible current of excitement crackling between them, which was impossible for an outsider to know. After all, who else in the room suspected that she and Sébastien were tuned in to each other with a vibration of the senses which made them conscious of every move that the other made. Without turning her head she could feel his awareness of her as something almost tangible. Mentally they were locked in an embrace of devastating intimacy. Physically they must never touch each other again except in the most conventional of handshakes or the customary cheek-kissing of friendship in greeting when the occasion arose, but nothing more. Ever.

The evening came to an end at last. Rosella noticed how grimly Armand seized his wife's arm above the elbow to hasten her away. Sophie looked sullen and defiant, knowing that the time of cross-questioning, which she had postponed, was about to burst forth in a deluge the moment they were on their own in their homeward-bound carriage. Philippe Aubert did not delay his departure either. After kissing Marguerite's hand he turned to Louise and had a few words with her, but when he came to Rosella it was not merely to say good night as she had expected.

'You know where I live, Rosella,' he said, with no risk of being overheard in the chatter of the other departing guests. 'If you need help at any time, or find yourself in any kind of difficulty or danger, send for me. Or come to me. Remember that. In the meantime, I look forward to our next meeting. Good night.'

He left her staring after him. Difficulties she could expect in full. But danger! What had made him think of that? She would ponder over it later, but now Sébastien was in the hall, seeing his guests on their way, and she could retire to her own wing. She bade good night to Marguerite, who was already on her way to bed, but Louise did not bother to answer, pretending to be busy handing her mother over to the care of the maid waiting to escort her mistress to her apartments at the opposite end of the château.

Marie was waiting in the tower room to help her undress. It was bliss after the long, exhausting day to have her clothes put away for her, as well as having her hair brushed until it hung down her back in a soft flow. She tumbled into bed, collapsed on to her stomach with her face against the pillow, and was asleep before Marie had time to turn out the lamp and go from the room.

When the deepness of her sleep was disturbed she did not waken, although she stirred restlessly. Slowly she was dragged nearer the surface of consciousness and she tossed her head on the pillow in protest, her hair tumbling about her, giving a little moan. Abruptly her eyes flew open, realization flooding into her mind of where she was and what she had heard. Or had she heard anything? The velvet silence of the tower beat against her eardrums, and only in her mind did an echo seem to linger of a long, harsh, sobbing cry.

She sat bolt upright in bed, her heart thudding, and scooped back her hair from her eyes with both hands.

84

Rolling over on to her side in the nest-like warmth that she had created, she lit the lamp at her bedside and looked about searchingly when the wick flickered into life. The room was as neat and tidy as Marie had left it. Nothing was misplaced. Nothing had fallen over to awaken her.

Had she been dreaming? She was vaguely aware of having uttered some sound, and perhaps it had been her own half-smothered whimper that had jerked her from sleep. Then came a thought that filled her with a sick dread, chilling her through, and making her palms turn cold and clammy. Was it a danger signal that tension and distress and anxiety were starting to play tricks with her sanity as they had done in the tower room once before? Had she made a great mistake in returning to the same surroundings in the west tower wing? But how else to conquer her terror of the château except at the very core of where it had all begun!

Swiftly she threw back the bedclothes and picked up the lamp. The opaque glass of its globe-shaped shade cast a diffused glow over her face and hair, holding her in a little cameo of light, throwing her multiplied shadow in all directions. She went out of the door and stood listening. The silence pressed in on her. Holding the lamp higher she went to the head of the staircase that curved down out of sight.

'Is anyone there?' she demanded in a voice that wavered slightly.

Not a sound. Beyond the radius of the lamp the darkness on the stairs lurked black as water in a well. With a shiver she returned to her room and closed the door behind her. She leaned against it and tried to find some explanation for having started from sleep in alarm. If it had been the first time she would have dismissed it instantly, but it was as though the clock had been turned back and once again the tower had become strangely alive.

Were there eerie manifestations beyond comprehension, beyond belief? Could it really be possible that the tower had caught and held in some awful, unimaginable way the long-ago echoes of a trapped woman's horror, anguish, and despair? Was that the reason why the west tower wing had been locked up with its secret? Or did it need human habitation before centuries-old cries could be heard again?

Taking up the negligée that Marie had put ready for her, she slipped her arms into it as she sat down on the bed. She was determined to think out everything logically and calmly, if that were possible. She could have been dreaming tonight and she accepted that fact. But how did it explain the soft murmurings and whispers that had sighed about her all those years ago when she had lain between waking and sleeping in this same bed? Then the sounds had been dreamlike, and although they had made her increasingly uneasy whenever she gave thought to them during the day, they had seemed too much a part of her natural sleep for her to question them. And if she had, would it have occurred to her child-mind that they could have seeped out of the stone walls behind the pink silk panels to penetrate her consciousness? Only later did she realize that they had all been part of a complex gathering of some inexplicable force, which had come to a climax on the night when she had been torn from slumber by an ear-splitting scream that had seared round and round her as though the tower room had started to spin like a top! Her own hysterical screaming had blended with that piercing shriek, and she had hurled herself from the bed to throw open the door and rush in panic-stricken flight down those curving tower stairs, the stone icy cold to her bare feet.

Like a little white moth in her fluttering nightgown, gripped by the screams emitting from her own throat, she had raced blindly out of the west wing and down the long corridors, her reflection flying with her in the tall pier

86

glasses on either side. Sébastien, no more than seventeen at the time, handsome as a prince in evening dress, had been coming up the grand staircase, returning from some nocturnal outing of his own, and at the sight of him she had hurled herself from the top stair into his arms.

'Rosella! Little one, what is it?' he had asked, seeking to soothe her. His breath was sweet and heavy with wine, but his voice, although slightly slurred, had been more amused than impatient. She had continued to cling to him like a limpet, her eyes rolled up in fright, half strangling him with her clasp about his throat.

He had carried her into the library where he had seated himself with her in a winged chair, her screams having given way to tearing, rasping sobs.

'What has frightened you?' He had disentangled her arms and set her on his knees where she sat straight-backed in the white cloud of her nightgown, shaken by each huge, tearful gulp. Then he had leaned back in the chair and set his hands on the end of the velvet-upholstered arms, watching her. 'A bad dream, was it? Too much dessert for supper, I suppose.'

Still unable to speak, she had shaken her head vehemently, her hair swinging in soft curly strands, but his twinkling smile showed his disbelief. Taking his handkerchief from his sleeve he had tossed it to her, and she, burying her face in it, had soaked it with her tears. Eventually she had raised her head, rubbing her eyes, her chest still heaving, and he had brought his face forward on a level with hers.

'There!' he had said with a chuckle. 'That's better. You had a nightmare, that was all. And no wonder, the way that young brother and those two gawky sisters of mine have been playing tricks on you. If they had not gone to the festival far away at Nevers, staying the week out with Aunt Lucille, I should have suspected them of some mischief done to alarm you.'

Her sleeve had fallen back from her forearm during the drying of her eyes and revealed pinch-marks as black as plums. He took her wrist with cool fingers and turned her arm to examine the bruises.

'Sophie has shown you no mercy, I can see that. I trust you pinched her back?' The sympathetic note in his voice had sent the tears welling up again and she could not answer him. Yet she had not had to, for he had answered the query himself with a shake of his head. 'But what chance have you had against her? Or Louise either for that matter? Both of them near enough to your age to make no difference, but both bigger and stronger. Louise has pulled your hair many a time, I know, and without doubt has given you a few sickening thumps in the spine with her fist, which is a favourite trick of hers. You have not been happy on this holiday, have you, little one?'

She was amazed that he had guessed all that had been going on. He had seemed so aloof and worldly to her ten years, and now he was showing her kindness at a time when she had never been more frightened in all her life.

'I don't like being at the château,' she had gulped. 'I never want to come back! Never!'

'Well, Cousin André comes to fetch you away again tomorrow, and if luck is with you, that will be the last you'll see of any of us.' He had pushed her gently from his knees and stood up. 'Now I'll take you back to the tower room —'

'No!' she had implored beseechingly, shrinking back. 'Don't make me! It's full of screams!'

With a sigh he had looked down at her. 'The time is two o'clock in the morning. You must go back to sleep. There's nothing whatever to be scared of in the château. Old places are full of creaking beams and squeaking doors.'

'But the lady screamed there!'

'What lady?'

'The lady who was shut up in the tower and starved to death. Jules told me the legend.' Her voice caught on a shudder. 'And tonight I heard her. I really did.'

'Jules,' he had answered without emotion, 'deserves a good kick up the backside. If I give you my solemn oath that you dreamed the whole thing, will you believe me?'

'Only if you don't make me go back to the tower room,' she had cried obstinately.

So he had taken her to his own dressing-room and made up a bed on the couch for her, covering her with a blanket and his morning-robe. Then he had closed the door on her. But she did not sleep for a long time. The whole château had been eerily turbulent that night. Boards had creaked. There had been the constant shiver of movement. She had had the spine-chilling sensation of being sought out by the lady who had screamed, as if that distraught ghostly figure had finally escaped from its prison and was wafting about trying to find her. She had buried herself under the blanket, holding on to the cord of Sébastien's morning-robe as though it were a talisman to protect her, and in the snug warmth she had finally slept.

It had been late when she had awakened. She had slipped out of the dressing-room and up to the tower, no longer afraid with sunshine lighting every corner, and had dressed herself in her travelling clothes ready for the arrival of André Cadel. He had not been due until early afternoon, but she had spent the intervening hours sitting on the entrance steps watching with impatience for the arrival of his carriage.

Fortunately, when he had come, he had wanted to leave again without delay, which had suited her very well. Her own farewells were few. The other children were still away, Pierre de Louismont had not returned from a business trip, Sébastien was absent, and Marguerite had been indisposed. So the servants who had attended her were the only ones to see her depart.

'Have you enjoyed your stay at the château, Rosella?' André Cadel had asked as the carriage bore them away down the drive.

'No, sir,' she had answered frankly, 'but Sébastien is the most wonderful boy in all the world! I'll never forget his kindness to me.'

Remembering those words spoken so long ago, Rosella rose from the bed and wandered slowly over to the window. She looked out at the dark sweep of parkland under the stars. No light shone from Philippe Aubert's villa. There were few stars. She barely noticed, caught up in wondering if that youthful praise of Sébastien given to André Cadel at that particular moment in the carriage had settled her fate. She recalled how she had always asked for news of Sébastien in letters to her grandfather and at subsequent meetings. It must have soon become obvious to him that her childish hero-worship had thrown out romantic shoots with the passing of time, and he had decided to ensure the perfect match for her. How perfectly her grandfather had planned everything. And all in vain.

She turned about slowly and thoughtfully regarded that gilded birdcage of a room. Whether the ghostly drawn-out sob had been in her mind or not, she had heard it. As she had heard screaming in the past. Could there be any truth in the legend that the lady in the west tower only made her spectral presence known when the shadow of some impending disaster fell across the château?

It occurred to her that, for all she knew, some misfortune might have overtaken the family after she had left the château. No word of it had ever reached her, but there was no reason why it should have done, being a child far away at school. Perhaps she should make some enquiries. But from whom? There might be a servant somewhere in the château who would be able to remember. But she must be careful how she found out. It must not arouse suspicion about the reason for her interest.

What did the manifestation mean this time? Was it a warning that the marriage between Sébastien and Claudine should not take place? Or did it go beyond that to some tragedy that had not yet appeared on the horizon?

Unhappily she realized that there was nothing she could do but wait. By being forewarned she must try to avert whatever disaster it was that might come.

CHAPTER FIVE

In the bright morning light Rosella made an exploratory tour of her apartments armed with a notebook and pencil. She intended to call in an architect later, but first she wanted to decide for herself what alterations would suit her best. Salons opened one into another and she discovered many small ante-rooms which she had not known existed. All were in delicate colours, holding the grace and charm of an earlier period, but although her eye appreciated the beauty around her she was unable to shake off a sense of dread each time she turned a handle to enter yet another room. It was the after-effects of the previous night, she told herself sternly, and it was foolish to conjure up a sinister atmosphere in these airy rooms bathed in sunlight.

Determinedly she concentrated on the business in hand and earmarked a butler's pantry to be enlarged to a sizeable kitchen where meals could be prepared both for herself and for occasions when she would entertain. It already had a shaft with a dumbwaiter, but she would have that blocked up, wanting no link with the main kitchens, and she would employ her own chef and be entirely independent.

She would have liked a private entrance into the wing from outside in order to be able to come and go without meeting any of the de Louismonts, but there was the aesthetic aspect to consider, for she would do nothing to change the château with any alterations that would detract from its original coolly beautiful design. It was a point to be discussed with the architect. In the meantime there were two ways out of the tower wing, which occupied the spread of floor above the main west wing, but both meant using the front entrance in the main hall; one way was through the tall doors through which she had entered in the wake of the housekeeper soon after her arrival at the château, and the other exit was down a small staircase with a prettily wrought balustrade that led to the rooms below and was not so convenient to use if these, which included the library and the portrait gallery, were in use. There was a third staircase, shut off by a locked door, which wound down to the base of the tower itself, and she decided to unlock it and investigate.

It was the last thing she wanted to do, but she would not shirk one corner of this wing that was to be her home. Taking a deep breath, she began to descend with a lamp in one hand to light the way, holding the skirt of her dress off the dusty steps with the other. The air smelt stale and undisturbed, and the walls, which were not covered with panelling as they were all the way up to the tower room, were dank and cold to the touch. An oaken door awaited her at the bottom of the flight, and she lifted the wooden latch and gave it a push. It swung slowly inwards with a protesting screech of hinges, sweeping a swathe of thick dust with it from the floor within the room. Nobody could have entered there for a very long time.

She held the lamp high and she saw that the circular room was exactly as hers must have been before being decorated, except that the bare stone walls, hung with cobwebs, rose to a much higher ceiling, the beams black and as ancient as the château itself. Whatever its original use had happened to be, perhaps a store of some kind, it had been taken over many years ago as a dumping place for broken and unwanted furniture. There was the glint of gilded woodwork, some older heavily carved pieces, and several chairs spilling stuffing out of age-blackened, striped silk. Paintings were stacked about wherever there was available space, some swathed in linen, others showing a dusty glaze in the lamplight.

She wrinkled her nose at the odour of mildew and neglect, deciding that there was nothing in the room that she would want, although she might look through the paintings before having all the rubbish cleared out at some future date. Upstairs again she turned the key once more on the tower base, shutting it away with its crumbling contents.

'Marie,' she said later where she sat at a *secrétaire* sealing a letter addressed to Sébastien, which she had written to tell him of the alterations she was planning to make to the tower wing, having decided that it was only courteous to keep him informed. 'I want you to deliver this letter to Monsieur de Louismont.'

'Yes, madame.' Marie took the letter.

'There's something else.' Rosella twisted round in the chair. 'Do you know if there are any servants in the château who have been here more than seven years – that's from the time I was last under this roof? '

'I have no idea, madame, but I can find out.'

'Be discreet,' Rosella instructed. 'I don't want anyone to know that I'm making enquiries.'

Marie showed no surprise. She was learning fast. Eventually she hoped to be taken into Madame's confidence, which was the privilege of ladies' maids who earned their mistresses' trust, and in the meantime she was determined to prove herself worthy.

It did not take Marie long to obtain the answer to her mistress's question. Within half an hour she returned with the desired information. Rosella was still at the *secrétaire*, having written another letter, a long one this time to

Monsieur Bataillard.

'There's not a member of staff who's been at the château as long as seven years, and only a few can tot up four or five,' Marie said, well pleased with herself for having found out all she wanted to know by simply asking, as a newcomer to the staff, who had been in the de Louismonts' employ the longest. 'It's Mam'selle Louise who is the trouble. Nobody can please her. She never stops complaining. They say Miss Sophie was bad enough, but her sister is the tyrant.'

Rosella was not surprised. But it did mean that Louise's ill-temper towards the servants had long since nipped in the bud any chance she might have had to find out if any misfortune had befallen the château after that eerie night of screams. 'Thank you, Marie,' she said, taking up her pen again to sign her letter. But there were footsteps coming along the corridor. A man's footsteps, firm and purposeful. She looked sharply towards the door. 'I have a visitor. Show him in.'

Sébastien had her letter in his bandaged hand. Marie vanished, leaving them alone. Rosella saw the conflicting expressions on his face. Anger mingled with affection, perplexity with hopelessness. He spoke to her in a dry and weary tone.

'Are we to discuss nothing?' He shook the letter at her.

She rose from her chair. 'Do you have some objection to my plans? You have only to say.'

'God in heaven!' He screwed up the letter and hurled it from him with force. 'You're only enlarging the butler's pantry! You can do what you like with it for all I care. It's yours. As the rest of the château is yours. But if you want to tell me your intentions, why write to me? Am I not under the same roof?'

She looked at his eyes and away again. 'I thought it best if we saw each other as infrequently as possible.'

95

He gave a sigh and crossed the length of carpet to reach her. 'And you think that's going to make any difference?'

'I don't understand you,' she said stubbornly.

'You know what has come about between us. Why are you pretending otherwise?'

She lifted her head, her face very grave. 'Nothing new has happened to me. My feelings for you have their roots in the past and can have no part in the present or the future. I am resigned to that and it cannot be otherwise. But you are associating me with your desire to possess the château, which is something entirely different.'

'That's not true!' he protested indignantly.

'It is the truth and you must realize it. I beg you to rid yourself of your confusion — for your sake, for Claudine's, and for mine.'

He took her face gently between his injured hands, his eyes loving. 'I cannot. Never shall I forget yesterday afternoon when you spoke my name and I turned and saw you on the stairs. Somehow I knew you had come back to me, never to leave again.'

'Don't say that!' she cried, frightened. In his words she heard the snap of a trap, the clang of a bolt shot home, the turn of a key that would never unlock. The château was closing its hold on her.

'But surely you realized that my forthcoming marriage to Claudine is one of convenience,' he said with some surprise. 'I'm fond of her and hold her in high esteem, but I don't love her as I know I —'

'Please!' Her fingertips flew to his lips to hold back with a light but frantic touch that which she wanted most to hear. 'You must not speak of love to me. You have no right to betray with words the girl you are to marry, and I have no right to listen to them.'

He encircled her wrists and drew her fingers down from his lips. 'I stand rebuked,' he said with a sad little smile. 'I will be silent. Yet you cannot stop what my heart will say to you.'

His arms went round her, not in violence as on the previous day, but with a quivering tenderness that brought her melting to him. She saw his mouth descending, but her strength seemed to have deserted her, and there was nothing in all the world except his loving nearness, the clean male scent of his skin, the smoothness of his coat as her arms slid about his shoulders to fasten themselves about his neck. His kiss was the sweetest experience she had ever known, a wonderful blending with his lips that sought to know the shape, texture, and mould of hers, not in possession, but as a prelude to unimaginable delights. It was as though their mouths were meeting for the first time and had known no previous encounter.

Only when the kiss came to an end did the world come crashing down on her again and she knew she had committed a great folly. All the ground she had gained was lost. She drew back from him, her hands going behind her to find the edge of the *secrétaire* to which she clung, leaning hard against it.

'That was a mistake and we must forget that it happened,' she said, concealing with visible effort the anguish that racked her. 'I was right in my decision that we should not see each other except in the presence of others, and from now on I shall not be swayed from that. You must not come to the tower wing on your own again. If you do I shall not be at home to you.' Her voice raised slightly in pitch. 'And if you care anything in the name of friendship towards me you will do as I ask.'

'I can make no promises, *chérie*,' he replied ruefully, 'but I will leave you for the moment. The last thing I want is to make you unhappy in any way.'

She thought he was departing without any further delay, but he did a very tender thing. He bent his head and

97

kissed her on both eyelids. Then he did go. She stayed for a long time where she was, hugging her arms, her head bowed in desolation.

That night the eerie cry disturbed her rest again. She lay locked in sleep, curiously unafraid in the dream state that held her secure from all outside it, hearing in the harrowing wail an echo of her own heartache.

In the morning she awoke to a realization of what she had heard. Not just a cry, but weeping. A rising and falling of sound in the irregular rhythm of despairing sorrow that knows no comfort, no hope. She felt her scalp prickle and her mouth went dry. When Marie came in with her breakfast on a tray, announcing that it was another beautiful day, she could not speak and took the cup of hot chocolate poured for her with shaking hands.

She determined to delay no longer in installing Marie in the wing, deciding that the presence of another human being within easy call would do much for her peace of mind and perhaps banish altogether that terrible spectral grief that was drifting to her from a woman who had suffered in that very room centuries before, caught like a lovely bird in a snare. Gradually, soothed by the flavour of the delicious chocolate and calmed by the sight of Marie bustling about in the sunny room, she reached the conclusion that the haunting – for that was what it was! – was due to her solitary state in the tower wing, which was making her too receptive, too vulnerable. Being so shut off from the rest of the château was having its effect. A pull on the bell-rope meant a delay of six or seven minutes before anyone came from the cellar kitchens and longer from anywhere remotely distant, such as a maid or footman coming from Marguerite's apartments in the east wing or the chapel in the north wing or even from the main hall itself. Perhaps sheer inconvenience as much as the legend had caused the west tower wing to have been used so little in the past. She guessed now that she had been accommodated in the tower room on that childhood visit to make sure she was kept in her place and did not make her presence obvious in a household where she was both unwanted and unwelcome.

When Rosella was dressed she left Marie folding away her nightgown and went to the room that she thought would be most suitable for the girl. She had intended that it should be redecorated, for the hand-blocked wallpaper was discoloured and faded, but that must wait for the time being. It was ideally situated, being close to the stairs up to the tower room, and was the right size, being neither large nor too small. She guessed it had been used for music practice in the past, for it contained a harpsichord, which proved sadly out of tune when she ran her finger along it, and in a cupboard she discovered stacks of music sheets, yellow with age. Glass doors opened on to part of the paved walk, which ran parallel to the salons on that side, giving a magnificent view over the battlements. Marie would never have cause to use that paved walk, but it would give her a sense of freedom, and she might like to sit outside her room sometimes on what was virtually a small private patio, for the curve of the tower on one side would be a wind-break and a buttress on the other would shield her from the sight of anyone even a few feet away along the walk.

As Rosella had expected, Marie was delighted at the prospect of moving into the tower wing, feeling that as a lady's maid she should no longer be expected to share quarters with the housemaids. She was excited to see the room chosen for her, and her relief that it was not ornate or grandiose was transparent in her face.

'You should be comfortable here,' Rosella said, standing in the middle of the room. 'The shelves can be removed from the cupboard to provide hanging space for your clothes, and a bed will fit well into that alcove when the harpsichord has been taken away.'

'Might I move in today?' Marie asked breathlessly, darting about on a round of inspection.

Rosella nodded, thankful that she did not have to spend another night alone in the tower wing. Not that she intended to call Marie to her except if she needed help in a dire emergency; nevertheless it was as though a weight had been lifted from her. She summoned the housekeeper and made arrangements for the furniture to be moved into the room that same morning. She also gave instructions that a bell must be connected that same day between the tower room and Marie's new accommodation.

The housekeeper departed. Rosella, who had discussed the matter with her in the salon where Sébastien had come to see her, remembered that the letter to Monsieur Bataillard still lay unsigned on the *secrétaire* where she had left it. Putting her signature to it, she decided to order a carriage and drive into town to post it. There she would consult an architect at the same time.

Lunchtime found her taking some light refreshment at a round table under a striped orange awning outside a café near the market square. All her business was done and the architect, who had showed interest in her ideas for the tower wing, was to visit the château to see it for himself the following day. While she ate she watched the passers-by, many of whom were country folk who had come into town with produce for the market, their faces weathered by hard work, their hands gnarled and horny, and the *sabots* on their feet click-clacked noisily on the cobbles. There were local businessmen with gold watch-chains looped across their waistcoats, pausing to have a word with each other on the corner. A tall priest hurried by, black robes flapping. Delivery boys pushed rumbling hand-carts or carried foodstuffs in large baskets on their arms.

Housewives out shopping gossiped together as they strolled along, and a cluster of little girls in be-ribboned hats went running past bowling hoops.

Suddenly one of the passers-by stopped, recognizing her with a scowl. It was Armand Montargis, Sophie's husband. He came towards her, threading his way between the tables. When he reached her he sat down opposite her without invitation and did not have the grace to raise his hat. He slapped both yellow-gloved hands palm-down on the table and glared at her.

'You played your cards well, I grant you that, Rosella! Not only did you filch the château away from Sébastien, but you saw to it that not a franc went to anyone else!'

She was taken aback by his rudeness, but determined not to be riled by this unpleasant man. 'I gather that Sophie provided you with the information about the will that you tried to discover from me. I have no comment to make. You must think whatever you wish, but in all honesty nobody regrets more than I that things have turned out as they have.'

He gave a derisive snort. 'Don't try to tell me that. I wasn't born yesterday. I know your sort. Out to grab all you can get!'

'Monsieur Montargis!' Rosella gasped. 'How dare you speak to me in such an uncouth manner! Leave my table!'

'Not until I've finished what I have to say.' He leaned across, lowering his voice, aware that he had caused a few heads to turn towards him from the other tables. 'You can put it right for the de Louismonts, particularly as you claim to be so distressed about inheriting all the money.' He rubbed his thumb and forefinger together significantly.

'What do you mean?'

'Give them their rightful share of it. Sophie is entitled to it – after all, the expectation of it was part of her dowry.' His tone became grudging. 'I suppose you'd have to give

Louise the same amount, as well as forking out to Sébastien too, not that I have any time for either of them. Jules and Madame de Louismont need not be considered – she is a foolish spendthrift, which is where Jules gets his weakness over cards and horses, so it would be throwing money down the drain to give anything to either of them. But Sophie –'

Rosella was aghast at his audacity. Had André Cadel anticipated something like this forthcoming from some direction, and was that why he had tied everything up so securely? Until she married or came of age, any amount of money above a normal requirement had to be approved by Monsieur Bataillard. 'I asked you to go from this table,' she said, interrupting him. 'There is nothing I wish to discuss with you.'

An ugly crimson crept up his jowls and spread across the bridge of his nose. Slowly he wagged a threatening finger at her. 'You'll regret getting the wrong side of me! I want Sophie's share of the Cadel inheritance and I mean to get it.' He flung the chair back from him as he sprang to his feet, scraping the legs across the tiles with a screech. Swinging his heavy frame round he thumped away from her back to the pavement and was soon lost from sight in the crowd.

She told herself that his threat was an idle one and there was nothing he could do. But he was a dangerous man and unscrupulous too. The remaining portion of the omelette on her plate was cold and her appetite had gone. She paid the bill and gathered up her gloves and purse. Armand was unaware that she had posted a letter that day to Monsieur Bataillard asking him about the chances of being able to recompense the de Louismonts for their disappointment, but if it could be arranged she had no intention of leaving out Marguerite or Jules no matter how they chose to dispose of their money.

She barely slept that night, keeping the lamp alight and starting up in bed at every creak of furniture or floor-board, but the tower gave forth no uncanny sound to her acutely listening ear. It was almost as though the tower were holding its breath. Watching. Waiting. Biding its own menacing time. Only temporarily set back by her no longer being completely alone in the wing.

The architect, when he came, soon decided that the alterations were simple and straightforward, presenting no problem. She discussed having her own front door to link up with the staircase that went down to the main wing, but he was openly reluctant to replace a window with a door, pointing out that it would spoil the perfect symmetry of the west walls outside, and she was forced to agree with him. In any case she doubted that Louise would care for it, for the location of it would be near her salon windows, and Rosella had no intention of enforcing her own authority on an issue that could cause endless trouble. She must let it ride for the time being.

While she and the architect were discussing the matter at the foot of the stairs near the window in question, she saw Philippe Aubert come across the lawn from the direction of the woodland and the river where he must have crossed by his usual route of the stepping stones, which he had mentioned to her that evening in the garden-room. She wondered when the opportunity might arise for that talk about her grandfather, which he had promised later on that same day. Although she was paying attention to the architect's talk she continued to watch Philippe through the window out of the corner of her eye. He was carrying a small bunch of purple violets.

Even as she watched Louise appeared, hurrying to meet him. He did not raise the violets to present them when Louise drew near, but kept them dangling in his hand. Only when she came level with him, making some exclamation over the nosegay did he lift it instantly and give it to her. She buried her nose in its fragrant depths, acting coquettishly, giving little ripples of laughter. When she linked her arm in his and they continued on towards the château together Rosella had the impression that he had not intended those violets for Louise, but innate good manners had prevented him from disappointing her. Couldn't Louise see that Philippe was not a man to be chased? She herself knew little enough about men, Sébastien having been the only man she had ever kissed, but she was discovering that she had an instinct in such matters. Philippe was too vital and strong-willed to want a woman ever seeking to control and dominate, which was Louise's whole aim with whoever she met, no matter how hard she might try to hide it from any one person whom she was particularly eager to please. Philippe would meet on equal terms in love, but the pursuit must be his and he the captor.

The two of them passed from Rosella's sight. The architect was saying that the work could not take long to complete.

'Nevertheless I do not want to commence until after Monsieur de Louismont's wedding,' she said, retracing her steps back to the tower wing at his side. 'The presence of workmen always causes a certain amount of upheaval, no matter how minor the operation in hand.'

'When is the marriage to take place?' he enquired.

She had heard the date mentioned for the first time by Louise at the dinner party. Sébastien had glanced quickly at her under his dark lashes, and it was as though that utterance by his sister continued to vibrate in the air between them. Like a death knell.

'It's in a week and a day,' she said. 'On May 30th.' And she knew it was a date that she would remember all her life.

Unexpectedly she found Jules waiting to see her when the architect had departed. He had sprawled his long, bony body in a winged chair, one leg hanging over the arm of it, hands behind his head, cigar in mouth. She saw at once that he had been drinking heavily.

'Want to buy a horse?' he asked bluntly without any preliminaries, speaking with the careful articulation of the very drunk.

'I'm not sure,' she said cautiously.

'You ride, don't you?'

'Yes, but – '

'Then you need a horse.' He removed the cigar from his mouth and the ash crumbled down his waistcoat. 'It's no good thinking you can take your pick of the stables. There are limits to what is yours in this establishment, y'know. Apart from the carriage horses, all the nags in the stables are Sébastien's own. He's bred them. You'll find no finer horses in the whole of France.'

'And the one you have for sale?'

'The prettiest bay you've ever seen.'

'Who owns it?'

'I do. I've had it a couple of months, but it doesn't suit me. Not enough spirit. I like a fight on my hands when I take on a new horse.'

That de Louismont streak of cruelty. That lust for domination. For complete possession. Rosella recalled what Marguerite had said about the de Louismont males. Even Sébastien had inherited the same explosive temperament.

'I'll look at the horse,' she said.

'No time like the present.' He lurched up from the chair and stood swaying slightly. 'Why not change into something you can ride in and try it out.'

It would be pleasant to have her own horse and have the freedom to explore the surrounding countryside at will.

'I'll put on my riding habit,' she said.

When she walked with Jules to the stables she saw a little group gathered near the trees on the lawn. Philippe and Louise were sitting with Marguerite at a garden table on which coffee and cakes had been served. Sophie was also there, making her daily visit to the château to see her mother.

The bay was beautiful and she loved it on sight. Its mane and tail wafted when Jules brought it from the stall, and its coat was as glossy as red-brown silk. He walked it round for her in the yard, but he was not at all steady on his feet and dragged at the bit, causing the animal to jerk its head unhappily, eyes rolling, hooves dancing. Jules swore at it viciously, and she shuddered to think what he must be like in the saddle with a whip in his hand. She knew she had to buy the bay, if only to free it from its present owner.

'What's his name?' she enquired, patting the splendid neck. The velvet nostrils were flaring wildly.

'Talleyrand.'

'How much?'

He named a high price, but she did not bargain. Monsieur Bataillard would not quibble over it. Jules helped her into the saddle and she settled herself, talking to Talleyrand, knowing that the highly-strung horse was upset and nervous. It swung its head up and down and side-stepped, and she guessed that Talleyrand associated a rider with ill-treatment and rough hands. Its superb physical condition was no credit to Jules, for it would be Sébastien's grooms who were responsible for that.

There was an oddly malevolent grin on Jules's face as he hung swaying on the bridle, looking up at her. 'Enjoy your ride, Rosella.'

'Thank you. Let go of the bridle, please.'

'With pleasure.' He lurched back. 'I'll give you a send-off!'

Before she realized what he was doing he gave a great yell, flashing a whip out of his coat-tail pocket, which he brought down with a tremendous cut across the horse's rump. It hurled itself forward with a snorting leap that nearly threw her from the saddle, but she had had a similar experience once before in Kent when a boy, using a rattle to frighten birds off the fruit-trees, had created a sudden clatter that had caused her horse to take fright. But that had been a much older horse, chosen for a schoolgirl to ride because of its age and docility, and it had had less speed and taken less alarm than Talleyrand.

Out of the stableyard thundered the bay, mane and tail streaming, scattering two grooms who had come from a coach-house to see what the noise had been about. Across the lawns it raced, sending up clods of green turf, while Rosella hung on to the reins, desperately trying to gain control. Out of the corner of her eye she saw the consternation of the little coffee-party at the sight of her. Philippe leapt to his feet, shouting something that she could not hear, and the three women rose too in airy flutter of chiffon and shady hats.

The formal gardens approached. Flowers and leaves were ground back into the earth as Talleyrand bolted through, ignoring the pulling hands on the reins as though he were riderless. Rosella's hat had gone flying off, and her hair, which had tumbled in a cascade down her back, was whirling out behind her. She was extremely frightened, but she kept her head and concentrated on keeping her seat and ducking down with a lightning reaction whenever a branch looked too low for safety. Only when she saw a narrow arm of the lake spreading out its carpet of water-lilies ahead did she see a new danger being added to the hazards of the nightmare ride. The placid gleam of the water swept towards them with a terrifying swiftness. She felt Talleyrand preparing himself for a jump, the steely muscles and sinews gathering together for a leap that could not possibly take them to the other side.

'No! No! No!' she screamed.

There was one dazzling second of hope when she thought they were going to make it, but Talleyrand fell short with an explosion of water, rolling over in the shallow depths where the bank sloped, throwing her into mud and water-lilies and weeds. She lay stunned with the impact of the fall, the upper part of her body in the squelching mud, her heavy skirt spread out under the surface of the water, rippling in the churning wavelets caused by Talleyrand's thrashing about as he struggled to regain his footing. Once up, he lost no time in reaching the grassy summit of the bank where he stood with water dripping down him, his muscles trembling, his head low. Making an effort she stirred herself, but found her waterlogged skirt almost impossible to manipulate, and she was frustrated by her weakness.

Other hoof-beats drew near. Philippe, having met a groom setting out in pursuit of the run-away, had taken his horse from him, ordering him to fetch another, and had come after her. He hurled himself out of the saddle and scrambled down the bank to her.

'You're ruining your shoes,' she said, half-laughing, half-crying.

He was overwhelmingly relieved to see that she appeared to have suffered no hurt beyond a few bruises, for there was no evidence of any broken bones in her attempts to rise.

'I'll help you. Put your arm around my neck. That's right.' He lifted her bodily and set her on the grass, scrambling up after her.

She was on her feet at once, her thoughts only with

Talleyrand, and she soothed and patted him, speaking softly and reassuringly all the time. Finally she leaned her cheek against the wet curve of the bay's neck. 'Nobody is ever going to hurt you again, Talleyrand. I swear it!'

The groom had arrived and he came to see what he could do to help. When she heard Philippe say that he should lead Talleyrand quietly back to the stables, Rosella intervened.

'No!' she stated firmly. 'I'll walk him back myself.'

Philippe did not argue with her. He handed over the reins of the horse he had ridden to the groom and fell into step at her side, matching her leisurely pace. 'Why were you riding Jules's horse? He's had a lot of trouble with it, I believe.'

'I'm not surprised,' she answered. 'He's the sort of man who should never be allowed in the saddle. But he won't be able to ill-treat Talleyrand again. I've bought him.'

Philippe raised a thick brow. 'Have you indeed? What made him bolt?'

She released a little sigh. 'Jules gave him a whack and yelled like a banshee. It was his idea of a joke. He has a most perverted sense of humour.'

'A joke!' Philippe exclaimed incredulously. 'You could have ended your life a few minutes ago with a broken neck!'

She did not want to think about that and tried to turn it aside with a light if somewhat macabre remark. 'Then Sébastien would have inherited the château and everybody would have been happy.'

The significance of what she had said hit both of them at the same time. She slowed her already slow pace almost to a standstill and their eyes met on a shaft of uneasy doubt.

She dismissed it instantly. 'It was a joke,' she repeated. 'I know Jules of old. And he had been drinking.'

They wandered on, but the thrust of Philippe's frown did not leave his brow. 'Drinking or not,' he said with an anger directed towards the absent practical joker, 'there is no excuse for such irresponsible behaviour. I'll speak to him about it.'

'I'd prefer that you didn't, Philippe. I don't want an issue made of it. Please.'

'Whatever you say,' he acquiesced reluctantly. 'But I wonder if you realize that you've landed yourself in a wasps' nest, Rosella?'

She smiled grimly to herself at his comparison. She had thought of the de Louismonts as caged tigers. But in their own way wasps could be just as deadly. 'Don't worry about me. I became immune to wasps' stings when I was here before.'

'I hope so.'

Only then did it dawn on her that he had included Louise in his overall description simply by not making an exception of her by name. It was hardly what one would expect from a man emotionally entangled. Or was it that the romantic feeling was all on Louise's side and his neighbourly friendliness had been misconstrued?

'I shall ride Talleyrand again tomorrow – if he's none the worse for his ducking,' she said, changing the subject. 'Or at least as soon as I can be sure that he trusts me.'

'What time would you set out?'

'I haven't thought. In the morning perhaps.'

'May I ride with you?'

She misunderstood the reason for his request. 'That's most kind of you, but I'll be perfectly all right. Talleyrand won't bolt again. He'll be quiet enough when he's treated properly.'

Philippe looked amused. 'I do not doubt it, but that was not why I asked. It's your company I want to share. As a matter of fact I intended to see you sometime this afternoon.'

'Did you?' she said casually, but she was remembering the violets. Could he have meant them for her?

'I'm arranging a party to go to the races the day after tomorrow and I'd be honoured if you would join us. Not that you haven't done a full share of racing yourself this afternoon!' he added wickedly.

They laughed together. She was sorely tempted to accept, but the party would most certainly include Louise and perhaps even Sébastien. 'Thursday,' she said ruminatively as though her days were crammed with commitments.

'Do say you'll come. We always have a picnic with champagne and cold game and usually round off the day having dinner together somewhere.'

She was filled with longing to go, but she dared not. Then she remembered that she did have an engagement. It was one of the invitations that had come by post after the dinner party. She was to attend a ladies' gathering.

'I cannot, Philippe,' she said with a regret that was genuine. 'I have a previous engagement.'

His face reflected his disappointment. 'I'm sorry. At least say that we can go riding in the morning.'

That was something else she must not do. He and Louise must sort out their own affairs. She would not become involved. 'I cannot promise. I must see how Talleyrand reacts to me. If he is still in an unpredictable mood it would be folly to take him out.'

'I agree, naturally,' he said, accepting the rebuff good-naturedly.

They had reached the lawn where the three de Louismont women waited at the garden table. They had received an account of what had happened from the groom who had returned with the spare horse, and Louise, seeing Rosella's bedraggled appearance, hid a laugh behind her hand and turned to Sophie to make some tittering comment. Fresh coffee had been served, but Marguerite was the only one to offer it.

'What a fall you had, Rosella!' Marguerite clasped her hands in agitation and rose to leave her own chair vacant. 'Sit down. Have some coffee.'

'I must get changed, Madame de Louismont,' Rosella said. 'The lake was icy cold.'

'Yes. You are quite right. You could catch a chill. Even pneumonia.' Yet she did not move aside, continuing to stare with distressed, dilated eyes at Rosella. 'I was thrown once through taking a fence that was too high. It was a terrible fall. They said such falls are often fatal.' She gave a shuddering sigh. 'It was for my poor mare – Pierre had to shoot her.'

'I'm so sorry,' Rosella said sympathetically.

Philippe touched her arm. 'Let me see Talleyrand into his stall. The grooms will take care of him. You go and put on some dry clothes.'

She gave him a grateful smile and left Talleyrand in his charge, hurrying across the lawn and up the steps into the château as best she could in her soaked outfit. Of Jules there was no sign. She supposed he was sleeping off his drunken state somewhere.

Talleyrand seemed none the worse for his misadventure the following day, but Rosella decided it would be wiser to postpone an outing for a few days in order that he could get to know her. She took him sugar lumps and stood in the stall talking to him, stroking his soft nose, certain with each visit that she was making progress. Jules was completely forgiven for his unpleasant joke, simply because he had been instrumental in enabling her to become the owner of such a beautiful animal.

She had come down the main staircase on her way to the stables again when Louise appeared in the doorway of one of the salons, the light behind her catching the sheen of her patterned gown.

'Rosella! Could you spare a moment?'

Rosella followed her into the salon, a light, enchanting room with Watteau frescoes, the furniture fragile in its eighteenth-century elegance. Louise picked up a large, white envelope, which she tapped against her fingers.

'Firstly I have to tell you that there will be a seat in the carriage for you with *Maman* and myself on the wedding day. We shall ride to and from the church together.'

'But I cannot go,' Rosella protested, appalled at the thought of having to attend. 'I should be an intruder.'

'Nonsense! Everyone will expect you to be there.' She handed over the envelope. 'This special invitation to the wedding is for you. Claudine came over in a carriage with it herself.'

'She's here?'

Louise nodded. 'She went to find Sébastien, but she wants to see you before she leaves.'

'I should think I'd be the last person she'd want to meet.'

'On the contrary. Claudine is not one to bear malice. She will eventually inherit enough wealth to keep her and Sébastien in luxury for the rest of their days, but she understands that it goes against his pride not to be able to match those expectations with the inheritance he had always assumed would be his. It must have been hard for him to break the news to the Comte, for there is no liking between them. Needless to say, there'll be no helping hand forthcoming from the Comte to provide some other mansion for my unfortunate brother and his bride. It is as well that you decided to content yourself with the west tower wing and want no more of the château than that.'

'Has Sébastien no fortune at all of his own?'

Louise's face relaxed into a mirthless smile. 'None of us has two sous to rub together. Papa was involved in a disastrous business gamble when a heart attack killed him, and his debts took a long time to settle. After that Sébastien ploughed everything that came in back into the estate. Even Sophie was counting on benefiting handsomely from Cousin André's will. Her lack of a sizeable dowry was buoyed up by what she thought she would receive, and in any case Sébastien would have allotted a generous portion to each of us if we had not been mentioned individually and the whole of Cousin André's fortune had passed entirely into his hands.' She gave a snort. 'Never did we imagine that things would turn out so disastrously. Armand has not taken kindly to the present situation. He is an avaricious, parsimonious devil.'

'Why did Sophie marry him?' Rosella asked.

Louise shrugged. 'Like most men – particularly widowers – he was not tight-fisted when he played the suitor. His first wife died childless two or three years ago, and I understand he was much sought after by husband-hunting ladies of his own age. But Sophie, being young and pretty and a de Louismont into the bargain, was much more to his liking. The man has no breeding, you know. A merchant who has made enough money to buy a position in certain circles of society and thought to clinch a more elevated place by marrying into one of the oldest families in France.' She let her shoulders rise and fall again. 'But there. She would not be talked out of marrying him, and having made her own bed she must lie on it. Or perhaps I should say,' she added with unexpected frankness, 'that she lies on it when she must. Sophie is disillusioned by marriage. It is not what she expected.'

As Louise finished speaking a girl's clear voice called out in the hall, easily heard through the half-open doors of the salon. 'Sébastien! I've been looking everywhere for you.'

Sébastien answered on a surprised note, his footsteps coming down the stairs to her. 'What are you doing here, Claudine?'

'I came to deliver Rosella's invitation. But tell me, how are your hands?'

'Almost completely healed.' Together their footsteps approached the salon.

Louise turned to face the doors. 'Now you can meet Claudine, Rosella. The new bride-to-be of the château.'

Rosella stood very still. The moment she had dreaded had come. She saw the double doors thrust open wide by Sébastien's arm reaching in front of Claudine, and they entered side by side. Sébastien's eyes met Rosella's instantly, and there swept into them a look as dark and tormented and tragic as that which lurked in her own. Then Claudine innocently broke their locked gaze, coming between their line of vision in a shy little rush of movement towards Rosella, a hesitant smile on her face, which was as delicately coloured and as classically moulded as that of any of the Watteau ladies who frolicked genteelly on the walls around them. She had the same starry daintiness, her pale arched eyebrows suggesting surprise at life's goodness to her, her pearly-fair hair drawn back smoothly into a cascade of ringlets under her rose-trimmed bonnet. She was beautiful and young and touchingly vulnerable.

'We need no introduction, Rosella,' she said in her soft tones. 'I've been looking forward to meeting you ever since I heard that we are to reside under the same roof. I trust that we shall be good friends.' She leaned forward and kissed Rosella on both cheeks.

Rosella felt a rush of grateful warmth towards her. There was no doubting Claudine's complete sincerity. Louise had been right in saying she would bear no grudge, but such generosity of spirit could only denote a truly exceptional character.

'I welcome your kindness to me,' Rosella said sincerely, 'all the more since you have every cause to resent my presence here.'

Claudine's light blue eyes expanded. 'But *you* are the one who has shown such overwhelming goodness of heart towards us! We have so much to thank you for. I shall never forget that you have allowed my dear Sébastien to go on living in the château that means so much to him. For that alone I am for ever in your debt.' She touched with an outstretched fingertip the unopened invitation, which Rosella still held in her hands. 'Knowing you are at our wedding will add to my happiness that day. Tell me you'll be there.'

A sickening lurch of misery tightened Rosella's throat and her answer came haltingly. 'I'll be there.'

Out of the corner of her eye she saw Sébastien's bandaged hands fall limply to his sides. It was an unconscious gesture of complete resignation to fate's deviousness.

'That's settled then,' Louise said briskly. She slid an arm through Claudine's with a show of friendliness that shut out Rosella. '*Maman* is waiting to see you. We shall take a cup of lemon tea with her in her salon in the east wing.'

'How is she?' Claudine fell into slow step with her future sister-in-law.

'A little tired after the final fitting for the gown she is to wear at your wedding. But I don't doubt that the dressmaker and her assistants are equally exhausted. Whenever *Maman* makes demands in that fragile, disarming way of hers, everybody falls over themselves to please her, even – as in this case – if it means practically remaking the whole gown.' Louise gave a wry laugh. 'When my father was alive it was exactly the same – he doted on her.

She has no idea what it means not to be loved and adored.'

'Madame de Louismont is most fortunate,' Claudine agreed without envy, her attitude that of one wholly secure in love herself.

Louise's eyes slid towards her brother. 'But Sébastien is the only one she adores and dotes on in turn.' Mockingly. 'Isn't that so, Sébastien?'

'You exaggerate everything, Louise,' he replied with a frown. '*Maman* has always cared for each one of us.'

'I'm sure she has!' Claudine was too wrapped up in her own happiness to see the old friction between brother and sister. She turned and held out a hand to Rosella. 'You're joining us for tea, aren't you?'

'I'm on my way to the stables,' Rosella said in tactful refusal, knowing that Louise did not intend that she should be included in the tea-party.

'How are you after your unfortunate experience yesterday, Rosella?' Sébastien asked her.

'Completely recovered,' she answered.

'What happened?' Claudine enquired with concern.

'My horse bolted. I ended up in the lake,' Rosella told her with a smile.

'I'll tell you all about it over tea, Claudine,' Louise said, dismissing the incident. Then she paused with her in the doorway to address Sébastien, who had made no move to follow them. 'Aren't you coming?'

'Of course.' He tore his gaze away from Rosella and went after them.

Slowly Rosella opened the envelope and took out the wedding invitation. The Comte de Vailly requested the pleasure of her company at the marriage of his daughter to the man she loved. And who loved her. The invitation and the envelope sailed gently to the floor. She stood with both hands covering her face, tearless, but needing to be shut in with the anguish that racked her like a physical pain.

In the night Rosella was jolted from sleep, in spite of the velvet silence prevailing, knowing instantly that the ghostly weeping had occurred again. Was it caused by her own emotional distress? Were her own heart-pangs linking her empathetically with that long-ago occupant of the tower room who had met death there alone and in despair?

She lay, frightened and chilled, wishing desperately that when day came there could be someone in whom she might confide her terror of the unknown. But there was no one that she could turn to, not even pleasant little Marie who waited on her so efficiently and willingly, happy almost to the point of having her head turned, her pride in her new position giving her a self-confidence that had been lacking before. Rosella was determined not to have that new assurance undermined by any fear of the tower, even though the haunting cries seemed directed for her ears alone.

When dawn broke she rose and went down to the stables, surprising a sleepy groom dousing his head under a pump, who ran wet-haired to saddle Talleyrand for her. She rode out on the bay for the first time since he had bolted, his coat a glowing copper in the sunrise. It was a perfect ride. She felt that Talleyrand was her only true friend in all the world.

On the eve of Sébastien's marriage to Claudine, Rosella postponed going to bed and wandered restlessly in and out of the salons in the west tower wing. In a few hours Sébastien would be gone from her. Gone from her to a bride whom he did not love. She pressed her clenched fists against her cheeks, admitting to herself at last that she had cherished a rebellious hope that he would come to realize that he could not go through with it. Yet she knew Sébastien better than that. His word was his bond and it was not the threat of scandal that held him to it, but his own sense of honour, no matter how great the personal sacrifice that resulted from it. Perhaps in years to come men would scoff at such high ideals, but the world would be a poorer place for it.

'Would you like a hot drink, madame?' Marie enquired, appearing in a doorway.

Rosella turned in time to see her maid hastily stifling a yawn and took pity on her tiredness, becoming aware of how late the hour had grown. 'I need nothing, Marie. Go to bed. I will go when I am ready. There is no point in your sitting up any longer.'

When Marie had gone, thankful to be released from duty, Rosella went out through one of the pairs of glass doors that opened on to the paved walk along the battlements. It was a night full of stars. Only a soft breeze played with the trees. Tomorrow was destined to be a balmy day for the wedding ceremony.

She sank down on one of the white wrought-iron chairs set out on the paved walk and rested her elbows on a lower part of the castellated wall, her chin in her hands. Sébastien. Sébastien. Sébastien. Her heart throbbed out her love for him with every despairing beat.

How long she sat there she did not know. She did not look at the clock when she eventually went up to the tower room and undressed and climbed into bed, but it was already far into Sébastien's wedding day. She lay on her side, her cheek resting on the back of one hand set in the softness of the pillow, and looked with wide-awake eyes at the patch of starry sky revealed by the window, doubting that sleep would ever come.

Then she heard it. At first it was no more than an almost inaudible whimper, making her think it was her imagination. But gradually the unmistakable sound of the mournful weeping grew more pronounced and she knew for certain that it had not been a dream on those previous occasions, and neither was it her own imagination now. It was there! In the room with her!

She lay perfectly still, scarcely daring to breathe, her pulses racing, while she strained her ears trying fearfully to locate exactly the direction of that spine-chilling lament. But it seemed to hang trembling in the air all about her, almost palpable, creating the illusion that if she dared to lift her head it would brush clingingly against her face and drape itself on her hair like floating cobwebs. Ice-cold.

Frantically she crushed down that particular horror and slowly raised herself on one elbow. The tragic wailing did not abate. Silently she put her feet to the floor and rose from the bed. She did not light the lamp, but waited until her eyes had adjusted to the dark azure gloom of the night before moving cautiously into the centre-point of the circular room. There she gave an involuntary gasp, pressing her hands over her thudding heart, when the weeping reached a little crescendo and then faded away to silence.

'Don't go,' she whispered falteringly. 'There must be something I can do to help you find peace and rest.'

Somewhere away in the trees an owl hooted, the pale curtains at the open window stirring gently in the warm night breeze, but the weeping was stilled. It was as though the tower had folded its secret into itself once again. Yet Rosella did not move from where she was standing, her taut senses telling her that some new turbulence was silently abroad in the quiet night.

Motionless she waited. Seconds ticked by. Then she almost fainted with shock and gruesomeness of what she heard. The shivering scratch of a fingernail ran down the wall outside her door!

She could not move her shuddering limbs, her mouth and throat curiously dry. Then with an effort of will she did not know she possessed, she forced herself haltingly forward to answer that terrifying summons. Reaching the door she slowly turned the handle and went reluctantly through into the deeper darkness at the head of the stairs.

'Yes? Where are you?' she heard herself whisper. But nothing stirred and the silence held her in a vacuum.

Putting her arms out to guide herself with palms flat against the walls on each side of her, Rosella began the descent, pointing her toes to lower her feet on to one stair and then the other. And suddenly the next stair in the black well was no longer there. Her foot went down and down into a void until she jerked it back instinctively, throwing herself backwards in an effort to keep her balance, pressing her weight against her hands. But it was too late. She fell, crashing against the curving wall, slithering in a crumpled heap to the other side, and then down, down, down, her arms thrown up to protect her head until she landed at the bottom of the flight, hurled by the force of her fall into a sprawling heap on the floor, her bruised cheek coming to rest on the polished boards.

Then she screamed and screamed.

Somewhere a door opened. Dancing lamplight banished the darkness as Marie came rushing from her room. 'Madame!' she shrieked at the sight of Rosella lying in a twisted tangle of limbs and nightgown. She came flying to throw herself down on her knees beside her mistress. 'Dear God! What happened?'

Rosella clutched at her maid's arm and struggled to sit up. 'Marie, I fell. I fell!'

'Not the whole flight!' Marie exclaimed in acute alarm. 'Don't move. Stay exactly as you are. I'll summon help.'

'No!' Rosella cried. But she was too late. Marie had sprung up and was tugging hard at a nearby bell-rope.

'A doctor must be sent for, madame,' Marie said, crouching down beside her again. 'This fall coming so quickly after your being thrown from your horse could have unforeseen consequences. The footmen shall carry

121

you back to bed – '

'No!' Rosella thumped the floor with a fist in her agitation. 'I don't want anyone to know I've had this fall.' She began an attempt to rise.

'Oh, please, madame!' Marie begged, trying to restrain her. 'No one shall see you in your nightgown. I'll fetch a robe.'

'Didn't you hear what I said?' Rosella demanded with rising impatience, thrusting Marie's pressing hands from her shoulders. 'You must obey me in this matter. Assist me to my feet. At once.'

'You might have broken some bones. Have patience. It could be dangerous.'

Rosella gritted her teeth obstinately, dragging her limbs together, and without Marie's assistance which she kept at bay with an outstretched arm, she staggered to her feet. No sharp dagger of pain told of a snapped rib or a cracked bone, and she sighed with relief although she ached with bruises from head to toe.

'There!' she said with satisfaction. 'You see. I'm perfectly all right. Now I'll sit down out of sight while you send away whoever comes to answer that bell. Afterwards you shall help me back to bed.' She turned to stumble away towards the double doors of the nearest salon.

'What excuse shall I make for ringing?' Marie asked, close to panic. She had not lost her awe of the footmen, even though she had seen them below stairs in their humble fustian jackets going about other less exalted tasks than that of springing to answer bells in a straightening of white bow tie and a flash of dark-blue coat-tails. She did not think that any of those on night-duty would be less than truculent at being summoned from a comfortable doze to cover the stairs and corridors up to the west tower wing for no good reason at all.

'Use your imagination,' Rosella answered wearily, putting a hand to her throbbing head, 'but be careful what you say.'

In the salon she sank down into the first chair, leaning back against the brocaded upholstery and closing her eyes, trying to analyse her fall. She had slipped. She had misjudged the distance between the stairs in the darkness. There could be no other explanation. But thrusting itself forward came the chill thought that she had been lured into a death-trap set by a presence that had become hostile to her. But why? What had she done? And what trouble was she storing up for herself? But whatever happened she would not move from the tower room. She must face out the danger that lurked there.

Marie's voice reached her. A footman had arrived. 'Fetch some brandy. Madame isn't feeling very well — oh! and some ice.'

'Ice? With brandy?'

'She has a headache. I'm going to make an ice-bag to put on her forehead. Bring plenty of it.'

Rosella opened her eyes, waiting for Marie to widen the triangle of light that showed through the door, and was suddenly afraid to be alone in the shadowed salon. Darting wary looks about her, she sprang up from the chair, ignoring the pains that tore at every muscle, and made for the door.

The sight of Marie calmed her again and she nodded thankfully, putting her hand on the maid's arm. 'You did very well. Bring the lamp. I'm going back to my room.'

Rosella looked at every step when they went slowly up the flight together. The old stairs were uneven, the stone worn almost saucer-shaped, but she would not have fallen if that terrifying sensation of space opening up under her had not caused her to lose her balance.

'When the ice comes I'll put it against your bruises,' Marie said, helping her into bed. 'There is nothing better.'

123

But in spite of Marie's ministrations there was dark bruising on Rosella's arms, legs, and body when morning came. Thankful that she had managed to protect her face during the fall, she decided that she must wear a gown other than the one with short sleeves, which she had intended to wear to the wedding. At least she was not too stiff in her muscles to walk, as she had feared she might be, and nobody would suspect what had happened to her.

'But are you sure you feel like going?' Marie asked doubtfully, lifting away the breakfast tray.

'I must be there,' Rosella said, propped against her pillows. She had made a promise to Claudine and she would keep it.

Marie stood with the tray in her hands. 'Could I say something, madame?'

'Yes?'

'I've heard the legend of the tower. Every new servant hears it, although the housekeeper likes to keep it hushed up, and it's more than anyone's job is worth to mention it in her presence. I think I understand why you don't want word of your fall to leak out. You have no wish to start foolish rumours circulating about your being struck down while running in fright from your room or anything like that, and never shall I open my lips on it. But please tell me, did you see anything?'

'No, Marie.'

'Did you hear anything?'

'Yes, Marie. But I wasn't running away from — whatever it was. I was hoping to meet it.'

'On the stairs?'

'I don't know. Perhaps I did in a way. I cannot be sure. In fact, I'm not sure of anything. Atmosphere lies heavy in this part of the wing. Why do you ask?' Rosella felt a sinking of the heart. 'Does it mean that you no longer wish to stay in the old music room near me?'

Marie raised her eyebrows in surprise at the question. 'No, madame. The lady in the tower would harm no one.'

Rosella leaned forward curiously. 'Why are you so sure?'

'I've seen her. Days before you arrived from Paris. On my first evening at the château.'

Rosella sank back again into the pillows. 'Put that tray down.' She indicated a chair. 'Sit down and tell me about it.'

Marie told her. Apparently it was an established practical joke among the servants to regale a newcomer with a horrific version of the tower legend and then send that person into the west wing with a candle on some trumped-up task, such as testing the bells.

'I was scared. I don't mind admitting it. A kitchen-boy as scared as I was had been given a duplicate key to open the wing for me. The whole place was shuttered. I had to pull each bell-rope, and they were watching in the kitchen to make sure I didn't miss one. The tower room was included, of course. I found the bell there, gave it a tug, and left again. I reached the bottom of the stairs and I don't know what made me, but I glanced back. And for a second — no more! — there was a shadowy figure of a man in a kind of cloak half-way down the flight with a lady in his arms, but she wasn't dead. The nobleman came back in time to save his wife. I'm sure of it, no matter if the legend is told otherwise.'

'A trick of the candlelight, Marie. Your imagination heightened by the tales you'd heard.'

Marie shook her head, her smile serene. 'Oh, no. Below stairs they'd told me that she'd starved to death with her tongue hanging out and all kinds of horrors. But that's not true. There's nothing to be afraid of in the wing itself or the tower. I know. I never told the others what I'd seen, but I had my own joke on them, seeing how surprised they were when I returned to the kitchen as calm as you like and said it would take more than their tales to frighten me.'

'You saw what you had wanted to see,' Rosella said quietly, knowing Marie's romantic turn of mind, her insatiable appetite for novelettes of the more lurid kind. Knights and ladies frequently appeared on the covers.

'Perhaps I did,' Marie admitted, 'but better that than to scare myself out of my wits.' There was an implied reproof in her words. 'If you allow yourself to think there is evil at work in the tower, then you must find some other reason for it than the lady in the legend — and what else is there? If there'd been any other horrible tale connected with the wing I'd have heard it that night when the servants sent me up here, you can be sure of that. Oh, no.' She shook her head firmly, picking up the tray again. 'You had an ordinary fall last night. No doubt at all about that. Why not stay in bed this morning and rest? Then you will feel more ready to face the wedding and all the excitement this afternoon. Is it to be the almond pink chambray gauze with the silk floss embroidery? I'll come back and see if it needs a last-minute press. You'll put the bride in the shade in that, madame!'

CHAPTER SIX

When the marriage ceremony was over Rosella stepped up in the open landau and took her seat again opposite Louise. Marguerite, although she had accompanied them to the church, had been whisked off to the reception at the side of the Comte de Vailly in his carriage, which had been the first to follow in the wake of the bride and groom.

Louise, nodding and giving little white-gloved waves of recognition to other guests awaiting their own carriages, settled back for the short journey to the de Vailly mansion. She made no attempt at conversation with Rosella, keeping her eyes coldly averted, and they rode in silence, their parasols, which dipped gently up and down with the movement of the landau, streaming frills and ribbons.

Rosella had anticipated such a show of animosity, knowing that the family's resentment and bitter jealousy must surely reach new heights on Sébastien's wedding day, which was to have been such a triumphant occasion for both the de Louismonts and the de Vaillys. Sophie had acknowledged her in church for the sake of appearances, giving her a cutting smile, and Armand had bowed with a belligerent politeness before taking his place beside his wife in the pew. Jules, acting as Sébastien's *garçon d'honneur*, had not as much as glanced in her direction. It was the first time she had set eyes on him since the day he had sold her Talleyrand, and she was certain that the swift payment, which she had requested from Monsieur

Bataillard, not wishing to have the offer withdrawn, had gone through, or else Jules would have come to her to know the reason why.

Marguerite, dignified and gentle-mannered, had behaved towards Rosella as on any other day, but she was withdrawn behind that vague, slightly unfocused gaze that had seemingly become natural to her over the years, the beautiful planes of her face serene as though she had put all that she found distressing and disturbing completely away from her. Rosella, filled with compassion, understood that she had given herself up to the pleasures of the day, not daring to allow herself to dwell on the dark and terrible aspects of it, which denied the chance of any real happiness to her much beloved son.

Sébastien himself, grave, composed, turning her heart over with the breadth of his shoulders and the way his blue-black hair curled down his neck, had kept his gaze ahead, even when making his vows. Claudine had not taken her adoring eyes from him, radiant in ivory satin embroidered with pearls, her elaborate bustle extending into a shining train, her veil falling from a coronet of wax orange blossom.

The gates of the de Vailly mansion stood wide open. Local people, who had not gathered outside the church or lined the route, stood each side to enjoy the spectacle of carriage after carriage sweeping into the grounds. The bride and groom had received a cheer, the Comte bows and the bobbing of curtsys, but the guests themselves were fair game for comment and criticism, a murmur of appreciation rising from the women when a particularly beautiful hat or bonnet went gliding past.

The wedding breakfast for about five hundred guests was served on long tables set in an E-shape on a lawn that stretched down to a lake where swans drifted. Garlands of flowers had been looped between the trees and on a dais musicians played, sunshine tipping the violin bows and reflecting back from the broad flanks of cellos. Champagne flowed and sparkled. Laughter and chatter rose on all sides.

From where Rosella sat at the head table she could only see the bridal couple by leaning forward, and it was not until Sébastien rose to his feet to reply to a toast that she was able to get a good view of him. His speech was faultlessly given, serious, courteous, but with a restrained, slightly disdainful attitude towards the whole assembly. At least, that was how it appeared to Rosella, although nobody else seemed to be aware of it, applauding him heartily when he came to a close. And as he went to sit down again his glance rested by chance on her face turned towards him. Although she looked away at once it was not quick enough to avoid seeing the burning look that flared up in his eyes.

When everybody rose from the tables the musicians struck up music for dancing, but it was some time before anybody moved towards the circular floor, which had been laid down for the occasion under a pink domed canopy hung with white tasselled cords. Sébastien and Claudine took the floor, her shimmering train caught up with a loop on her little finger, her veil swirling with them in a misty flow. It was the signal for others to follow suit, and soon the bride and groom were surrounded by dancing couples.

When the dance ended Sébastien surrendered Claudine to her father, who led her into the next waltz. Without a glance in any other direction, showing that he had been aware all the time he had been dancing of the exact spot where she was standing in conversation with a group of people, Sébastien came straight to Rosella and took her without invitation into his arms, sweeping her on to the floor.

They danced without exchanging a word, but he made

blatant love to her through the pressure of his gloved hand in the small of her back, which held her too close to him, the caressing touch that held her fingers, and in the looks he gave her whenever their eyes met. When the dance ended he did not let her go, his arm hardening like an iron clamp about her, and he signalled with a nod to the musicians that they should begin again without a pause.

'No, Sébastien!' she protested urgently. 'We must not dance a second time together – '

But it was as if he did not hear. He crushed her to him as they rotated in another waltz. The faces of the spectators at the edge of the floor began to turn towards them with curious glances, and whispers started to follow them. Once she saw Claudine's sweetly puzzled expression fly by in an aura of bridal veil, but otherwise the other dancers became part of that whirlpool of colour in which she and Sébastien danced on as though they would never stop.

'Please let me go,' she begged when the dance neared its conclusion, but he would not have released her then if Philippe, whom she had not noticed in church or at the wedding breakfast, nor had given any thought to, had not stepped on to the floor as the last notes faded, holding his arms out to Rosella and giving Sébastien no chance to retain his claim on her.

'This next dance is mine,' Philippe said, addressing her, his determined air showing that he had no intention of allowing Sébastien to brush him aside. Reluctantly Sébastien bowed to her and stepped aside.

'I'd like to rest,' Rosella said. It was not only that she wished to escape as quickly as she could from the stares directed towards her, but because she was suffering from the full effects of her fall down the stairs; every step she danced had racked her.

She turned to leave the floor, but Philippe, who had

taken hold of her hand, did not release it and brought her round to face him again. 'I don't doubt that you would like to rest,' he said coolly, 'but you're going to dance with me – and you'll go on dancing with me until every gossiping tongue in this place is wagging about us – and that scandalous little contretemps with the bridegroom is overshadowed and forgotten!'

'I'll not do that!'

'Do you want the bride to start this unhappy marriage with suspicions already formed?'

'They'd be groundless!'

'Then let us ensure that there'll be nothing for her to brood over on her wedding night, and that it stays that way. The music, Rosella, has started.'

She danced with him until she feared she might drop, all her bruises from her fall aching without respite, her strained muscles a physical protest. He flirted openly with her, causing glances that had been sharp and censorious when she had danced with Sébastien to become amused and tolerant, interested and inquisitive. The kiss he appeared to steal did not go unnoticed, causing eyebrows to raise, for such behaviour at a wedding party was tantamount to an announcement that another would soon be forthcoming.

Among the spectators Louise watched jealously. She had expected to spend the whole reception in Philippe's company once her obligation to sit at the top table with family and guests of honour was over, and had sought him out immediately. He had seemed slightly preoccupied, his attention not wholly on what she had been saying to hold his interest, and again she had had the uneasy feeling that he was bored. How dare he be bored! She didn't have to spend her time with him. There were plenty of other fish in the sea – but that wasn't what she wanted. She wanted him.

She had wanted him the minute she had set eyes on him last summer and for a while her hopes had run high. But he had gone again in the autumn, back to Paris and all the excitement of life there, leaving her in the château with *Maman* treating her as though she were no more than a well-liked, obliging servant, Jules, whose current *ami* she had loathed even more than the others, and Sébastien, wrapped up in courting Claudine.

It had been an endless winter for her. She had swallowed her pride and written to him, but he had replied in a courteous, friendly manner as if his letter had been intended for the others as well, giving no indication of whether or not he ever gave thought to the few kisses they had shared. But then, why should he? It was not only she who had sought to be alone with him in a shadowed conservatory or succeeded in drawing him into a moonlit garden when music had floated from the open windows into the scented night. Men like Philippe were too much in demand. At times she almost hated him for eluding her power to captivate, which she could exert when it suited her, knowing that he was not like the average man who found her dramatic de Louismont beauty and strong personality too daunting a combination for comfort.

Watching him flirting outrageously with Rosella made her burn inwardly. When he had moved towards the dance floor she had thought he had intended dancing with her, but instead he had made some polite excuse and left her talking to some people who had joined them, and the next thing had been that it was he and not Sébastien who was dancing with André Cadel's bastard granddaughter. Admittedly Rosella did not appear to be responding. She looked white-faced and strained, her tight little smile forced, although to others not knowing her it might not appear to be like that.

Another dance came to an end, and this time Louise saw

that they did not intend to resume again when the music started up once more. She hurried forward, planning to be in their path when they left the floor, for already they were moving across it, Rosella limping slightly. Philippe said something to her and they changed direction. It had not been deliberate, for Louise knew Philippe had not seen her waiting, but it did nothing to ease her seething jealousy. She started to weave her way through the guests gathered around the canopied floor, holding on to a glimpse of his tall, burnished head and Rosella's rose-trimmed hat in the distance, but people whom she knew waylaid her, and when she reached the other side they were nowhere to be seen.

Jules had followed her. He had drunk a great deal of champagne, but he had observed the fixed direction of his sister's gaze and seen what it was on the dance-floor that had made her face go taut and pale and her mouth set in its hard, discontented lines.

'You'd better watch out, Lou-Lou,' he mocked, using his childhood name for her, 'or else Philippe will be slipping through your fingers — that is, if you ever did have any grip on him.'

Had they been in any other place she would have raised her hand and hit him hard across his thin, taunting face with all the force of her pent-up wrath. Instead, she kept herself fiercely under control and spoke in a low voice with vicious undertones: 'Go to the devil!' And she flung herself away from him.

Rosella sat down in exhaustion on a stone seat in a sunken garden where a few other guests were strolling about. Philippe had taken two glasses of champagne from the tray of a passing waiter, but she would have refused it if he had not urged her to drink it.

'You look as if you need something to put the colour back into your face,' he said, sitting down beside her. All

133

trace of his flirtatious approach had gone, dropped completely now that they were no longer observed, his face serious. 'I had no idea you were genuinely exhausted by the dancing. Not until I felt you stumble did I realize that you really did need to rest. What's the matter? Are you ill? Do you feel faint?

She had taken a sip of champagne and she shook her head. She was thankful that she had managed to stay on her feet as long as she had done, for she had been quick to see the sense of diverting attention away from Sébastien's behaviour, which could have caused Claudine much unhappiness if it had continued. And how she would have escaped from his embrace without Philippe's intervention she did not know.

'Normally I should have been able to dance for hours — goodness knows I longed for the opportunity often enough during the dancing lessons at the seminary — but last night I fell down a flight of stairs.'

'Where?'

She had not intended to elaborate, but in her present state of tiredness it seemed easier to answer than to evade. 'In the west tower. I have the room there.'

'The haunted tower?'

She smiled wanly. 'You know the story too, do you?'

'Your grandfather told me the legend while talking about the château one day during my last visit to Martinique when I went to have a look round the island again. I've always regretted having to sell my father's land and old home there, but at the time I needed to expand in shipping, changing from sail to steam, and I had to raise money in all directions. That's why I became interested when I knew André intended to sell his property. I stayed at his house for most of the visit. He was an extremely hospitable man.'

She twisted the stem of the glass, looking down at the

dancing bubbles. 'I used to cherish the hope every time he came home to France that he would decide to take me back to Martinique with him, but he never suggested it and I did not dare, not knowing then that I was more than his ward.' She lifted her head. 'How did he look when you saw him? Was his health telling on him even then?'

Philippe nodded reminiscently. 'He was much thinner than the last time I had seen him, and although he tried to hide it I could tell he was depressed. Three generations of Cadels had managed that plantation and lived in the house with its columned veranda and many rooms. I know the thought of leaving it all was painful to him. He knew that once he left Martinique he would never see the islands again.'

'I know, of course, from the letter you left at the hotel that you knew of my existence. Did he ever say anything about me to you?' She sat back against the stone seat. 'This is what I've been wanting to ask you ever since you said you'd talk to me about him one day.'

He took the champagne glass from her, seeing that she would drink no more of it, and set it down on the flagstones beside his own emptied one. Then he rested his arm along the seat behind her. 'André did mention you. Several times. He had a number of photographs of you, but none recent enough for me to associate the camera-rigid child with the beautiful girl I saw on the hotel staircase that day – and again on the balcony.'

She paid no heed to the compliment, her mind concentrated on her grandfather. 'My mother ran away with my father from Martinique. I suppose that was why he would never have me there.'

'Did she? I should think you're right. André seemed concerned that you were still confined to the seminary, but when I asked once why he didn't send for you he shook his head and said the islands were no place for a young girl.'

'Do you think I was the chief reason for his decision to return to France?'

'He most certainly had your welfare very much at heart, but he was also failing in health. You must not start believing that he would have lived longer had he stayed where he was. In fact, I had the unhappy impression that his days were numbered when I parted from him. Naturally I was always in constant touch because of all the business I handled for him in Paris, quite apart from our own transactions, and when he wrote most cheerfully to say that he would soon be on his way home to France, giving the date of his arrival, I hoped the tone of his letter meant that he was much improved. *Hélas*! That was not the case.'

'I'll never forget the nightmare of waiting in vain for him to arrive,' Rosella said gravely.

He leaned forward. 'If only I had not been in such a foolish rush to depart from Paris! We would have met then – on that very day when I chose to leave the letter instead of waiting to see you, but I expected you to be a well-chaperoned, immature little schoolgirl who would know nothing more about André's time of arrival than I did. But I was in the embarrassing position of having offered country hospitality to a fellow ship-owner and his wife – a lady whom I had never met – who wanted to find a residence in the Loire valley and I could delay no longer. As it happened, Madame changed her mind and I received word that they had decided on Provence instead.'

He grinned good-humouredly as though the capricious action of the unknown lady had caused him no inconvenience. Rosella found what he had told her illuminating. So she had been right. It had not been an uncontrollable desire to see Louise again that had made him leave Paris with such haste.

'Provence is inviting,' she said warmly. 'I visited Saint-Tropez and a few other places once with my grandfather. Most of all I remember the scent of rosemary, lavender, and thyme that drifted from the rocky hills, the black cypresses, and the vivid colour of the sea. I agree with the ship-owner's wife in preferring Provence to the Loire valley.'

'I wonder why?' he remarked with interest, bending his arm on the back of the seat to prop his chin in his hand. 'Is it because the Loire valley to you means the Château de Louismont? And the château means unhappiness?'

She nodded. 'When I visualize the map of France I see one section of it darker than all the others. That is the region which I had hoped never to visit again. I never imagined that fate would intervene so unexpectedly and drag me back to it.'

'It is a tragedy,' he said with intense seriousness, 'that you should feel such animosity towards one of the most beautiful areas in all of France.'

'I can see its grandeur with my eye,' she explained sadly, 'but my heart is set against it.'

'Therefore you really see nothing,' he said, regarding her with a half-curious, half-puzzled air. 'What is it that binds you so tightly to the past? What makes it impossible for you to view life as the adult young woman that you are? When are you going to escape your cage?'

His words struck deep. He was right. She was a prisoner of her own emotions. Yet she alone knew that the tower room symbolized all that held her captive – love, fear, all that had gone before.

'Maybe I've lost the key,' she faltered. It could be that the château would hold her until the day she died. Perhaps freedom of choice had already flown from her. If the walls of the tower room ever closed in and crushed her she would know terror at her end, but not surprise.

137

'I think not, Rosella.'

She lifted her head slowly, brushing back a stray tendril of hair that had fallen to curl down past her cheek, and knew herself to be heartened by that note of complete confidence in her which she had heard in his voice. Was it possible that in Philippe she had found someone in whom she could truly confide? Someone she could turn to as the friend she had longed for and never hoped to find?

For the first time she noticed that, while they had been talking, the day had been fading into a glorious sunset, turning the sky to palest lemon, and in every tree coloured lanterns were twinkling. She felt she could have stayed in that peaceful garden all night, hearing the music in the background, inhaling the perfume of the flowers, which filled the quiet air.

She smiled at him, almost shyly. 'You give me encouragement.'

His whole face registered his pleasure. 'That's good. I'm glad.'

All around them there came a ripple of movement. Guests were passing through the sunken garden, making their way back to the mainstream of activity. At the same time Louise appeared in silhouette against the pastel sky at the top of the flagged steps.

'There you are, Philippe.' Her voice held a brittle lightness that did not ring true to Rosella's ears. 'The bride and groom are leaving. Coming to say *au revoir*?'

Rosella rose to her feet with Philippe. Louise chatted to him while the three of them joined the other guests streaming towards a carriage waiting in the drive. When everyone had gathered in a merry, excited throng, Sébastien and Claudine emerged from the mansion together into the evening sunlight. Claudine, who had changed into a travelling outfit of peacock green, swooped forward like a lovely little bird to kiss Marguerite on both cheeks and to be embraced by the closest of her friends, turning to her father last of all. Sébastien bade farewell to his mother, and shook hands with a number of people, but his eyes were busy, searching the crowd.

Rosella hung back, trying to conceal herself behind other guests, knowing for whom he was looking. But when he and Claudine took their seats in the carriage he happened to be on the side nearest to where she was standing. She would have drawn back even further, but Philippe had taken advantage of the crush to put an arm about her. Sébastien snapped an order to the postillions, impatient to put an end to the waving of hands and the casting of petals, and with a dancing clatter of hooves the four matched greys set off amid cheers and applause along the drive.

The carriage passed within a few feet of Rosella, and Sébastien saw her. Saw her with a dark promise in his eyes that all was not over between them, no matter how much she might fight against it. Then with a flash of Claudine's green feathered bonnet and a last glimpse of her rapturous face the carriage was gone, lost from sight beyond the trees.

'I'll drive you home,' Philippe said in an expressionless voice at Rosella's side. When she turned to him she saw that he had witnessed the look that Sébastien had cast her way. And she saw something else too, and her hopes of a friendship with him came crashing about her. Philippe wanted more than friendship and he had no intention of surrendering her to Sébastien or to anyone else. He meant to have her for himself.

Never had the château been more bleak and empty. Rosella realized how much she had relied on catching glimpses of Sébastien, each time a tiny recompense for having conscientiously avoided a deliberate meeting, which she could have managed so easily.

She wondered how many hours he had paced the floor at night before his marriage, knowing that his love for her was growing stronger instead of lessening, no matter how he tried to will it otherwise. What she found truly alarming was that he had suddenly cared nothing for the principles to which he had adhered so rigidly, but had cast sense and caution aside in the abandoned way he had danced with her for all to see. She could only hope that he would come to care more for his bride than he had anticipated during those first weeks of intimacy, otherwise he would return with renewed determination to lay siege to her, a thought which she found frightening in the portent of disaster that stretched out before her.

Marguerite gave her news of the honeymooners sometimes in her detached, distrait manner when they met by chance in the château or out in the grounds.

'Sébastien has left Switzerland with his bride and they have gone to Baden-Baden. Is that not correct, Sophie?' she said one morning, turning her head in the shade of her parasol towards her younger daughter, who was at her side.

'The other way round, *Maman*. It was last week they were in Germany. Now they are in Lucerne for two or three weeks.'

'Indeed, yes.' Marguerite's voice held that edgy note which it always did when something one or other of her daughters said jarred upon her nerves. 'So much travelling. Here, there, and everywhere.'

She strolled on in the direction of the formal gardens, Sophie in tow. Rosella, bound for the stables, frowned thoughtfully as she continued along the path, wondering if Sophie, or Louise for that matter, saw how their mother had deteriorated in Sébastien's absence, almost as though the prop on which she leaned had been snatched from her.

140

With a sense of shock Rosella had noticed that Marguerite was wearing odd gloves, one cream and the other white, and pinned to her bodice were two ornate jewelled brooches which normally would never have been worn until evening. Small matters perhaps as far as anyone else was concerned, but to an elegant, Parisian-born woman such as Marguerite, who had always been impeccably attired, it was indicative of a new and deep disturbance. When not taking a daily stroll with Sophie, Marguerite had taken to sitting for hours in the shade of the garden trees where she could see down the curving drive as if waiting for her son's return, her hands idle in her lap, looking for all the world like some charming figure in a painting, motionless against the background of rich, green foliage.

On the basis of these scraps of information as to the honeymooners' whereabouts, for Sophie never spoke directly to her and Louise ignored her existence except when forced in company to address her, Rosella followed the travels of Sébastien and Claudine on the large globe in the library, turning it to pin-point their current location. When she heard that at Nice they had chartered a yacht, she looked at the blue patch that was the Mediterranean and gave the globe a slow and gentle spin, as though speeding them smoothly on their way and at the same time trying to stretch and break the invisible bonds that kept her emotionally tied to Sébastien. But the bonds took the strain. And held.

Monsieur Bataillard made his visit to the château to see how she was settling in and to deal with financial matters. He shook his head in disapproval over the share of the income from the estate that she wanted Sébastien to have for himself and for those he numbered as his dependents.

'Too much! Too much! Do you realize what you're asking me to do?'

She had nodded determinedly. 'Let it be as I have said, Monsieur Bataillard.'

He departed, still disapproving, saying that he would come again as soon as Monsieur de Louismont had returned from his travels.

The alterations to the west tower neared completion. To escape the noise and banging, Rosella often rode out twice a day on Talleyrand, capturing a sense of liberation in being free of the château, able to find scarcely used bridle paths and to come across wide vistas of hills and forests without another living creature in view. Talleyrand was still highly nervous, quick to shy or start at an unexpected sound, but she knew that he enjoyed their expeditions and her arrival at his stall always brought forth a whinny and gentle nuzzling in his impatience to be saddled and away.

Philippe had ridden with her twice, but that had been by chance, for he had spotted her at a distance when out riding himself and had caught up with her. She had also met him at several *soirées* and a number of garden parties, but each time she had had her own carriage and politely refused his offer of escort home again. Usually Louise was present at the same functions, and she skilfully monopolized his company, making it difficult for him to extricate himself, usually gathering other guests into the silken web of social etiquette that kept him entangled. His frustration would show in the many glances he cast in Rosella's direction, particularly when she was being attentively entertained by other males. She did nothing to encourage or assist him in his determination to spend the greater part of each occasion at her side, but she could tell he did not intend to let matters drift on in such a way indefinitely. He finally confronted her with an invitation to a summer ball, which was a challenge issued to settle matters between them one way or another.

He had come into the château grounds by way of the

stepping stones across the river and reached the forecourt when she was bidding adieu to three ladies who had called on her. She had had refreshment served in a shady arbour in the rose garden and had enjoyed their visit. As their phaeton departed she turned to go back to the garden to sit a little longer among the roses, and there was Philippe blocking her path, feet apart, hands low on his hips in the eternal male stance when facing the possibility of some kind of conflict, verbal or physical.

'Louise is not at home,' she said, deliberately assuming the reason for his presence. 'She went out in her carriage about half an hour ago.'

'I did not come to call on the de Louismonts,' he said, his smile serious. 'It's you I wish to see. There's something I must say.'

'Oh?' She moved towards the rose garden and he fell into step at her side. 'What is it?'

'I thought when we talked on the day of Sébastien's wedding that a very special relationship was developing between us. I felt you trusted me.'

'I do,' she said. 'That has not changed. Have you imagined it is otherwise?'

'Since that particular occasion you have taken pains to avoid me whenever possible. Have I done or said anything that has offended you?'

She came to a halt, dismayed that he should have been brooding over some slight he imagined he had inflicted. 'No, indeed! But – but circumstances – ' Her voice trailed off and she was at a loss to know what to say.

He took her hand and kept it within his as they wandered on again, and he spoke with careful emphasis. 'I know of no circumstances that could possibly keep us apart. We are both free to see whom we choose and to be with whom we choose. Since I came to the villa a few days before you arrived at the château I have gone alone to every social event. I'm bored with it! You know that well enough. And you also know that I've wanted to take you every single time, but you have given me every kind of pretty excuse whenever I've tried to inflict my company on you.' He gave her a sidelong glance under a lifted brow and saw the half-smiling look she gave him. 'I think you know that I've wanted to lay claim to you ever since you stepped into the garden-room on the day of your arrival – or, to be strictly truthful, ever since I first saw you on the stairs in the Hôtel du Louvre.'

They had reached the rose garden and were shut away within the box hedges with a riot of crimson blooms. She withdrew her hand from his and walked slowly to the sundial that stood in the middle of the rosebeds, where she rested her fingertips on the sun-warmed, lichen-streaked stone. Philippe had told her what she had known all along: that if she wished it, the summer was theirs to spend together and, if she refused, nobody else would gain by it, for there was nothing between Louise and Philippe, any more than there was with any of the other girls whom she had seen coquette with him on so many occasions. His step sounded on the path. He had picked two roses, and one he threaded by its stem into her hair, the heavily scented blossom coming to rest above her ear. The other he put into his buttonhole, smiling at her.

She smiled back at him, amused. 'I could scarcely have accepted any kind of invitation from a stranger in a hotel lobby, but we are quite well acquainted now.'

His smile widened into a grin, and he rested both arms on the sundial opposite her and lowered his height to look full into her face. 'There is to be a summer ball in aid of some charity or other. Come and dance till dawn with me, Rosella.'

'I accept – gladly,' she said.

He nodded his approval, still looking his fill of her. He

was paying compliments with his eyes. She put up her hands to tuck the rose more securely into her hair, elbows raised high in an unconsciously provocative movement, her sleeves sliding back in a folding of muslin frills. He stepped round the sundial and set his hands on her waist. She remained perfectly still, watching him, knowing he was about to kiss her, her fingers motionless on the rose. His mouth descended and took hers in a kiss that was warm and ardent. A kiss with open desire in it. A kiss to put the seal on an unspoken commitment to spending the rest of the summer in each other's company. A kiss to warn that she could no longer slow down his pursuit of her. A kiss of love.

He lifted his lips slowly from hers, so slowly that even the last touch of them was a caress. His hands left her waist to take over the fastening of the rose in her hair. 'Let me do that,' he said softly, his eyes not leaving hers.

She had the fleeting thought that for the rest of her life the scent of those particularly velvet-dark roses would remind her of that kiss, this man, and the sun-dazzled enclosure within the black box-hedges.

They talked for quite a time in the shady arbour. He told her more about Martinique and in her mind's eye she could picture the white plantation house where her mother had grown up. Only when he strolled with her back to the main entrance did they refer to the ball again and made arrangements about the time he would come for her when the evening arrived.

They parted at the steps, and when she entered the château she thought back to his first words of invitation to the event. Even if she had not wanted to accept it would have been extremely difficult to turn down an opportunity to spend a whole night away from the château. Not that she had heard anything more in the tower room since that terrible night of her fall, but her awful dread that the turbulence would return, lay over her constantly.

She was unable to get a full night's rest, for ever waking with a start and listening, her heart pounding against her ribs, her hands clutching the sheet. She kept the lamp burning all night, but the dancing wick often created shadows, making a cowled monk out of drapery, a hand out of a hanging ribbon, a waiting woman in the closet door left slightly ajar. Now she would have nothing left out of place at night, not even a negligée laid ready for her to put on or slippers for her feet. She found herself quick to lose patience with Marie if her orders were forgotten or as much as a drawer left slightly open, which created new shadows. She knew that Marie understood the reason for such tense agitation and did her best, but she had fallen in love with the young groom who tended Talleyrand, and happiness made her blissfully careless and forgetful at times, which resulted in Rosella continuing to suffer unnecessary alarm from time to time, adding to the constant harassment of her own apprehensions that did not ease.

'You have been in the rose garden for over an hour with Philippe!' It was Sophie's accusing voice that rang down from where she stood half-way down the grand staircase.

'I suppose I have,' Rosella answered calmly, starting to ascend the stairs.

'Alone!'

'I scarcely think that gives cause for questioning.'

'I disagree! And you've a rose in your hair – like a trollop!'

Rosella ignored the insult, not realizing that the quiet composure of her expression served to exacerbate Sophie's mood. She drew level with the girl and would have passed her, but Sophie's hand shot out and gripped her arm above the elbow, jerking her to a standstill. The rose slipped from her hair and fell on to the stairs in a flutter of limp petals.

Sophie's heel stamped down on it and ground it into the carpet.

'Sophie!' Rosella exclaimed in angry protest.

Sophie shook her arm furiously. 'Why can't you keep away from Philippe? Louise told me how you enticed him on Sébastien's wedding day into another part of the grounds to be on your own with him. And you are for ever getting him to dance attendance on you at parties.'

'That is not how it has been.' Rosella pulled her arm free.

'You're lying!' Sophie cried hotly. 'Louise fell madly in love with Philippe last summer. She lived for his return. You have ruined everything for her.'

'I am aware that Louise will believe that.'

'Don't pretend innocence to me. You've schemed to get him away from her.'

'That's not true!' It struck Rosella again that her mental image of the de Louismonts as a pack of caged tigers was as true as ever. They fought and clawed each other mercilessly all the time, but they united instantly to face a common enemy.

'You don't care that Louise is utterly miserable about it all!'

'There is too much unhappiness in the world. I care that anyone has to suffer.'

'Then stop running after Philippe!' Sophie's voice rose to a high note of sustained temper. 'His tenancy of the villa comes to an end in the autumn and he is not renewing it. If nothing is settled between Louise and Philippe before he leaves she will have lost him for ever!'

'I did not know that he had no plans to come back to the villa again. I thought he owned it – '

'You fool!' Sophie mocked viciously. 'It's *your* villa – it's *your* property. Did you imagine that a few acres out of all the château's land adjacent to the grounds would belong to somebody else? You don't even know what you own, it is so much!'

'I admit that I have read none of the deeds and papers yet. Monsieur Bataillard intends to go through everything on his next visit.'

Sophie threw up her hands with a contemptuous laugh, leaning back against the banisters. 'The irony of it! Sébastien knows every stick, stone, and vine-leaf. Yet you twisted old Cousin André around your little finger to make him bequeath it all to you.'

'You are making another untrue accusation.' Rosella was determined not to be goaded any more. 'It has never been my wish to deprive you or your family of anything. You have all lost everything you expected from my grandfather's will, but Monsieur Bataillard intends to see Sébastien whenever he returns and do whatever is possible to ensure that you are not left completely empty-handed.'

Sophie's whole face congested and she thrust herself forward from the waist. 'Damn you!'

Rosella, deeply upset, bit her trembling lip and continued up the stairs, realizing that the well-meaning financial arrangements which she had talked over with Monsieur Bataillard, would only increase the resentment of each of the de Louismonts towards her. Even if by some miraculous development of affairs she could hand the château over to Sébastien himself he would feel emasculated by the gift, hating her for it as much as he would despise himself, the terrible de Louismont pride mortally offended. Taking the château from her through marriage would have been an entirely different matter. It was both legal and customary for a husband to assume charge and possession of his wife's fortune and properties. But fate had denied him that opportunity.

Turning in the direction of the west tower wing, Rosella's thoughts dwelt on all that Sophie had said.

Heaven knew only too well that she herself understood what it meant to love in vain. But did Louise love Philippe? Really love him? With heart and mind? The looks the girl gave him were sultry enough, and at times there was a passion-starved gauntness to the splendid de Louismont features that made up her unusual beauty. But there was something else too -- a kind of desperation of charm and calculated appeal that was like that of a plain spinster for whom there was no hope of a match. With none of the other gentlemen whose company she attracted did she bother to exert herself, but they were all from the district, many of them eldest sons with good prospects, as yet unaware that Louise's dowry would not be what they imagined it would be, and it was possible that Louise saw only in Philippe a man who would take a woman for his wife because he wanted her, unswayed by the scales of financial gain or lack of it. Her pride would suffer no humiliation or setback through him.

Rosella paused, struck by another aspect of the situation. Could it be that she herself was not the only one longing to be released from the bonds of the château? Did Louise also crave to be free of it and the family and the whole Loire valley itself? Did she yearn to break the filial bonds that kept her tied to a sickly, selfish woman who was so used to attention that she never noticed the self-sacrifice of her daughter that went into countless errands run and small tasks performed every day to suit her slightest whim? Did all these reasons combine to make marriage to Philippe the only feasible route of escape?

And Sophie? What of Sophie who tried to disguise the fact that she was wearing the same gown yet again with a shawl or sash or an added frill of another colour? Why had she married a man much older than herself, rich and prosperous, but parsimonious to the extreme, humourless and greedy, unless it was to escape? But unfortunate

149

Sophie must have soon discovered that she had fled from one cage into another; Rosella thought it probably explained the reason why Sophie returned daily to the château, which was at least gracious and spacious compared with the house that was said to be exactly as her husband and his first wife had furnished it and where Sophie was not allowed the smallest extravagance or permitted to change a thing.

Marie came forward to meet Rosella when she entered the wing. 'The painters have just finished, madame. They are packing up their pots and brushes. The alterations are complete.'

'That is good news,' Rosella said. 'I shall go and view the new kitchen immediately.'

Now there would be no more lukewarm food coming that long distance from the main kitchens. At last she would be able to entertain, to give luncheon, dinner and supper parties. It was a pleasing prospect.

As the days went by Rosella found herself looking forward far more than she had expected to the ball, which was to be held in the grounds of another château some distance away. She had discovered that many of the people whom she had come to know would be attending, and a veritable cavalcade of equipages would be setting out from the district when the evening arrived.

It was very much in her thoughts when she reined in Talleyrand on a wooded hillside one gold and azure afternoon and rested her hands on the saddle-bow. She could see the white ribbon of a road that everyone would follow. Then her gaze swept away from the road and towards her own château, its four pepper-pot roofs rising high above the lush tree-tops of its surrounding parkland, and she could see beyond it to where the de Vailly vineyard reached the boundary of the land that was hers. It struck her afresh how ideal a marriage between

Sébastien and Claudine must have seemed to those who had no idea how fate was to intervene.

Talleyrand was cropping the tender grass under the trees, his bridle jingling against his moving jaw. She straightened up in the saddle and gave the reins a little tug. 'Come, Talleyrand,' she said on a lingering sigh. 'We must be getting back to the château.' She never referred to it as home, not even figuratively. It was a destination. A place to live in. A prison.

Half an hour later she rode at a leisurely pace up the drive, but when she came within sight of the château's forecourt her face drained of all colour. An empty carriage was being driven away from the main entrance towards the coach-house. She recognized it instantly. Sébastien and Claudine had returned!

CHAPTER SEVEN

In the hall Rosella found the luggage of the returning honeymooners being carried up the stairs. A footman on door duty came forward as soon as he sighted her. 'Madame, there is an urgent message for you. Madame Claudine de Louismont wishes to see you without delay.'

Rosella, puzzled, made her way to the south wing where Sébastien's apartments had been re-decorated during the honeymoon to suit Claudine's taste. She could not imagine why Claudine wanted to see her in such haste. A feeling of trepidation seized her. Would Sébastien be present? If he should be, she must guard against any change in her facial expression when she saw him again. She must crush down the inward surge of love that would take possession of her.

When she reached the double doors she hesitated before tapping, her knuckles hovering within an inch of the mahogany panel, assailed by a new uncertainty. Suppose – suppose Sébastien had been foolhardy enough to make some confession to Claudine! She knocked quickly. Whatever had happened, she must know the worst.

Claudine answered in a weak voice from within. 'Enter.'

Rosella opened the door and went in. Claudine was alone, standing by the open window as though desperately in need of air. When she turned to see who had entered she dispelled all Rosella's fear that Sébastien might have spoken out of turn by the warmth with which her name was spoken.

'My dear Rosella! How good to see you!' Claudine made a few shaky steps towards her with hands outstretched.

Rosella, concealing her dismay at the sight of Claudine's drawn face, her pallor and shadowed eyes, took the girl's hands into hers. Claudine had lost her healthy bloom. And gone was the radiance, the spontaneous joy, the lightness of spirit. 'This is a surprise,' she said as they leaned forward and kissed each other's cheek. 'I had not heard that you were on your way home.'

'Nobody knew. It was all decided in a hurry. I was not well.'

The reason for that was obvious. Her body was swollen and extended in a pregnancy that must have been far advanced on her wedding day, but a skilful dressmaker and the abundant use of fashionable tucks and swathing had hidden the fact most successfully. It explained very clearly to Rosella why Sébastien had been fully aware that his change of circumstances would alter nothing: the Comte de Vailly would not have cared if Sébastien had become a pauper with a begging bowl as long as his unfortunate daughter was respectably and honourably married to the father of her forthcoming child.

'How are you feeling now?' Rosella enquired, taking Claudine's arm and helping her across to the chaise longue.

'Thankful to be home! I've been travel-sick the whole time.' She sat down weakly. 'The long ride in the carriage was the final humiliation.' Her hand fluttered across her eyes as though to blot out the memory of it.

Rosella bent down and lifted Claudine's feet up on to the chaise longue. 'There! That will be more comfortable for you. I'll ring for some lemon tea.'

'I knew you'd look after me.' Claudine sank back thankfully against the cushions that Rosella tucked behind her back. 'Madame de Louismont barely greeted me. She had eyes only for Sébastien, exclaiming how well he looked, how tall, how handsome — as if it were seven years we had been away instead of seven weeks. How strange she is! I do not believe that she even noticed that I was *enceinte*. But then all she could think about was asking Sébastien if he would do this for her and that for her — and he still in his travelling clothes! The only time she is not vague and strange is when she is concentrating on him.' A resentful note had crept into her voice. 'He went with her — she had her hand on his arm as though she had no strength to walk without him. He forgot all about me.'

'When is your baby due?' Rosella asked, wanting to bring the subject on to a happier plane.

The glow that started up in Claudine's eyes was doused at once by a deep, brooding sadness. 'In the early autumn,' she said evasively.

Tactfully Rosella did not press the point. 'That's a good time to have a baby — when the heat of summer is over.'

'Yes,' Claudine said dully.

The lemon tea arrived then. Rosella poured it and Claudine seemed to revive a little when she had emptied one cup and was ready for another.

'This is delicious. I cannot begin to tell you how awful it was feeling ill all the time in those foreign hotels. Normally I adore travelling. Papa and I have been almost everywhere together, but this time I could not fancy any strange foods — in fact, everything I ate seemed to upset me. I spent hours lying in shuttered rooms with an aching head while Sébastien went climbing or sailing or riding on his own. There were the gaming tables to keep him entertained in the evenings at most of the resorts, but on the whole it was all very tedious for him. And yet he kept postponing our return home. The cruise settled the matter in the end. The sea was smooth enough and I felt quite well if I kept out of the sun, but then I was afflicted with such cramps and pains that I was terrified I might lose the baby. That's when I declared that I would return home whether he came with me or not!'

Rosella guessed why Sébastien had extended the trip in spite of his wife's continued indisposition. He had wanted to stay away from her, perhaps long enough to overcome his feelings for her. She hoped that this would prove to be the case. No matter what he thought or expected of her, anything that might have existed between them had been ended by his marriage. On that she was resolved.

'Everything will be all right now, Claudine,' she said reassuringly. 'You'll have the best of attention at all times.'

'I hope it's a girl.' Claudine said fervently.

'Do you?'

Claudine put the cup and saucer aside with a little clatter, her eyes brimming with tears. 'Sébastien might find it in his heart to care for a daughter, but he will not allow me to mention the possibility of the baby being a son. It would be a final humiliation to have an heir who would never inherit his beloved château.'

A stricken look passed over Rosella's face. Was the next generation to suffer even greater deprivation through a will that had already set so many lives awry?

When she left Claudine she wandered slowly back to her rooms, her riding hat and crop dangling in her hand. Through an open door Louise's strident voice reached her, upbraiding a servant.

'How dare you let your mistress appear in a morning gown at this hour of the day! And with jewels!'

'There was nothing I could do, mam'selle. She will not listen to me any more. At times she sits before her looking-glass and puts on every piece of jewellery she possesses.'

'There's nothing unusual in that,' Louise insisted hastily. 'She gets a little bored sometimes. In future you will see that the right garments are put out and the rest are – er – kept right out of the way.'

Louise's voice faded out of earshot as Rosella turned up another flight of stairs. So Marguerite's daughters were aware of her decline and the lady's maid at a loss to know how to handle her mistress. Perhaps with Sébastien's return Marguerite would rally mentally again.

Rosella entered the west tower wing and her shadow moved at a leisurely pace in and out of the rectangles of evening sunshine thrown across the corridor by the tall windows. She did not call out to Marie, who was always waiting when on duty, knowing that it was hardly time for the girl to have returned from her afternoon off in the company of the young groom with whom she seemed to be forming a permanent attachment. But when Rosella reached the part of the wing flanked by salons on either side, she saw through open doors that she was not alone as she had imagined. Her cheeks went hollow. Sébastien was waiting for her.

She came to a halt. He had risen from the chair where he had been sitting, and a half-smile lit his features. She took a few steps into the room and placed her hat and crop on a side-table. Not a word passed between them. On the wall a clock ticked loudly. He approached and stood facing her.

'I made an attempt to forget you, Rosella, but it was impossible.'

'You must not say such things to me!' She withdrew slightly and her hand came to rest on the back of a chair as though she might thrust it between them should he reach out for her.

'Why not? Few people can have been as completely honest with each other as we have been. It's too late for it to be otherwise. On the strength of our mutual candour I can remind you that you were the one to suggest that we

156

might marry.'

'I did not know then that you were betrothed — or that Claudine was already compromised.'

'Nevertheless, you must admit that your offer was extremely unconventional — and I learned enough about you that day in the woods to know that we are right for each other.'

'Not any longer! You are married to Claudine.'

'Since when has a marriage of convenience offered any barriers to people of our temperament?'

'To her it is a marriage of love!'

His face hardened. 'I have honoured my obligations. The child will be born in wedlock. That is enough.'

'It is not enough! You should never have gone through such a travesty of vows with someone as gentle and sensitive as Claudine.'

'Don't talk such nonsense to me.' He threw up his hands in exasperation and took a few paces across the room before swinging back to face her again. 'Have you any idea of the scandal that would have resulted if I had not gone through with the marriage? The social ostracism I should have had to endure? The barrier of silence? What's more, the Comte de Vailly would have called me out, for no matter what new laws are passed there is still only one way for gentlemen to settle such matters. He is no mean shot, but I am the better, and without doubt I should have killed him. Voluntary exile for a number of years would have been unbearable. God knows how long it takes to get a pardon these days! I would have had no wish to return as an old man to the Château de Louismont.'

She bit back the reminder that after such a span of years that he had envisaged her own son might be installed as the owner of the château, which she pictured as a giant millstone destined not only to weigh down herself, but her children and her children's children, as though all must

157

inherit her own aversion to it. How tragic it was that Sébastien should love it as much as she feared it. And it was a greater tragedy that he did not love Claudine as much as one grey stone among all those that made up that tall edifice of towers and battlements.

'Claudine will die if you do not cherish her!' she cried.

'I respect Claudine. She is my wife. I would not willingly cause her a moment's distress, but I cannot deny any longer my need for you. These weeks away from you have been the longest in my whole life. Tell me that it has been the same for you.'

'Sébastien,' she answered in a tremulous but determined voice, bringing her two fists together on the back of the chair and holding them tautly balanced there in emphasis, 'I had hoped that this time apart from each other would have made sane, sensible persons of us, able to meet on terms of friendship with no more thought of what might have been between us. I have reached that brink of no return. Nothing you can say or do will make me change my mind!'

He went very white, but he had no chance to reply, for while she had been speaking a door somewhere had opened and closed. Light heels came tapping along the corridor outside.

'My maid is coming,' she said quickly.

'Send her away!'

'No. You must leave. I can trust Marie to hold her tongue, but if any other servant finds out you have been here on your own with me, whispers will start. You must never come here alone again.' She spun about, hearing Marie draw level with the open doors. 'Marie!'

The maid would have passed by with her gaze politely averted, but she was pleased to be summoned and tried to hide her curiosity under guarded lids. 'Yes, madame?'

'Was there anyone near the entrance to the west wing?'

'Madame Sophie brought two ladies with her this afternoon and they are viewing the portrait gallery before leaving.'

'Then show Monsieur de Louismont down the staircase past the area where the new kitchen has been installed, and go ahead through the door that leads to the rest of the château to make sure he is unobserved.'

Marie withdrew tactfully to await Sébastien. He put his hand over Rosella's on the chair with a loving pressure. 'There are other ways to enter the west tower wing than by doors and stairways. Rest assured that we can meet whenever we wish. Nobody else need ever know.' Taking up her hand he put the palm to his lips. 'I'll be back.'

In dismay Rosella watched him go. He had not only refused to see that she had no intention of venturing into a deeper relationship with him, but he had informed her that he could appear at any time in her apartments through some secret passageway that existed.

Her anxious glance swept round the salon in which he had left her. Like most of the salons in the château, which had been re-designed and refurbished sometime early in the eighteenth century, there were panelled walls of silk or tapestry framed by ornate carvings able to hide the existence of any number of concealed doors, very much as the carved garlands in her tower room masked the existence of a door handle in the cause of symmetry.

The tower room! Surely she would be safe from any surprise visit there. The basic shape of the original mediaeval tower had been only lightly veneered with rococo hangings, allowing no space or corner for any concealed passageway.

She hurried from the salon, wanting to set her mind at rest, and hurried up the tower stairs. But when she turned a curve she stopped abruptly, startled. A man blocked her way. It was Jules.

'What are you doing here?' she demanded, flustered. She wondered how long he had been lurking in the shadows. And how much he had overheard.

He obviously guessed her thoughts, for his expression was sly. 'I've been waiting to see you, dear Rosella.'

'What do you want?'

'To be blunt, a loan. I'm being pushed by my creditors, and there's an outstanding debt incurred during a game of cards that honour compels me to settle without further delay.'

'Come with me,' she said, continuing on up the stairs. She had some money on hand that she could let him have. Out of the corner of her eye she noticed that before he followed her he glanced sharply back at the stair on which he had been standing. But she thought nothing more of it and led the way up the rest of the flight into her room.

'Now,' she said, turning to face him, 'you'd better tell me the exact amount that you require.'

He named a sum that made her eyes expand. 'Why do you look like that?' he questioned blandly. 'It's nothing to you. And I need it. Urgently.'

'But so much!' she exclaimed. 'I haven't anything like that amount to hand. I should have to ask my lawyer for it, and I doubt whether he would grant it for me to settle your debts for you.'

'Then don't tell him. Make up some tale about wanting a new carriage, clothes, jewels – anything.'

'Even if I were prepared to lie for you, Jules – which I'm not! – he would expect to settle the bills. Not just to hand over the money.'

'You had better get it for me – and quickly! – or else I shall repeat to Claudine every word that Sébastien spoke to you not ten minutes ago.'

He made the threat in the same quiet, low-toned voice, his unconcerned expression quite unchanged, which had

160

the effect of giving it a truly deadly ring. She blanched, but did not lose her composure. Face the tiger! Never show fear or turn your back!

'You are capable of the meanest trick — as I know full well,' she said evenly, 'but Claudine is a newcomer to your family. She would do no harm to anyone. Would you really try to destroy her peace of mind if I cannot raise the money that you want?'

'Recall old times,' he advised silkily. 'Did I ever shun the chance to get some amusement at the expense of anybody else's finer feelings? I haven't changed. But circumstances have. It isn't a joke any more. I want that money and I intend to have it!'

'I'll have no truck with blackmail!'

He shrugged easily. 'Take your choice. Claudine thinks you are her friend, doesn't she? Either pay up or prepare to see her suffer complete disillusionment. About the two of you. I should not be surprised if the shock brought on a miscarriage.'

It was true. Terribly true that any kind of shock might have disastrous effects. But paying money over to Jules was not the answer. He would come again and again to threaten and cadge, never satisfied, the insidious danger steadily growing. She must find some way to bluff him into silence. Once and for all.

She gave a little laugh, thankful that she had shown no sign of weakness. 'Go to Claudine then! Tell her what Sébastien said. Go on! Do you think she will believe you? She is besotted over him — and she knows you for the man that you are!'

'What do you mean?' Sudden anger thickened his voice.

She laughed again. 'Sébastien must have grown weary long since of settling your debts, and he has most surely given Claudine good warning against any attempts that you might make to obtain money from her.'

It was a shot in the dark, but it had not missed its target. She saw by the bitterly resentful flicker in Jules's eyes that she had touched on the raw truth in the matter of his elder brother refusing to settle any more of his debts.

'That doesn't mean she won't believe that you and Sébastien aren't lovers!' he blustered. 'I can be very convincing.'

Rosella grinned in his face. 'She will think you've stooped to the basest of all types of revenge. And she is well aware you have every reason to resent my being here. Like Sophie and Louise, you would have received your own income for life from the Château de Louismont and its lands once it had become Sébastien's property. I understand that he had intended to be more than moderately generous to each one of you.'

It was no time to tell him that she had tried to amend matters on that score for all of them, for she had a final knock-out blow to deliver, a flash of inspiration having shown her how to settle every aspect of the dangerous situation that had arisen so unexpectedly and devastatingly. At the same time much good could come from her solution. 'I shall invite Claudine to use these apartments as her own. She has already confessed to a fear of loneliness and boredom, her pregnancy naturally preventing her from taking part in any social activities for the time that is left. To know she is welcome to come and go in the west tower wing as freely as she pleases, and to see me at any minute or hour that she desires to chat or play cards or drink coffee – by night or day – will dispel completely any trace of suspicion that you might try to implant in her mind.'

She knew that she had won. Jules had been bluffing in his turn as much as she had. No doubt he knew better than to risk crossing Sébastien on such a scale. He made a self-mocking gesture of surrender, the narrow, sardonic smile returning to his thin-lipped mouth.

'Forget all that I said, Rosella. Give me what money you can spare. Make it a gift. I'm in serious trouble this time.'

She went to a drawer and out of a box she took all the francs she had. 'Do not ever ask me for money again,' she said, holding it out to him.

He snatched the francs and counted them greedily. With obvious relief and some surprise that she should have much more than he had expected in her immediate possession he nodded, giving no thanks, and stuffed the money into his pockets.

'It's a pity you didn't marry Sébastien,' he said conversationally. 'It would have lifted a burden off everybody's shoulders. Still, you never know your luck. Childbirth can be hazardous. Claudine might die. Think of that! With her out of the way Sébastien would marry you, get the château, and everything would be fine for all of us.'

'Get out!' she gasped. 'Get out! Get out!'

She slammed the door after him and leaned against it, her eyes pressed against her raised forearm, experiencing a physical sensation of nausea at his callousness.

Thundering back to her came the awful suspicion that had crossed her mind after Talleyrand had bolted with her. Had Jules really tried in his drunkenness to get rid of her? Had he consumed so much wine on that day to boost his courage for a deed that even his vicious nature must have found appalling? Not realizing that she could ride as she did, but believing her to be inexperienced in the saddle, having no more ability than the average young girl fresh from a seminary – institutions that rarely encouraged advanced horsemanship. It was fortunate for her that Mademoiselle Delagranges had believed that every social accomplishment should be well taught.

But now to Jules – and to who else? – Claudine had

become the stumbling-block between Sébastien and possession of the château, which could be obtained through another marriage – to herself! She put a shaking hand over her mouth. If Jules had tried to cause her death that day on Talleyrand, would he turn his eyes towards Claudine, planning some accident for her? The château was full of flights of stairs, high windows, battlements – a hundred places where an innocent, unsuspecting person could be thrust down.

But what was the right thing to do? Rosella wandered restlessly around her room, pondering the dreadful problem. Claudine was not well. Such a warning could prey on her mind and perhaps affect her unborn child in some harmful way. Surely Sébastien was the one to tell, but would he take such an accusation against his brother seriously? He would not believe Jules capable of attempted murder without some proof. And what proof was there? Only a whip-slash across a horse's rump in a stupid moment of drunkenness, which was typical of Jules's savage sense of humour. A practical joke. Nothing more.

Rosella had stopped her pacing by the window and she looked out towards the roof of the villa that showed among the distant trees. Philippe! Philippe would listen to her. But what could he do to protect Claudine anyway? He was not even in the château itself. She alone must keep watch for anything unusual that might indicate danger towards Claudine. Only then could she act – and accuse.

Late that night Rosella woke to a long drawn-out wail of sorrow that hung trembling in the lamp-lit room. After all the tension of the day, which had followed that awful period of fearing night after night that the sound would return, she gave way to panic, drowning the ghastly lament with her own screaming.

'Marie! Marie!' She sprang out of bed and threw herself at the bell. Wrenching the door open she rushed out on the landing, but there a new horror engulfed her. She dared not go down the black well of the stairs, remembering how it had melted under her before, casting her down and down.

Marie, running in answer to the bell, hearing her name screamed out over and over again, thought her mistress had had another fall. Instead, she found her standing with her back pressed against the wall at the top of the stairs, shaking her head hysterically.

'Madame! Dear God! What is the matter?'

Rosella collapsed into her arms. 'The room is crying!'

'Listen for yourself!'

Marie rushed to the open door of the tower room. It was as she had expected. Silence reigned. She entered to make sure. All she could hear was the distant hooting of an owl through the open window. 'You *were* dreaming, madame,' she said, turning back again. 'There is no crying to be heard. Not a sound in there.'

Rosella scooped her hair back from her frightened face with her fingers and kept her hands pressed against her head. 'Am I going mad, Marie? Oh, tell me I'm not going mad!'

CHAPTER EIGHT

Monsieur Bataillard stayed for three days at the château going through all the papers and documents with Rosella. But hardly had they settled down to business when he asked her if she had met a certain Monsieur Armand Montargis.

'Sophie's husband? Yes, of course,' she replied.

'Well, he has been trying to make a nuisance of himself. His lawyers have been in touch with me several times. When they discovered that there are no grounds whatever for contesting the will they switched their tactics to another line. Monsieur Montargis has put in an absurd claim for his wife's dowry to be paid out of my late client's estate.'

She remembered Armand's threat to make trouble. 'Is he entitled to it?'

'Dear me, no! He is threatening to take the matter to court, but he might as well throw his francs in the Loire. Do not concern yourself. It is little more than a cunning trick to extract money from you in the hope that you will want to avoid dragging the family into any legal tussle. Put the matter from your mind. It will never get any further and we shall hear no more about it. His lawyers have more sense than he has. Now! Let us attend to more important items.'

Monsieur Bataillard proved to be far from approving when she mentioned the large share of revenue from the château's property, land, and vineyards that she wanted

166

made over to Sébastien. He begged her to reconsider carefully, but she was adamant, pointing out that the tight supervision and strong control of it all was entirely in Sébastien's hands and she wanted it to stay that way. Seeing that there was no chance of persuading her to change her mind, the lawyer said he would draw up the necessary papers.

Sébastien received Rosella and the lawyer in the library. He listened to all that Monsieur Bataillard had to say and made only one objection, which was to the word *salary*. As a gentleman he found the word utterly unacceptable in connection with himself. The document was re-phrased at once to suit him by the clerk whom the lawyer had brought with him from Paris. Then Rosella and Sébastien both put their signatures to the paper.

When the wearisome business was at a close Sébastien followed Rosella from the library. 'Only a woman who loves greatly would do what you have done for me,' he said, smiling a warm, wondering smile.

She made a swift little gesture of deprecation. 'Please do not put any exaggerated importance on it,' she said anxiously, but glad to have brought happiness to his eyes. 'It is in order that your mode of living should not be changed – or that of your dependents.'

'I think it means more than that – much more. No matter how you deny it.'

They were in one of the open salons between one room and another, and the hour being late all the candles in the sconces were lit, holding the two of them in a golden glow. He made to draw her towards the shadows of an alcove, but she resisted, thrusting herself from him.

'Monsieur Bataillard is to dine with me. I must go.'

'Then I shall come to you later?' he said, smiling.

'No, Sébastien,' she implored frantically, 'you must not!'

'You cannot stop me,' he said lovingly, amused by her flurry.

'I can! Has Claudine not told you that I have invited her to come and go as she wishes in the west tower wing – at any hour of the night or day?'

The smile faded from his face. 'Why should you do that?'

'Jules was in the tower wing waiting to see me that day you returned from your wedding tour. He overheard what you said to me and threatened to tell Claudine. It was only an idle threat!' she assured him hastily, seeing anger distort his face. 'But I had to ensure his silence. No wife has an open invitation to rooms where something might be amiss.'

'That was clever of you,' he said bitterly. 'A little too clever in my opinion. It would have been better if you had let me deal with Jules. When he comes back from Paris again I shall settle that matter with him once and for all. In the meantime you can retract that invitation to Claudine.'

'I shall not do that.'

'In God's name, why not?' he exclaimed in exasperation.

'There was another reason for it – although I'm not sure that it would have occurred to me right away if Jules had not put the idea into my head. Claudine is unwell in her pregnancy and she is lonely. She had hours of loneliness abroad and she finds the same state of affairs here. You are out all day – oh, I know you have much to deal with on the estate after a considerable absence – but she does not see you in the evenings either! I have found her in tears several times. I had a long talk with her in the morning before Monsieur Bataillard arrived. That's when I invited her to luncheon that day to meet him – not exactly exciting company, but she jumped at the opportunity. That's why she's dining with us this evening – because she expects you to be out again. When I told her she could seek me out whenever she felt particularly depressed, no matter whether I had visitors or not, it did much to cheer her – and I'll not take that privilege from her!'

'All this talk of loneliness is absurd,' he argued irritably, showing unwittingly that he knew he was at fault, but was loath to admit it. 'She has friends and acquaintances – '

'She told me that she does not want to receive any of them – or go calling either – when it is obvious to all that her pregnancy is far, far in advance of the two months that it should be!'

'They will know when the child is born anyway,' he stated with a certain phlegmatic male logic.

'It will not matter to her when she has a baby to love and fuss over and show off. And who is to know that it was not a premature birth? She would not be so self-conscious now if she was happy – there are gowns enough that would disguise her condition – but at the moment she cannot face the world. Why do you desert her when she needs you?'

His face darkened. 'You dare say that to me! I need you, but am I not deserted?'

'I am not your wife!'

The bitter unhappiness showed again in his eyes. 'Claudine and I soon discovered that we are strangers to each other.'

'Then the fault is yours!' She flung the accusation at him angrily, hiding her own misery within it.

'I do not deny it. I have nothing to say to her. It is you whom I love.'

He had said it. The words that she had determined should never be said. She felt no joy, no triumph, only desolation. Unwisely she took a step towards him, not quite knowing why. And then she was in his arms, yielding to him, and for a few moments of surging, untameable passion his mouth possessed hers while he held her locked

169

to him. Then suddenly Monsieur Bataillard's voice addressing his clerk reached them through the opening library door, forcing him to release her. They fell apart and faced each other, a little distance apart, he flushed and triumphant and exulting, she pale with remorse at having allowed her feelings to carry her away.

'Never again, Sébastien!' she cried. 'Never, never again.'

She turned on her heel and ran from him. Ran and ran until she reached the tower room and threw herself heedlessly across the evening gown that Marie had laid out in readiness. She lay dry-eyed, her chest still heaving from the speed at which she had run, despairing at her own folly in failing to keep at a distance the man who could never be hers.

There were to be short periods when Claudine was to feel quite well, but on the whole she was condemned to ail with every kind of discomfort throughout her pregnancy, and often she was forced to take to her bed. Rosella did what she could to ease the boredom of these times, reading to her, playing chess or backgammon, and repeating whatever entertaining scraps of gossip she happened to have heard.

After what Rosella had said to him, Sébastien did make some effort to spend more time in his wife's company, which had the effect of lifting her spirits when she saw him and plunging them down again when he failed to appear, and the switchback of emotion that resulted did nothing to help her condition.

Whenever she had a spell of feeling better or rose from her bed to what she thought of as 'a good day', Claudine would wander along to the west tower wing, knowing that she would always be welcome. She had no liking for her own company, being by nature garrulous and extrovert, used in the past to living solely to an accompaniment of praise, flattery, and adulation. Her mother and then her father had indulged her, and she had never known a harsh word until she and her father had become estranged during her betrothal. She had foolishly imagined that, after being told that she was unfortunately *enceinte*, he would bring forward the wedding date, but this he refused to do, white-lipped with rage, pointing out that a union between two families as important as the de Vaillys and the de Louismonts, involving the coming from far afield of many already invited distinguished guests, could not be treated as though it were a marriage of peasants at the point of a shotgun.

Sébastien's loss of his inheritance had been the last straw as far as her father was concerned. Immediately after the wedding he had closed the de Vailly mansion and gone abroad once more. She was not sure exactly where he was – and at a time when it would not be many weeks before his first grandchild was born. It was an additional burden to bear and she was thankful that she could talk to Rosella about him sometimes.

'I miss riding. Papa and I always went riding once a day wherever we were,' Claudine said one afternoon to Rosella. She had entered the west tower wing at the very minute that Rosella had returned from an outing on Talleyrand.

'I'm sure you do,' Rosella said sympathetically, taking off her riding hat and peeling off her gloves.

Claudine went across to the open glass doors and looked across the battlements at the view. 'I longed to be back here all the time I was on my wedding tour, but now I feel shut in. It's because I'm out of touch with the outside world.'

'What about a drive?' Rosella suggested. 'It will not take me more than a few minutes to change my clothes.'

Claudine wrinkled her nose doubtfully. 'Where? I do not

feel like going far.'

'We could go round by the road and pay a call on Philippe.' Rosella had noticed that Claudine was always relaxed with him, knowing him well from his being in and out of the château so often.

'I should like that!' Claudine said, brightening. It was turning out to be 'a good day' in more ways than one. Not only had Rosella suggested the only outing that could have appealed to her, but she was feeling well and, what was more, Sébastien had lunched with her, which was a treat in itself, and he had talked to her at length about some new method of raising certain crops, a topic he had found absorbing, and she had been at pains to listen keenly and try to understand it all. But when he had risen from the table he had apologized for being such boring company. She had protested that she wanted to know all he was doing on the estate, but he gave her one of those curious, half-fond, half-pitying looks which no man ever gives to a woman he really loves. Yet when she had raised her face for a kiss he had put his lips against hers, although he had restrained with a gentle grip about her wrists the arms she would have put around his neck. There was one question she wanted to ask, but did not dare. She loved him, but she could not confide in him. She could only trust that, after the baby was born, he would come back to their marital bed, which he had left during her sickness on the honeymoon, and had never once shown any sign of wishing to return to it.

When he had seduced her during their betrothal he had been tender and loving beyond her wildest dreams, but from the wedding night everything had changed, leaving a stranger violent and morose in his passion, whose desires had seemed to spring from some terrible frustration. Bewildered and violated and afraid, she had used every excuse to keep him from her until finally he had left her alone by night and by day. In hot and stuffy shuttered hotel rooms she had lain sick and ill for many solitary hours, longing for home and an end to the wedding tour which had turned out to be such a disaster. During that time she had had plenty of time to think, ponder, and remember, trying to pin-point that indefinable moment when somehow his attitude must have changed towards her.

She had recalled again the evening when he had ridden with injured and bandaged hands to her home to break the news that he had lost his inheritance to Rosella. He had been tight-lipped and restrained, not responding to the embrace of comfort that she gave him, but she had put that down to a state of shock at the blow to his pride and his heart. In the days that followed he appeared to have become his usual self again, being no less affectionate and gentle in his speech to her, although a certain hollow-eyed look of sadness at the loss of the château had remained with him. Once he had wanted to make love to her, but since her father had been informed of her earlier wanton behaviour he had seen to it that she was never out of sight of a hawk-eyed chaperon. But she should have slipped out of the house and met Sébastien in the moonlit garden as he had begged her and given him solace and release and balm within her enfolding arms. Perhaps that was the last time he was ever to turn to her in a true and loving need that would have saved them both from this terrible dissolution of all they had been to each other. And she had denied him.

Now she was home she had to face the possibility that she had lost him beyond recall, and she held herself entirely to fault. She had deliberately put from her mind that memory of Sébastien dancing with Rosella at their wedding as though she were the bride and he half-mad with desire, but she could not blind herself to the present way he looked at Rosella with his heart in his eyes. She did not blame him for that, knowing that she herself looked sickly and pale, her hair dull and lacking sheen, and her figure swollen to a size that she could only think of as grotesque. But she did not intend to give up trying to win him back, and the only chance to do that was to seize whatever opportunity that came along to be as light-hearted and loving and beguiling as she could be under the circumstances, which should make him see that when she was slender and pretty and healthy again she would be the same Claudine in whose arms he had once lain with satisfied contentment, murmuring endearments while he retraced with caressing fingertips the contours of her body that he had then so newly discovered and possessed.

With her thoughts dwelling on Sébastien, Claudine was quiet when she and Rosella started out, but soon the excitement of going beyond the château gates took over and she became pink-cheeked and merry, waving to some farm children who ran after the carriage until one of the younger ones tumbled and yelled over a cut knee. Then Claudine had the carriage stopped and got out herself to examine the damage and bind up the wound with her own freshly unfolded lace-trimmed handkerchief.

She enjoyed every minute of the time spent with Philippe. The three of them sat together in the shade, and during the afternoon he showed them his albums of sketches and water-colours and even photographs of Martinique. She noticed how enchanted Rosella was with the views of the immense bays, the old plantation houses and sugar-mill towers, the dark-skinned fishermen in their odd peaked and brimmed straw hats, and the endless variety of exotic trees and flowers. She supposed her friend was looking at them with her grandfather and mother in mind, knowing they must have seen those same scenes and walked on those deserted beaches, but she herself considered the highlight of the visit to be Philippe's interest in her and what she had to say during the conversation that flowed between the three of them with such ease and amiability.

His whole attitude towards her was good for her morale, making her feel she was still attractive and desirable and not as lumpy and plain in her pregnancy as she had supposed. It encouraged her to think of venturing out on other expeditions, not, of course, to mingle with female acquaintances whose sharp eyes would be undeceived by a carefully arranged shawl, but she could watch horse-racing from an open carriage, a play from a theatre box, and listen to a concert from a seat behind pillars. Even the forthcoming summer ball, which Philippe and Rosella had been discussing, could be viewed from the seclusion of one of the trellised alcoves that would be erected around the open-air dance-floor. She made up her mind to be there.

On the evening of the ball Rosella, coming from the west tower wing, met Claudine on the alcove-studded landing at the head of the grand staircase, and they duly admired each other's gowns.

'Are you sure my shawl is concealing enough?' Claudine whispered anxiously as they made their way down the flight to where Philippe, who had arrived in good time, and Sébastien awaited them.

'Don't worry,' Rosella answered reassuringly. 'Nobody will notice. In any case it will be dark with only the lights of paper lanterns.'

'I wish we were going to be with you and Philippe,' Claudine said in another whisper, 'but Sébastien said we must join up with Sophie and Armand.' She made a little face. 'Louise is coming too with some young man I have never met, and Madame de Louismont said she wanted to be included.'

'Is *Maman* ready yet?' It was Louise who spoke, coming from a salon leading off the hall where she had been showing her escort a portrait of herself while waiting for the others to gather.

'I do not know,' Claudine answered. 'I have not seen her.'

Louise, attempting to conceal her impatience with both her mother, who was obviously going to be late, and Claudine who – in her opinion – should not be making a public exhibition of herself, began to introduce the tall, fair-haired young man at her side. 'I should like to present Monsieur Marcel Berthier – ' She broke off, aghast, catching sight of her mother at the top of the stairs. *'Maman!* Dear God! What on earth – ?'

They had all swung about to follow her shocked and horrified gaze. Marguerite, innocently unaware of the incongruous sight she presented, had arrayed herself in an age-yellowed satin gown that must have been fashionable when crinolines had reached their widest and most unwieldy size. The rosebuds around the *décolletage* and catching up flounces of the hooped hem were crushed and tired, accentuating the absurd youthfulness of the style which contrasted devastatingly with Marguerite's mature looks, lovely though they were. Her hair, which she must have had dressed by her maid before changing on her own into the crinoline, had been hastily rearranged into a ringlet that rested on one bare shoulder, and the result was untidy and unkempt, tendrils of her soft hair flying out in all directions. She had forgotten her gloves, but had tied ribbons about her wrists and throat, and on every finger she had pushed all the rings that each could hold.

Sébastien was the first to move. He checked Louise when she would have outpaced him with a warning touch on her arm. Then he mounted the stairs without haste to take his mother's hand and put it to his lips.

'You have been the belle of the ball in that gown, I do not doubt,' he said to her, smiling, 'and I am sure no woman ever looked more beautiful, but this evening I had hoped to see you in a particular gown that I believe suits you more than any other you have had for a long time.'

She smiled in vague surprise at him. 'Which one is that?'

'The new velvet. Had you forgotten it? It came from Paris only last week.'

Her be-ringed fingers flew to her mouth in confused recollection. 'I had forgotten it! Do you really think it suits me better than this one?'

'I do indeed. You chose that shade of blue to set off your sapphires.'

'So I did!' She glanced down towards those who stood like statues in the hall, unable to take their gaze from her. 'But I will wear that gown another time. Everybody is about to leave —'

'Sophie and Armand are not here yet,' he said in the same calm and easy tones. 'I want them all to have a glass of wine before we start off. Louise will call your maid — ' he raised his hand slightly in a signal to his sister while giving his mother an arm to lead her back in the direction of her apartments again ' — and when you are ready you shall ride in my carriage and at my side with Claudine.'

They disappeared from sight, Sébastien still talking as though nothing untoward had occurred. Louise, crimson with restrained temper and embarrassment, muttered something to Monsieur Berthier about her mother being enchantingly forgetful at times, and hurried off to find the negligent lady's maid who was about to find herself dismissed with only time to pack her bags.

Monsieur Berthier, no less embarrassed than Louise, cleared his throat. 'Splendid evening for the ball, is it not?' He took a handkerchief from his sleeve and surreptitiously wiped his brow with it. 'Good weather and all that. A little too warm, if anything.'

Philippe talked about Marguerite's strange behaviour to Rosella when they were alone in his carriage, driving ahead of the others. 'Louise told me once that Madame de Louismont had suffered a nervous breakdown some years ago. I gathered from what was said at the time that she had never fully recovered, although Louise implied that she played on her frailty to make everyone obedient to her whims. I must say that Sébastien knew exactly how to handle her without upsetting her into a scene.'

'Marguerite adores him. I think it was his absence on his wedding tour, coming so soon after my turning up to take the château from him, which preyed on her mind and brought about the recent change for the worst in her. It is as though she does not feel safe when he is not at home or near at hand.'

'You mean he has become a tower of strength to her since her husband died?' He gave a nod of understanding. Then his attention was caught by some coloured lights in the distance. 'We're almost there!'

It was a night of music and starlight, ices and champagne and long buffet tables loaded with every kind of delicacy. Everybody was there. Rosella found herself much in demand, but Philippe had taken the precaution of writing his name across the whole of her programme from midnight onwards to ensure that after that time they would not be parted. She danced twice with Sébastien. He had not crushed her to him as he had done on his wedding day, but held her at the conventional distance. Yet his eyes did not leave her face and in that twirling, rotating forest of dancers he told her again that he loved her and would not be silent, although she implored him not to say it again to her.

Claudine, half-hidden in her alcove behind a bank of

flowers, watched them and saw them again as they had been on her wedding day. For a moment she thought that her heart must stop with the shock of realizing what had not occurred to her before: they were in love with each other, her beloved husband and her dear friend. She felt no anger, no jealousy, no hatred, for such vindictive emotions were alien to her, but she knew an unbearable heartache and anguish that set her hands trembling violently in her lap while Marguerite, who was sitting with her, tapped a toe to the music and smiled towards her son while she wafted an ostrich feather fan.

Claudine was amazed that she found herself able to think with absolute clarity, in spite of what she was enduring. She knew that she could not stop loving Sébastien any more than she could like less Rosella who had been so good to her. Were they having an affair? With the odd clicking into place of her stunned mind that made her feel like a wound-up automaton she doubted that they were, which made their anguish as great as hers, and she pitied them. She also had one floating straw at which to clutch, believing it stout enough to sustain her: she was his wife and he could not – and would not – leave her, which gave her a slender, fragile chance with the passing of time to make their marriage whole again. On this thought she must dwell or else she might become as deranged as her cruelly possessive mother-in-law.

When Sébastien came back to the trellised alcove after returning Rosella to Philippe, Claudine asked him to take her home. They left with Marguerite a few minutes later and nobody noticed them go.

It was dawn when the last waltz whirled Philippe and Rosella around the floor in the company of over a hundred other couples who were seeing the night through to the end. She gave a final deep curtsy to his bow, and then, smiling at each other, his arm about her, they left the still

179

colourful scene to have his carriage summoned for them.

In the golden early-morning sunlight they sat side by side with the hood down, the trotting horses and a yawning coachman taking them back through the stirring countryside. Everywhere birds were singing and on the river bank there were delicate festoons of sparkling, spray-laden cobwebs. His arm was close about her. Now and again he kissed her, bending his head to put his mouth softly on hers. It was in keeping with her mood, for he kept thoughts of Sébastien completely at bay and she was deliciously dance-weary and languorous.

Not until the château appeared round a bend in the road did she tighten inwardly, the old dread in the pit of her stomach hitting her as it always did. Philippe saw how she raised herself away from his arm and sat stiffly, looking towards the west tower wing. He let his hand rest on her creamy back, which was revealed by the low scoop of her gown.

'There is no need to return to the château yet, is there? Before I left the villa I ordered breakfast for us on the terrace.'

She turned to look at him with bright, relieved eyes. 'How clever of you! I adore breakfast out of doors. I have it served on the battlements sometimes.'

'I know. I've seen you up there sometimes from my window when I've been getting up myself in the mornings. You are quite an early riser.'

She looked away from him. 'I don't sleep well.'

Dancing seemed to have given them both a tremendous appetite and they did justice to the basket of hot croissants, the strawberry jam, the refilled pot of strong black coffee and the bowl of fresh peaches.

'Show me the way back to the château across the stepping stones,' she said when he would have called the carriage again. 'I have often wondered exactly where they were.'

'Promise not to fall in the river,' he teased, laughing, and she declared she would not.

They came through the trees and there were the stepping-stones, broad and flat, some slightly a-wash with water. She took off her satin dancing slippers and he tucked them in his pockets. 'Mind your dress,' he warned. She held her ruffled skirt high by its attached silk loop on her little finger and put her other hand in his. He went ahead of her, helping her from stone to stone. The sun struck warm on their heads and on her bare shoulders, but when they reached the bank the cool shade of the trees fell over them again. He stooped down to put her slippers back on her feet.

'That's it,' he said, straightening up again, and then he indicated a track in the grass. 'Here's the path that I follow. You will see that it joins the one where I found your shawl that day I came back from the château – '

He stopped, realizing what he had said. She drew back from him, the skin straining over the bones of her face. 'When you came back?' she echoed in a jerky voice. 'I thought you had found it later in the evening when you returned again to go to the dinner party. Did – did you know that Sébastien and I were nearby in the glade?'

He nodded, reluctantly, his expression sombre, and he measured his words. 'At first I did not realize you were there. I sometimes avoid the path and keep to the bank of the river – as I did that afternoon – and the noise of the water covered all sound until I branched back to the path when I spotted your shawl. Suddenly I could hear your raised voices. I snatched up the shawl and went.'

'What did you hear?'

'Very little. It was only a matter of seconds – '

'I want to know!' Her voice throbbed vehemently.

'Rosella – ' he protested unhappily.

'You heard me propose marriage to Sébastien. You did. I can see you did. Oh! Oh!' She put her hands together, pressing the edge of them against her mouth. 'I cannot bear it!'

Before she could move away from him he enfolded her swiftly into his arms, holding her close in comfort, in reassurance, her face buried against his shoulder, his hand cupping the back of her head. He spoke soothingly to her. 'It does not matter what I heard – or what you said. It's not important. You were offering him the château – and that's why you said what you did. It's all in the past – over and forgotten.'

'It's not!' she moaned. 'He loves me. He wants me. And I have loved him all my life.'

He held her from him, looking into her face. 'All your life? Now you are being fanciful. It's only a handful of years since you made that one previous visit to the château. And then you went back to the seminary with a headful of romantic dreams about Sébastien de Louismont. Is that it? Am I not right?'

He was right. She knew he was right, although she did not want to admit it. It was too soon to discard something she had held close to her mind and heart for her growing-up years. In the confined and suffocating atmosphere of Madame Delagranges's establishment, denied outside company of any kind, closeted only with girls, it had been natural that her youthful longings should have been directed towards the only boy with whom she had ever been in close contact, whose handsomeness had remained vividly in her mind, who had soothed her fears. He had become her knight in shining armour. Philippe had brought her to the brink of seeing all she felt for Sébastien in a different light for the first time, but she would go no further towards that revelation. Not yet. She did not want to see, she did not want to know. She would not have something so dear and precious snatched from her and shattered beyond recall.

'Don't say any more,' she begged in a whisper.

But he ignored her plea. 'When are you going to grow up, Rosella? Throw away that sentimental yearning! That's not love. Not as you are capable of loving. Neither is it love with Sébastien. Else how could he not have kept in touch with you? How could he bear the thought of marrying another woman? He lusts after you because you represent all he cannot have – and he has never been denied anything before in his whole life.'

It was the truth – she recognized it now – and she was forced to surrender to it. It enveloped her and invaded her and swept her infatuation from her. He saw her eyes break on the pain of it and knew she would never be quite the same person again. Yet he was also aware that he had only hastened the inevitable, putting into words what some part of her must have known all along, and he regretted nothing. He loved her and he had longed to smash the way open for her to love him, knowing that she could ruin and blight her whole life if she let the years slip by in a hopeless yearning until it was too late. He had meant to have her from the start – and not in any other man's shadow. He had hurt her, but he had set her free. Whether she would turn against him he had yet to discover, but it would make no difference in the end. Not even the château itself should stand between them.

In silence she drew herself out of his arms. 'I know my way out of the woodland from here,' she said huskily, no longer looking at him. 'Don't come with me. Please.'

He watched her go, a shimmering figure with her evening finery at odds with the bright sunlight. So she had turned from him. Disappointment and anger and impatience surged upwards at the prospect of the long task ahead of him to win her round to him again. So much time

183

wasted when it could have been spent in love and loving. Suddenly he could not bear the thought of it.

She was almost out of sight. He sprang forward and ran a few yards along the path after her until he was within earshot. 'Rosella!' he called, slowing down to a standstill.

She paused, looking over her shoulder in reluctant enquiry. 'Yes?'

'Let me see you later today!' he implored.

A matter of moments passed before she gave a nod and continued on her way. He gave a deep and satisfied sigh. It was all right after all. The cut he had dealt to release her had been sharp and swift and clean. It would heal. She held no grudge against him.

She disappeared from his view. The sun's heat was beating down on him between the trees. He pulled free his white evening tie, loosened his collar, and took off his coat, which he slung over one shoulder as he turned back to the river.

He was smiling to himself. He would teach her what love could be. She whom he loved as he had never loved before.

CHAPTER NINE

Rosella drew up a chair to the *secrétaire* and opened her diary to make another entry. Her face was pale from lack of sleep and the hand that held the pen quivered slightly.

'Last night the turbulence in the tower room returned again for the third time this week. I am losing courage and yet I will not give in and retreat before this hostile force that seeks to overpower and dominate, for I have this compulsive belief that I must face it out, no matter what happens. I can no longer summon up the strength of will to speak out and challenge whatever awful manifestation it is that oozes out of the walls to hang suspended over and around me. Yesterday I had the bell, which is connected to Marie's room, moved from the wall near the door to within reach of my hand from the bed, but when I rang for her during last night's disturbance the weeping had faded away by the time she had rushed into the room. There is no pattern or timing to these visitations, no link with anything that happens in the château, no connection with anyone's coming and going, for I have kept a record. Everything points to the obvious conclusion that it is my disruption of the de Louismont household and therefore the peace of the château that has summoned up this spectral antagonism against my presence under this roof and not necessarily because I occupy the tower room itself. It could be that I appear to be as alien and invasive as those enemy

soldiers who once stormed the château in the noble lord's absence and brought about the death of all its occupants and finally – although inadvertently – the self-imprisoned lady herself, which offers one possible explanation as to why I am being haunted – for haunted I am, and I live in terror that one night the tower room will scream again as it did when I was a child and then I shall look upon some horror that was concealed from me at the time. What my fate will be when that occurs I dare not contemplate, which is the reason why I am setting everything down in case I do not survive the ordeal.'

She put the pen back into place on the silver inkstand and took up a hand-blotter, which she rolled over the page with care. A footman came in through the door. 'Monsieur Aubert has called, madame.'

'Ask him to wait, Béraud.'

When the footman had gone again she closed the diary and put it into a drawer, which she locked, retaining the key. Picking up her lacy hat she tied its ribbons under her chin and went to find Philippe. He greeted her with a grin. 'Ah! You are ready, I see. Shall we go?'

He offered her his arm and she took it, but held back. 'Would you mind if we took Claudine with us to town? She has decided she must have a new gown for the family dinner party this evening – it is Sophie's natal day and the first time that all the de Louismonts will be gathered together since the wedding.'

'It will be a pleasure to take Claudine,' he answered agreeably.

Claudine, wearing a long cape to conceal her increased size, confessed her nervousness about the dinner party to Philippe while the open landau bowled the three of them in the direction of the market town. 'It is the first time that I shall be seated at the opposite end of that long table to Sébastien. The only other occasions when I have dined there were before we were married. I must – oh, I must! – look my very best this evening.'

For Sébastien, her heart echoed. And she thought she had never been fonder of Philippe, who was constant in his escorting of Rosella, almost as though he understood the triangular situation and wanted to win her away from it. If only Rosella would fall in love with Philippe and he with her! If only! she prayed.

Claudine was known in the emporium and there was no delay in her being served. She was ushered into a room set aside for customers of importance who were *enceinte*, where a host of flowing robes and full-waisted gowns were displayed for her inspection.

'What do you think of this?' Claudine asked Rosella when it had come to the point of her trying on those that she liked best. She was arrayed in a robe of bright cherry silk edged with a pleated frill, falling straight from throat to hem, but prettily tucked and gathered at the back to give an illusion of a bustle without any of the discomfort that would otherwise be involved.

'It suits you!' Rosella exclaimed.

'I think Sébastien will like it,' Claudine said. The striking colour flattered her and she felt she looked almost pretty in it.

A porter carried all the parcels to the landau. Philippe was waiting for them in it and he got out when they approached.

'There's a band playing in the park,' he said. 'Would you like to take some refreshment at the café there?'

'Yes. I love a band!' Claudine declared, exhilarated by the success of her shopping expedition. 'That will be fun.'

They found a table on the terrace under a striped awning. Claudine, who had developed a craving for sugary things, tucked into spiced cake and pastries, chattering all the time, while Rosella and Philippe sipped their coffee, smiling at her and each other.

Suddenly Rosella stiffened. Philippe turned his head slightly to see what had caught her eye. His mouth tightened and he glanced back quickly to her, giving a warning stare to indicate that at all costs they must keep Claudine's attention away from that direction. Both of them had seen Sébastien strolling under the trees towards the gates with a tall, beautiful woman with fiery hair, unmistakably of the *demi-monde*.

'Would you like something else, Claudine?' Philippe enquired. 'I'm sure you would. *Garçon!* Bring the *croque-en-bouche* I can see from here for Madame!'

The tall pyramid dessert was placed in the centre of the table, causing Claudine to giggle and declare that the sight of it was too much and it must be removed before she was tempted to start at the top and nibble her way down to the plate on which it stood. By the time she had been served a small portion and the rest of the dessert had been taken away again, Sébastien and the *demi-mondaine* had disappeared from sight.

Claudine, dressed in her new gown, swept into the west tower wing where Philippe had arrived to dine with Rosella. He had expressed a wish to see her in the new finery she had bought and she had promised to show herself off in it before she joined the de Louismont family party. Both he and Rosella acclaimed her appearance at once.

'Is it not grand?' Claudine sought more reassurance, swirling out the wide skirt of her cherry silk gown in a ripple of frilled pleating, its superb colour echoed by the rubies she wore in her ears and around her throat, which had been Sébastien's marriage gift to her.

'You look magnificent!' Philippe exclaimed with warm admiration from where he stood, glass in hand. And he raised it to her, receiving a ravishing smile in return.

'Wait until I make my entrance this evening!' she declared, clasping her hands together, her gaiety a little too exuberant. 'How they will stare at me! Louise will look down her nose, thinking my gown is far too flamboyant. Sophie will make some catty remark and chew her lip in envy while that miserable husband of hers will shake his head over my extravagance. Now what about Jules?' She tapped a finger with mock thoughtfulness against her cheek. 'I know! He will make plans to try to borrow money again. Even my mother-in-law cannot escape noticing this splendid colour and will be forced to see me as a real person instead of a pale shadow that has somehow appeared in the family circle.' She had gurgled mischievously, making her frills swing out again. 'Am I not wicked to speak so disrespectfully about my in-laws? But I don't care! All I care about is that Sébastien will feel proud of me.'

'He will,' Rosella cried in certainty, for Sébastien, no matter if his heart failed to be stirred, could not deny that on this particular evening Claudine with the new maturity brought about by her pregnancy looked — as Philippe had so rightly said — magnificent.

'I must go. I must not be late.' Claudine turned in the doorway and looked back at them, her eyes suddenly bright with suppressed tears, her smile a little crooked. 'Wish me good fortune.'

'I do.' Rosella rushed forward and they hugged each other briefly in perfect understanding.

'I echo that,' Philippe said, putting his arms around both of them and giving each a kiss on the cheek.

'Thank you,' Claudine said gratefully as though

strengthened by their good wishes, and with a swish of silk she left them.

The night was warm enough for coffee to be served out on the battlements. Rosella and Philippe went to sit in the chairs placed there for them.

'I wonder how Claudine has managed to get through the dinner party,' he said, taking the cup that Rosella had poured for him. 'Do you think she happened to see Sébastien before you did this afternoon by any chance?'

Rosella set down the coffee-pot, leaving her own cup unpoured. He had expressed the unhappy suspicion that had been lurking at the back of her mind. 'I was afraid she might have done, but on the other hand she was so merry, so full of laughter.'

'Personally I found her cheerfulness a trifle forced as it was this evening.'

Rosella's hands were limp in her lap. 'We don't know the circumstances,' she insisted. 'It could be that we all witnessed a chance encounter in the park today between Sébastien and an acquaintance from the past – and Claudine showed wisdom and dignity in ignoring it.'

Philippe stirred his coffee, sitting back in the chair. 'It could be,' he said impassively.

Rosella realized he held his own opinion about the meeting between Sébastien and the *demi-mondaine*, but he intended to keep it to himself.

She walked with him downstairs when it was time for him to leave. They went hand in hand towards the great hall, heads together, making plans for the morrow. Suddenly they heard raised voices. The doors of a salon burst open with a flash of gilded carving. Claudine rushed out, only to swirl about in their path, blocking their way, to address Sébastien, who stood in the room looking after her.

'Why did you trouble to return at all at this late hour?' she cried on a tearing sob.

'Calm yourself, Claudine!' Sébastien ordered in even tones, although his eyes were angry. 'You have an audience on all sides.' Behind him his sisters had risen from their chairs, Jules and Armand with them. Even Marguerite had swooped gracefully from the sofa to her feet, her expression shocked and startled, her eyes wide.

Claudine answered him hysterically, paying his admonition no heed. 'We waited for you to come home to dinner until it was pointless to wait any longer. I bought this new gown today specially to please you!' She flung out her arms and took a step back in a little action of self-display that was both poignant and tragic.

'It's a most elegant gown,' Sébastien said in the same even tones, but his hands were clenched tight, 'and you look beautiful in it.'

'But to no avail! And why? I will tell you. No! Do not come near me!' She flung up a hand to check Sébastien coming towards her. 'Although I'm your wife I'm not the mistress of the Château de Louismont and never can be! And that is all that matters to you. You felt no sense of occasion as I did on what was to be our first evening as married host and hostess to your family. And you care so little for my feelings that you failed to get back in time to take your place at the head of the table. I dined facing an empty chair.'

'I regret —'

'You regret nothing! Nothing except that you married me and not Rosella, who could have given you the château and an heir to inherit it!'

She dropped her face into her hands, all her strength spent, swaying on her feet. Sébastien swept her up in his arms and carried her away to their apartments.

191

When Claudine screamed out hysterically a few nights later Rosella, shut away in the west tower wing, heard nothing of the commotion or the arrival of the doctor fetched to ensure that no miscarriage resulted from such fright over an ordinary nightmare. Claudine was given a draught to soothe her. Although she told Rosella about it the next morning she declared she could not remember what she had dreamed except that it had been frightening, and then she made it clear that she did not want the matter referred to again. Everybody fell in with her wish, thinking the matter best forgotten. Nevertheless she remained unusually solemn and subdued for several days.

Rosella was deeply concerned. She believed Claudine had lied to her in saying she could not remember any details. All she could hope was that the turbulence in the tower room had not seeped out to other parts of the château on that occasion as it had done on that night in her childhood when Sébastien had given her sanctuary in his dressing-room. She herself had had almost a week of undisturbed nights, but often a period of quietness preluded a particularly horrifying visitation, and every day she dreaded the coming of darkness.

CHAPTER TEN

With a flash of colour a butterfly fluttered over Rosella's head and settled on her book, making her catch her breath with delight, the trembling underside of its wings black and brown in contrast to the glorious spread of orange and blue that she had seen in its flight.

'Don't move,' said Philippe's voice behind her, making her start violently.

Her strained nerves had reduced her to heart-thudding alarm at the slightest unexpected sound or movement. But she recovered herself and spoke in a whisper, watching the butterfly take tiny steps across the open page. 'What sort is it?'

'A peacock butterfly. See the check pattern on the dark underside of its wings? Perfect. Ah, there it goes!'

He dropped down on to the grass beside the hammock and rested one arm on an updrawn knee. Together they watched the vivid spread of wings dance away into the formal gardens. Then he looked up at her. 'I'm afraid I startled you. Sorry about that.'

She gave a shrug and eased herself against the cushions. 'I'm very jumpy these days.'

He rose to his feet and leaned over her, putting one hand on each side of the hammock. 'What's the matter? What are you worried about?'

He wanted to know. Desperately. He had seen her fade before his eyes over the past weeks. She was a mere shadow of the girl with the untouched bloom on her who had caught his eye in Paris that day; she had lost weight, and her skin had taken on a kind of transparent quality. If she were still yearning after Sébastien he must know it. But he was certain that there was something else that was troubling her — and troubling her greatly.

She had longed to tell him of her fears, but now that the opportunity had presented itself she hesitated to put everything into words.

'Blame the château,' she said evasively. 'You know I feel myself a prisoner in it.' Then she asked him a question that took him by surprise. 'When are you giving up the villa?'

'I've made no definite date. Why?'

'I have decided to take it over myself when you leave. It would be somewhere for me to escape to at times when I find the château too oppressive.'

'You need not wait until I'm not there. There is a guest-room that is always prepared for anyone who might come unexpectedly. You know the way. Across the stepping stones.' His eyes were very serious. 'I told you once before that, if ever you were in any danger, I was there to help you. Perhaps this is the better way. You can seek shelter under my roof if ever you feel that you need refuge.'

She lowered her feet to the ground in a flow of skirt and petticoats while he steadied the hammock for her. 'Danger?' she said irritably. 'I did not use that word. Oppressive — that was what I said.' Her parasol was leaning against the tree and she snatched it up, popped it open, and settled it on her shoulder, the frilled muslin moon of it framing her face and shining hair. 'So if you could let me know as soon as possible when you will be going away I can start working out my own arrangements.'

A spurt of anger darkened his face. 'You seem in a devilish hurry to be rid of me!'

She arched her brows, seeing that she had angered him,

and suddenly it offered a light diversion to tease him. not uncoquettishly. With a twirl of her parasol she turned from him and began to stroll along the path.

'Well?' he demanded, still standing where he was. 'Is that the truth of it?'

She did not answer him, knowing that he would follow her. When she heard his step behind her she quickened her pace. And so did he. She broke into a run with a ripple of laughter, and he gave chase. In between the flower-beds. Down through a sunken garden past a sundial and up again. She dodged round a fountain, giving him a tantalizing glimpse of her through the shining veil of water.

On she ran, her light figure darting ahead of him through the speckled sunlight of a long rose arbour. When an escaping thorny tendril hooked her flimsy parasol, whipping it from her hands, she swung about to catch it back again, but saw him coming and left it swinging there, heels flying.

She lost her way. She had plunged into an area that was unfamiliar to her. Marble statues strangled in ivy stared with blind eyes from lichen-covered plinths where nature had taken over the winding footpaths. But he was still coming after her.

He intended to catch her when he was ready and not before. She was breathless and exhausted, laughing as she had not laughed since coming to the château, running before him like an enchanting will-o'-the-wisp that he could ensnare the moment he wished it. Ahead among the trees and undergrowth beyond the statues was an old summer-house, ornate as a sugar-cake with its delicate rococo woodwork, paint flaking from its trellis-work.

She made some attempt to hide from him in it, collapsing on the slatted circular seat and swinging up her feet to lie full-length, her head resting on her arm. He paused under the arched entrance, resting his hands against the wooden pillars on either side of him, and when she saw how he was looking at her she raised herself on an elbow and there was no surprise on her face, only a dawning of self-awareness, and her lips parted softly.

He went across and dropped down to a knee to gather her to him where she lay, covering her mouth with his, laying claim to her at last, letting her know that there would be no more running away from him. Her response was joyous and avid and immediate, her kissing leaping into a wildness as passionate as his, her arms tight about his neck, her fingers buried in his thick hair. When one kiss ended another began. They found themselves unable to keep their lips from each other.

She knew a sweet aching akin to pain throughout her whole body, which she had never known before, and her flesh trembled with a life of its own under his loving hands which took one secret and then another from her. She knew she loved him. As she must have loved him for far longer than she realized, not recognizing the steady growth of a far deeper relationship when it had come to her, so immersed had she been in her feeling for Sébastien.

Philippe half-lay with her along the dusty seat. Her closed eyes shut out everything beyond the circumference of the summer-house. It was as though she were cocooned in love. Safe. Secure. In sanctuary.

'I love you,' he murmured, touching her face with his fingertips.

She let his words sink into her. Like the sun-rays that pierced the gaps in the curved roof above their heads. Warm. Golden. Beautiful. And she whispered that she loved him too, reaching her arms to him again.

They stayed in the summer-house for a long time. In stillness. In contentment. When at last she stirred it was as though she had wakened from sleep, her face rosy, her lashes heavy.

'How quiet it is here,' she said blissfully. She got up slowly and went to lean against a pillar, looking out into the wilderness of shrubs and trees, some of them having once been fine examples of topiary, but which had overgrown into grotesque shapes. He came and stood by her.

'Do you see the difference?' she said in a sad change of voice with a little wave of her hand towards the tangled greenery. 'In the summer-house everything is calm and full of light. Out there it's dark. Waiting for me. Waiting to swallow me up.'

He turned her sharply towards him, gripping her by the shoulders. 'Tell me!' he appealed. 'Tell me!'

'It's the tower,' she said with trembling lips, startled into confession. 'I know some evil lurks there, although how can I expect you to believe me? Even my maid insists that there is nothing that could harm me.'

'Go on.' He listened intently. He did not say whether he believed or disbelieved all she told him. It was enough for him that she was convinced she had heard the eerie sobbing, the scratch of a spectral fingernail, and had known the horror of falling down a flight of stairs into blackness.

When she had finished telling him she swayed into the closeness of his embrace, her forehead resting against his chin. He talked to her, urging her to consider whether her grandfather would have wished her to remain at the château in such unhappiness.

'He cared for you. He was concerned for you. Do you think he would want you to suffer such fear and misery?'

'You are right, I'm sure,' she agreed. 'It is that somehow I feel compelled to stay and see this terrible mystery through to the end – until it is a mystery no longer and whatever is there is revealed to me. No peace can come to the château – or to me – until that time.'

'Then move out of the tower and into another wing. God knows the place is large enough! The de Louismonts must rattle about in their section of it like dried peas in a pod.'

His description brought a wan smile to her lips, but the seriousness did not leave her eyes. 'I could not do that anyway. It would mean going back on the promise I made that they should have the rest of the château while I kept to the west tower wing.'

He tilted her chin and spoke very earnestly. 'Then promise me that you'll come straight to my villa any night that you are afraid. Bring your maid too if you mind about the gossip. But who cares? All that matters is that you are safe and that you should feel safe.'

'I will do that. But what if I should find myself alone in the tower room with Marie out of call? I have already failed once to find the courage to descend that flight of stairs again on my own in the darkness.'

'That is easily overcome. We will arrange some kind of signal. I can see the light of your tower window from mine.'

'And I can see yours.'

'Have you a red scarf or something similar that you could drape around a lamp — without setting fire to it? As soon as I see the light change colour I will come across to the château immediately.'

'I expect I can find something. I gave Marie the only scarlet dress that I've ever possessed, but there should be a scarf or sash among my things that would do.' A thought struck her. 'Suppose you happened to be asleep when I signalled?'

'I have not overlooked that. We don't want this private arrangement known, but I have a couple of menservants whom I can trust to keep watch in turn without talking about it to the rest of my staff, or anybody else, for that matter. But, first of all, before we go ahead with that, I'd like to look around that tower and every corner of the wing. You never know, we might be able to find some perfectly ordinary reason to explain the sounds you have heard. An echo, perhaps. A draughty chimney. A dumb-waiter shaft. Who can say? I want to look into it anyway.'

She put up her hand and placed it against his cheek. 'You have made me less afraid just by listening to me. For that alone I am more than thankful.'

He turned his face slightly and put his lips on her wrist. 'Let us go back to the château. Your tower has me to contend with now. It shall not alarm you again if I can help it.'

When they reached the west tower wing he made a thorough inspection of every nook and cranny, making a plan of it at the same time on a note-pad, which she had found for him. He also wanted to know exactly what rooms were situated on the floor below. In the tower room he tapped the walls and listened, thumped with his fists, and even found a tiny space amid the carved cherubs where the wood had warped, the penknife he dug into it meeting the clink of stone beneath the thin veneer. She hung on to his coat-tails in alarm when he leaned precariously out of the window to check that the domed ceiling moulded itself exactly into the very shape of the pepper-pot roof without a gap that could let the wind come whistling in.

Finally he stood stock-still in the centre of the room and let his gaze sweep once more around the circular walls.

'I cannot see any place where a draught could cause the sobbing sounds you have heard,' he said. 'The walls are solid enough under these panels as far as I can tell. What lies beneath this room?'

'Nothing, except at ground floor level where there's some kind of store-room. I looked in once, but it's full of

199

discarded furniture and I did not trouble to investigate.'

'Let's go down there.'

'We must take a lamp.'

She led the way down, but he went into the room ahead of her, holding the lamp, and he saw as she had done that nobody else had entered there for years.

'What do you think this room was used for originally?' she asked him, watching him rise from making a thorough check of the undisturbed, dusty floor.

'An arsenal most probably,' he answered, pushing aside some of the furniture to get through. The lamplight sent his shadow dancing up the walls. Then she saw he had spotted what she had failed to see on her previous inspection. Half hidden behind a tall cupboard, which he was starting to heave to one side, was a massive door.

'Where can that lead to?' she exclaimed, leaning forward across a rickety table to get a better look at it.

'Outside, I should think,' he replied, using all his strength to shoot back the rusty bolts. When he had managed to turn the key he hauled on the door. It opened with a screech of hinges to reveal a thick screen of leafy creeper through which the sun thrust needle-rays to brighten the whole room. He tore some of the creeper aside and revealed a view of the lawns and the distant willow-shaded lake.

'From out there I've looked at the tower hundreds of times and never noticed that there was a door in the base of it!' she exclaimed.

Philippe was scrutinizing the ceiling above his head. Then he went outside to stare up at the tower itself. Rosella followed him out into the sun and turned to follow his gaze upwards.

'I was looking to see if by chance the creeper might cover a window between the store-room and your bed-room,' he said, 'but it does not reach that high and you can see for yourself that there's never been any kind of aperture in those ancient stones.'

They went back into the store-room. He locked the outer door, but weighed the heavy key thoughtfully in his hand. 'I think I should have this key duplicated and that lock well-oiled. Then if you have cause to signal to me that you are frightened or alarmed in any way I can use my own short cut to reach you without any delay.'

'That's a wonderful idea!' She held up the key that she had removed from the door at the head of the stairs and brought down with her. 'You had better have a duplicate made of this one too. I keep the way to the tower base locked, partly to keep the dust and dirt shut away and partly to avoid any risk of an accident. It would be easy for a servant unfamiliar with my section of the château to open the door, thinking it was a cupboard, and come tumbling down.'

He took the key from her and pocketed it with the other. 'How many servants sleep in the west tower wing at night?'

'Only Marie. I'm served by the château staff in addition to my own kitchen staff, but all occupy the servants' quarters in other parts of the building. The west tower wing simply is not large enough to accommodate them.'

'Then we can dismiss any thought that it is some kitchen maid's lovesick weeping that reaches you.' His eyes narrowed thoughtfully at her in the light of the lamp that he held between them. 'Jules played a fiendish practical joke on you when he made the horse bolt — are you sure he is not at the root of all this?'

She shook her head with absolute conviction. 'He has been away from the château several times when I have heard those awful sounds in the night. He was also absent that terrible time, which I have already told you about, when I stayed in the tower room on holiday and heard the walls scream.'

'That could have been a dream,' he said gently. 'Not what you are hearing at the present time — that is real enough to you — but on that particular occasion it could have been a nightmare extension of the same disturbing sounds. Do you understand me?'

She nodded. 'It could have been, but I'm sure it was not.'

He took her by the hand, holding the lamp higher to illumine the stairs. 'How long is it since you last heard the weeping in the tower?'

She mounted the staircase at his side. 'A week and two nights.'

'Did it coincide with anything out of the ordinary happening in the château?'

'No. It was a perfectly normal day. As I have said, the phenomenon does not follow any kind of pattern.'

'Well, next time you hear it, give me our pre-arranged signal and I'll come at once.' They were back in her apartments and he grinned at her suddenly. 'You have dusty streaks on your face.'

'So have you!' she exclaimed, amused.

He looped his arms about her, drawing her close to him. 'Get your bonnet and we'll drive into town. A locksmith will make those keys while we pass an hour or two on a café terrace somewhere.'

She rushed to get ready, feeling as if a weight had been lifted from her. The duplicate keys would be in Philippe's possession before night came again. She no longer had to face the tower room alone.

When several more nights went by followed by a full week and then another of undisturbed rest Rosella began to hope that perhaps she had faced out the worst of the

202

tower room's torment, and she wondered again if it had been related to her own emotional distress, for being in love with Philippe had given her a new serenity, a new happiness such as she had never known before. One night she awoke to the last whisper of a long, heart-heavy sigh that hung about her where she lay, but although she strained her ears, ready to rush the bedside lamp forward to glow behind the red silk scarf that she draped every night across the window in readiness, she heard nothing more. She tried not to think that it might be a sign that the tower room had not finished with her yet, reminding herself that Philippe now stood with her against the unknown. Nevertheless, the chill of the thought lingered on with her, and she knew she had not been mistaken. That haunting sigh had been a warning knell of whatever it was that had yet to come.

Claudine, who was drawing near her time, had become increasingly listless, making it hard to interest her in anything. Since the night of the scene over Sébastien's absence from the family dinner party he had tried to make amends, staying in to dine with her and encouraging her to wear the cherry silk gown again for him on these evenings, which she did, but all her pleasure in it had gone. Sometimes after they had dined he took her with him to see Marguerite instead of going on his own, but she only went out of a sense of duty and a wish to fall in with anything he suggested, for it saddened her and added to her own dejection to see the steady deterioration of a woman who had once been a great beauty and an enchanting hostess to all the glittering social events that had been held in the past at the Château de Louismont.

It had been Sébastien's decision that, after the incident preceding the summer ball, the dismissed lady's maid should be replaced by a nurse who although she did not wear a uniform in order that Marguerite should not suspect her true duties — kept her under constant surveillance and saw to it that she was always properly dressed according to the hour of the day. Fortunately Marguerite did not resent the presence of the nurse, whom she looked upon as a companion appointed most thoughtfully by her dearest Sébastien in order that she no longer had to ring a bell to have someone at her beck and call; also — which was most delightful — she had a good listener to whom she could talk unceasingly about her wonderful son for hours and hours on end.

Only Philippe was able at times to cheer Claudine. He brought her light and amusing books to read, persuaded her into a gentle game of croquet now and again, and once made her laugh outright at the absurd gift of a monkey-on-a-stick, which he had bought in the market while in town. She was playing croquet with Rosella and Philippe on the afternoon when the weather changed after a particularly long and sultry spell. The breeze began to strengthen, suggesting that a late summer storm might soon clear the air, and it blew across the lawn where the game was in progress, dipping the wide brims of the girls' hats and fluttering into a pretty confusion the filmy folds and frills of their pastel-coloured dresses. When Claudine suddenly shivered and rubbed her arms while awaiting her turn to use her mallet on the ball Rosella paused before making her stroke and asked if she wished to go back into the château.

'Dear me, no!' Claudine answered, having become caught up in the game. 'I may win. I cannot throw that chance aside.'

'Then let me fetch the jacket that you left on the chair indoors,' Rosella suggested. 'You must not catch a chill.'

'Let me get it,' Philippe said, about to put his mallet aside.

'No,' Rosella said, raising her hand. 'I know exactly where she left it. There!' She had sent the ball spinning through the hoop. 'Now you two carry on with the game, and I shall be back in time for my turn again.'

The jacket was lying over the arm of a chair in the salon of the Watteau frescoes. She picked it up, and not until she turned with it did she see that Sébastien was also in the room. He had been sorting through some books in a glass-fronted cupboard and he stood with one open in his hand.

'Who is winning?' he asked with a smile, nodding his head in the direction of the window through which it was possible to see the figures of Philippe and Claudine on the croquet lawn in the distance.

'Claudine,' she answered, making a move towards the door. 'I must hurry back.'

But he put the book down and blocked her way. 'Even if it were not for the game you would be hurrying back – to Philippe. I've not been exactly blind over the past few weeks.'

She gave a deep nod, clutching the jacket to her. 'I've fallen in love with him. And he loves me,' she said simply, unable to lie to him.

'Will you marry him?'

'Yes,' she whispered, sharing Sébastien's hurt, knowing what her words meant to him.

'Does Claudine know?'

'I told her as soon as I knew myself. I wanted to put her mind at rest – about us. I felt after what she said to you about not being mistress of the château that she had doubts in her mind that should not be there.'

'When is the wedding to be?'

'Philippe wants me to marry him soon – tomorrow if I wished it. But I cannot settle on a date yet.'

'Then you are not completely sure in your mind about

him?' There was no mistaking the rise of hope in his voice.

It saddened her afresh to take that hope from him. 'I am decided. I want to share my life with no other man. He is — everything to me. But I'm not sure when I can leave the château.'

'What is there to keep you?' His tone was bitter.

She could not explain to him about the tower room. 'I shall know when the time is right.' She moved away. 'I must go. The others will be wondering what has happened to me.'

He made no further attempt to detain her, but held the door for her and he looked into her face as she went past him.

Outside the breeze met her gustily, making her hold on to her hat. Sophie was coming up the steps of the entrance, but she tilted her chin haughtily and passed into the château without giving Rosella a glance. She and Armand made a point of cutting Rosella deliberately since his failed attempt to contest the will and squeeze out the dowry he had claimed.

'You've been a long time,' Claudine said with mild surprise when Rosella came running up, holding out the flapping shawl to her.

'I can see it's my turn,' Rosella said, picking up her mallet. The game continued.

Rosella persuaded Claudine to spend the rest of the day with herself and Philippe, which she was glad to do, Sébastien being out at a local military function. After dinner the three of them spent the evening playing cards.

Philippe left shortly before midnight. The sky was full of lightning and the rising wind was tossing the trees. Rosella strolled back with Claudine to her apartments, making sure that she did not trip on any of the stairs in the fitful candlelight.

The first great drops of rain began to slash against the

206

windows when Rosella started on her way back through the château. Re-entering the salon where the three of them had been spending the evening she was surprised to see that the glass doors of the salon out to the battlements had blown wide and were crashing to and fro, the curtains whirling horizontally into the room. The playing cards, which had been left stacked on the table, were blowing everywhere. She rushed across to close the doors, but the wind beat against her and the rain struck icy cold on her face and head and penetrated the thin satin that covered her shoulders. She had to struggle to bring the doors together and flick the latch into place.

In the tower room she had expected to find Marie waiting for her, but the bed was not turned back and no nightgown had been put ready. She frowned, hoping that Marie was not starting to take advantage of her willingness to let her have free time to meet her sweetheart from the stables, with whom she was so much in love.

She rang the bell, expecting Marie to come hurrying to answer it with hands tying her frothy apron about her waist, ribbons flying from her cap. But no step sounded on the stairs. Rosella's last thought before she slept was that she would reprimand Marie in the morning.

When the sobbing woke her it resounded on a wailing shriek that coincided with a great crack of thunder that seemed to vibrate through the very stones of the château. With a gasp of terror she sprang from the bed, giving herself no time to think of anything except that Philippe must come to her. With shaking hands she set the lighted lamp on the table that stood by the window, knowing that its glow, penetrating the red scarf draped across the window, was a bright beacon in the dark, storm-torn night.

The shriek had faded with the rumbling away of the thunder, but she dared not wait for it to return with the next clap. Knowing that Philippe would be on his way to

207

her already gave her the courage she needed to face the stairs. She would wait with Marie, and together they would meet him.

There was no other lamp, but she lighted a candle, and protecting the flame with her trembling hand she hurried out of the room and down the narrow stairs. The thunder crashed and rolled again, but by then the room had been left behind, and if the walls shrieked she did not hear them. In her taut, nervous state it seemed to her that one stone stair quivered under her bare foot, and she wondered if fear could have brought her to the edge of hysteria, for never in all she had been through did she remember being so rigid with terror. When she reached the bottom of the flight blue flashes from the lightning flicked across the floor to reach the hem of her nightgown. She opened her maid's door and called to her.

'Marie! Are you awake?'

But the candlelight showed an untouched bed. Marie had not returned!

Anxiety stabbed at her. At the same time she became aware in a lull between the rolls of thunder that the glass doors of the salon were banging again.

She turned and ran down the corridor into the salon, but the protecting shield of her hand was not sufficient in the fierce draught of wind that met her, and to her dismay the candle guttered and went out. For a matter of seconds she was left in darkness, stumbling towards the doors that she was convinced she had latched securely, hearing from the tinkling of glass that they were broken.

Lightning showed her the stretch of parkland under a sky that had suddenly become a livid blue again. With overwhelming relief she saw the dark figure of Philippe racing towards the tower in the pelting rain, a lantern swinging in his hand. The raindrops hammered at her until she managed to push the vibrating doors closed, and she snapped home the latch for the second time, unable to understand how it could have slipped free. Unless some hand had loosened it? A chill ran down her spine, but she thrust the thought from her, knowing that very soon Philippe would be charging up through the tower store-room towards her.

She made a move to draw the inside shutters to keep out the weather, but she froze, seeing Philippe change direction and run to a spot directly beneath the battlements outside the salon. What had he seen there that was important enough to delay his rush into the tower? Was there somebody down there? Who or what could it be?

Without hesitation she unfastened the doors again and rushed out on to the battlements, heedless of the rain. Gripping the great wet castellated stones on each side of her she leaned over to look down.

She let out a scream. Even from such a height she had recognized the limp and lifeless figure that lay crumpled where it had fallen from the battlements. The scarlet silk dress shone like a pool of blood. It was Marie's poor dead face that Philippe turned towards the light of the lantern.

CHAPTER ELEVEN

For several days the police asked questions and made enquiries, but the result of their findings was a foregone conclusion. The inspector summed up what had happened on the night of the tragedy as clearly as if he had been present: the deceased, a little late for duty, had rushed in from her evening off and arrived in the west tower wing during the temporary absence of Madame Rosella, who had been accompanying Madame Claudine de Louismont back to another part of the château.

Before changing into her black dress and apron for duty, the deceased had thought to catch a last glimpse of her sweetheart from the battlements and wave to him, which she often did from outside her own room. But on this occasion, being in a hurry, she had chosen to dart through the deserted salon in order to save a few seconds of time. But the young man in question, caught by the rain, had made a dash to his quarters above the coach-house, not thinking that she would brave the elements on such a night. Disappointed, the unfortunate girl had leaned over too far in a vain bid to see him, lost her balance, and fallen to her death. Madame Rosella had returned and fastened the doors, unaware of the tragedy that had taken place. Why had the doors been open a second time? The storm, of course, was responsible for that. Remember what a storm had been raging that night!

It was very peaceful and still in the churchyard where Marie was laid to rest. Rosella had travelled with Philippe to the village in the Roanne district to attend the funeral and follow the coffin with the family and other local mourners. The young groom had been given time off to be there. Rosella, catching sight of him, saw that he wept unashamedly.

Jogging back across country in the carriage afterwards, her black veil turned back from her white, sad-eyed face, Rosella sat with her hand in Philippe's, gazing out unseeingly at the passing scenery. Every detail of that terrible night churned over again in her mind.

She herself had summoned help while Philippe had come tearing into the château, pale-lipped with fear that he might find that something had happened to her too. She had rushed into his arms and he had held her tight and hard, pressing her head against his shoulder, letting her give way completely to her grief. Neither of them had given a thought to the weeping she had heard in the tower room, and everything was silent there when eventually she returned to it at dawn, the sun rising on a sparkling day, all sign of the storm banished.

A tear rolled down her cheek. 'If only I'd looked down the first time I shut the doors,' she murmured in distress.

Philippe's hand tightened over hers. 'There was nothing you could have done to save her. It had been instantaneous. You yourself heard the doctor say her neck was broken on impact. She knew nothing of it. She suffered no lingering pain.'

It had been a tragic accident. Everybody in the château had been stunned by it. None had ever wished her harm. But Rosella wished she could be sure that it had happened as it was said and not because Marie had been frightened by something she had seen that had forced her back over the edge in a panic that had made her oblivious to all other danger.

The journey continued. They stopped overnight in an

211

old, mellow-walled hotel in a small town of cobbled streets and ancient pastel-coloured houses rimed by age. Next morning she packed away her mourning clothes and chose another garment for the last stage of the journey, not wanting to depress Claudine all over again with a sombre appearance upon her return. Claudine had been deeply upset by the accident, but had not wanted Rosella to go to the funeral.

'I'll get back as quickly as I can,' Rosella had promised, and she was keeping her word. But when the landscape became familiar in the gathering dusk of evening and the distance between the carriage and the château shortened with every prancing step of the horses, Rosella felt it would be all she could do to enter that sinister tower room again.

The market town, when they passed through it, was already ablaze with strings of coloured lights, banners, and bunting everywhere in honour of the annual wine festival later that evening. People were in a holiday mood, many decked out in carnival costume, and they rushed to the carriage windows to shake their be-streamered fairings and toss flowers in for Rosella to catch and gather on her lap. Brass bands thumped away on street corners, children danced and sang, and every now and again there would be the staccato crackle of firecrackers let off by riotous youths to enliven the proceedings.

Rosella tried to respond to the merriment, waving back to those who waved to her and smiling when a grotesque carnival head nodded against the window, but Philippe, watching her with the sensitivity that comes through caring deeply, knew what she was feeling.

'You should have a holiday,' he advised sensibly. 'Losing Marie has been a great shock for you, quite apart from other fears and anxieties that you have had to suffer. You need a complete change of scene and air.'

'Where?' she asked wearily, sitting back again as the town with all its festivity drew away, and she twirled the stalk of one of the flowers between a finger and thumb.

There was a pause. 'Martinique. With me.'

She turned her head slowly to look at him. 'Do you mean that?' she said longingly.

He slid an arm about her shoulders and drew her close to him, taking her hand in his, 'It will be a honeymoon you will never forget. No, listen to me,' he said, seeing she was about to make some protest. 'You have nothing whatever to keep you at the château. You have more than fulfilled your grandfather's wish that you should take up residence in the château, and marriage releases you from all obligations – your lawyer told you that himself. As for this compulsion to face whatever the tower room threatened you with, well – you can take the night of that most tragic accident as your time of confrontation. The walls shrieked, you said – the very sound you had always dreaded. You believed that it would foretell disaster and that disaster took place. It is over. Finished. You are free. I'll accept no more delays. Say you will set a date for our marriage – we'll go to Paris and be married there. You've never seen my house on the Rue St. Honoré – our home, my dearest.' He raised her hand that he held and kissed every finger. 'Say now that you will marry me.'

She could not refuse. Lost in loving she gave him the answer he wanted. 'I will marry you – '

'Rosella!' He kissed and hugged her, and while she was still pressed to him, her cheek against his, she continued what she had been about to say.

' – but I'm not free of the château. I never can be.'

He held her back from him, his grin exuberant. 'I intend to make you so happy that you'll never have a thought to spare for it! Not only will you have Paris to enjoy, but my offer has gone through for the purchase of your

213

grandfather's residence in Martinique, which I could never have made our second home if it had been included in his bequest to you. We can spend some part of each year there.'

'The house where my mother was born! And where she grew up! Oh, Philippe, how wonderful!' Then her face clouded again. 'But wherever I am and wherever I go I shall always have to return to the château at intervals. Monsieur Bataillard has told me that.'

'I suggest you keep the villa for those business visits, and then you need never stay in the château again. Or, if even being that near to the place disturbs you, we'll take rooms at the hotel in town whenever you have to view your property and lands.'

She nodded and drew herself from him, her gaze becoming abstracted as she plucked nervously at the gilt chain on the purse on her lap.

'There is something else.'

'Yes?'

'You were wrong in thinking the night that Marie died was the end of everything in the tower room. The walls did not shriek to warn me in time to go and save her. It happened afterwards – when she had been lying dead in the rain for two or three hours. The evil is still there. Her death was a final warning. Next time it will be me!'

'If that is how you feel,' he said, putting his fingertips against her cheek and turning her face towards him, 'you shall not spend another night under the château's roof. I will give you time to pack together whatever you need to take with you and then we can set off for Paris at once. Your other clothes and anything else you want can be sent on after .you. Your time at the Château de Louismont is over, my darling. I swear to love you and take care of you to the end of my days.'

'Oh, Philippe!' She flung herself across his chest and

buried her face against his neck in her relief that he was putting an end to her misery and opening a whole new life for her with him. His arms enfolded her and they stayed wrapped together until the carriage rolled through the open gates of the château.

The massive entrance came alongside the window and the horses came to a halt. The carriage door was opened and Philippe got out first to help her alight. She was reluctant that he should leave her and clung to him, but she knew he could not leave the villa without giving final instructions to his servants and collecting some luggage together. He kissed her reassuringly.

'I'll be back to collect you as soon as you signal with the lamp at your window,' he said, 'but are you sure you would not rather set a time for me to come?'

She shook her head. 'I don't know how long it will take me to reconcile Claudine to my departure, and I have to pack and make arrangements about everything. I may take one hour and I may take three.'

She stood on the steps to watch him out of sight. When she passed through the arched entrance into the château she was aware of the eerie sensation that it was reaching out to seize on her, determined not to let her go, and was drawing her in to lay bare its core of evil. The footman shut the doors behind her, and it was like the closing of a trap. To her surprise Louise came rushing to meet her at the head of the stairs and hustled her into the library where all the family was gathered, giving her some information that drove away contemplation of all else. 'Thank God you've returned! Since you left Claudine has stayed locked in her room, refusing to come out. Not even Sébastien was able to persuade her. We've had to leave food outside her door on a tray, which she took in whenever she was certain we had gone again.'

In the library Sébastien was the only one to greet her,

his expression one of deep concern. 'I did not dare have the door forced in case Claudine did the harm to herself that she threatened, saying that she would jump from the window if anyone tried to force an entry. She has flung the most extraordinary accusations at all of us.'

'What sort of accusations?' Rosella asked, removing her coat, which he took from her. She saw that Armand sat with Marguerite and Sophie was in attendance. Jules stood by the fireplace, looking at her with narrowed eyes through the smoke of his cigar.

'That one of us is trying to murder her!' he answered in despair.

'That's right!' Jules sauntered up, hands in his pockets, and addressed Rosella mockingly. 'She says each one of us has an excellent reason for wanting her out of the way because we'd all be better off if Sébastien could be free to marry you.'

Rosella gave him an angry look. 'You brought that subject up with me once before. Are you the one who put such a terrible thought into her mind?'

He shrugged derisively, not troubling either to confirm or deny accusation. 'Claudine is no fool.'

Rosella started for the stairs and the others all made as if to follow her, but she stopped them. 'None of you is to come with me,' she said firmly, pausing with her hand on the banister rail to look down over her shoulder at them, 'except you, Sébastien.'

He went with her up the staircase. 'Why should Claudine imagine for one moment that I'd do her any harm? She's bearing my child. She's my wife. Has her pregnancy turned her mind?'

They were out of earshot of the others and she paused, turning to him. 'I've no idea what can be at the root of this locking herself away, but something must have upset her badly. You will remember how she broke down in a way

216

most unlike her over your absence at the dinner party – she must have seen you in town when you were strolling in the park with – someone else.'

He thrust out his lower lip, raising an eyebrow thoughtfully. 'Oh. That was unfortunate.'

'Is that all you can say?'

He sighed elaborately. 'That most beautiful young woman had travelled all the way from Paris to see me. For the sake of old times she wanted money for a certain urgent matter that we need not go into. I gave it to her. I have not seen her since and do not intend to. You must appreciate that the nature of our past acquaintanceship was scarcely anything that I'd wish to disclose to my wife, but,' he added with a cynical glint in his eye, 'I can assure you that my behaviour has been exemplary ever since and I'm unable to think of anything that could have caused Claudine any special distress at this time.' He reached out and touched her arm. 'Not even to gain you would I have harmed one hair of the head of that pretty, silly little wife of mine, though how to convince her of that I don't know.'

'I'll do it. I don't know how, but I'll make her see the truth somehow,' she said, hurrying on again. Before they came near to Claudine's room she told him to wait while she went on alone, and tapped on the door. 'Claudine, it is I, Rosella! Please let me in.'

There was movement inside the room. Claudine spoke from the other side of the door. 'Is there anyone with you?'

'No.'

The key turned and the door opened a crack to reveal Claudine's wary eye. When she saw Rosella standing alone she swept open the door, caught her by the wrist, and pulled her into the room. 'I'm so thankful you're home!' she cried, bursting into tears. 'I've been frightened! Terribly frightened! Someone has been trying to kill me!'

'Hush, hush.' Rosella led the sobbing girl across to the sofa and they sat down together. 'Tell me about it.'

Claudine raised a tear-stained face. 'It started that night when I awoke screaming with fright. I had felt hands close about my throat! They said I'd had a nightmare, and the physic the doctor gave me made it difficult to remember everything clearly afterwards. But I did not dream that choking hold! It happened.' She gulped and plunged on. 'Then another night a board creaked in my room. I sat up and called out. And I saw that one of my pillows had been taken from my bed while I'd been sleeping. It lay where it had been dropped on the floor – and the door was open! Somebody had been about to smother me, but had taken fright and rushed out.'

'But you can't be sure. Nightmares can seem very real sometimes. And on the second occasion you could have knocked the pillow on to the floor in a moment of restlessness.'

'Right across to the opened door, which my maid always closes?'

'What else happened? Or is that all?'

Claudine gripped Rosella's hand tightly between her own. 'I had final proof the night Marie was murdered!'

'Murdered? What do you mean?' Rosella went pale.

'Marie didn't fall. I'm sure of it! She was nervous of heights and never went too near the edge of the battlements. I noticed how she shrank away whenever she put chairs on the terrace there for us, although she never said anything.'

'It's certainly true that she never sat out on her own section of the terrace as I had thought she might do,' Rosella admitted, 'but she was in the habit of waving to her young man from the battlements.'

'She didn't have to go close for that. And would she, who was nervous, go right to the edge in that terrible storm with a wind tugging at her? No! She stood back at a safe distance, but someone came behind and gave her a tremendous push that sent her toppling over.'

'But why? Why?'

Claudine lowered her voice in horror at what she had to say. 'Her murderer thought that she was me! Don't you see? She was wearing that red silk gown you gave her – and although it's brighter than my cherry gown by daylight there would be little chance to see the difference when she stood there on the battlements. She was my height and build – the difference in our figures at the moment could not have been seen by someone entering the room behind her.'

'But you are fair and she was dark.'

'She had a scarf over her head out there in the rain. It was found caught on a bush near where she fell.'

Rosella was silent, weighing up all that Claudine had said. It was a logical explanation for a previously inexplicable tragedy, but which of the de Louismonts would go as far as murder to gain their own ends?

'Why did you not tell the police what you suspected?' she questioned.

Claudine covered her face with shaking hands. 'I feared that it might be Sébastien who was trying to be rid of me.'

'Do you mean that you love him so much that even though you thought he might be attempting murder you could not give him away?'

'He loves you!' Claudine cried, her voice muffled. 'I know he loves you. I've seen how he looks at you – and his eyes follow you all the time.'

Rosella took hold of Claudine's wrists and pulled her hands firmly from her face. 'Listen to me!' she urged. 'You trust me and I have never lied to you, nor will I lie to you now. I did love Sébastien – it was an infatuation that sprang from young romantic dreams and had no more substance than that. I once – it was almost on the eve of his marriage to you – asked him to wed me. No! Let me finish,' she insisted, for Claudine had opened her mouth to speak, tears starting again from her eyes. 'But he rejected me, because he was betrothed to you. If he had really loved me he would not have let the threat of scandal or any other unpleasant outcome part us, but what he felt for me did not reach such a high level. He married you. You!' She gave Claudine's wrists a little emphatic shake. 'You are his wife. Sébastien has many faults, but he is strong in character and his code of honour will ensure that you remain his wife, the mother of his children, and no one will ever usurp you. He's waiting in the corridor. He wants to see you, to tell you himself that you have been wrong to fear him. He alone is your true protection in this world.'

'But who – who –' Claudine faltered '– has been trying to murder me?'

'I don't know. Perhaps we shall never know. There is a streak of ruthlessness inherent in the de Louismont nature that is right out of the jungle – untamed, violent, raw. But when it is tempered with the gentleness that is yours, Claudine, your children will be the finest de Louismonts ever to be born.'

'Why do you speak as if there is no threat to my life any more?'

Rosella smiled, her whole face suddenly radiant. 'Because I shall remove that threat for ever in a few minutes when I break the news to your in-laws that I am deeply in love with Philippe and that we are to leave tonight and be married without delay as soon as we reach Paris. The guilty person – whoever he or she might be – will know that there is no chance of Sébastien and I coming together and that you are not and never have been the barrier to any greedy gain. You will no longer be in any danger whatever. You are safe. My marriage to

Philippe sets a seal on it.'

'Dear Rosella. How happy I am for you! And for myself!' Claudine laughed a little hysterically in her relief, and then gulped, pressing her hand against her back. 'Oh! A twinge of cramp.'

'Are you sure it is only that?' Rosella asked quickly.

Claudine nodded. 'I know what you're thinking, but I get aches and pains all the time.' She settled herself more comfortably. 'I shall miss you.'

'And I'll miss you, but we'll write to each other. Now I must go, because I must pack a few things together and be ready to leave. Talk to Sébastien. Put the past from you. Start your marriage afresh. Look to the future, dearest Claudine.'

'I will!'

They embraced and kissed each other. Then Rosella left her. Out in the corridor Sébastien was leaning against a wall, arms folded, but he straightened up when she approached him.

'Well?' he asked anxiously.

'She knows now that there is nothing to fear from anyone.'

Relief washed over his face. 'Thank you,' he said simply.

'She loves you so much. More than you'll ever know.'

He gave her a somewhat wry look. 'People often fail to know how much they are loved. I'll go in to her.'

He went into his wife's room and closed the door. Rosella, turning away, realized that she had not told him of her own departure. She would go back downstairs to break the news to the de Louismonts and she would say farewell to Sébastien after she had packed her things.

CHAPTER TWELVE

In the tower room Rosella picked up a letter bearing a
Paris postmark, which had been placed on the table by her
bed to await her return. It was from Monsieur Bataillard.
She opened it almost absently, her thoughts busy with the
dramatic impact she had made on the family when, after
telling them that all was well with Claudine again, she had
announced her imminent departure and forthcoming
marriage.

She had watched their faces carefully. Louise had gone
white to the lips, sinking back into her chair and gripping
the arms of it. Jules had turned his back rudely and
arrogantly. With a bitter stare Sophie had stalked to her
sister's side and placed a hand in silent consolation on her
shoulder. It had been shaken off furiously. Only Armand
had spoken, but to Marguerite, explaining to her what had
happened, although not before Rosella had seen his face
congest into a look of savage enmity.

Abruptly Louise had created a minor sensation of her
own, springing to her feet. 'So you're leaving us, Rosella! I
speak for us all when I say that we're glad to see you go. In
fact, it calls for a celebration!' She had spun round to
address the others, flinging her arms wide. 'Let's all go to
the wine festival! Even you, *Maman*. Rosella can leave the
château as she came – without welcome and without
farewell. Come. We must get ready at once. The festivities
will have started hours ago.'

Rosella paused in unfolding the letter in her hand,

hearing the carriages drive away. They had gone. Moving nearer the lamplight she read her letter through. An involuntary gasp of astonishment escaped her. She would have read it again, wanting to be sure that she had not misunderstood it in any way, but a faint sound came from somewhere outside the door.

She stuffed the letter away in her purse, snatched up the lamp, and crept to the door. She whirled it open. 'Who's there?' she demanded. But the lamplight showed her the silent, deserted flight.

Had she imagined the sound after all? Uneasily she returned to her room and set about her packing. The scrunch of gravel under carriage wheels sent her to the open window to look out. It was Sébastien's calèche that was disappearing down the drive. His and Claudine's reconciliation must have resulted in a decision to go together to watch the fun of the wine festival. She drew the window closed again. It meant that she and Sébastien would not be exchanging any goodbyes. Perhaps when Claudine told him about her leaving with Philippe he had thought it was the best way. Returning to her packing she decided to leave a letter for him before departing. It meant spending a little longer in the tower room, but there were certain things she wanted to put down on paper for him to read as soon as he returned from the wine festival.

It was almost midnight when she sealed the letter. Going to the window she lifted the lamp and signalled to Philippe. Now he would start off to fetch her, giving her another ten or fifteen minutes to spare. She put on her coat and swathed a filmy scarf over her head and across one shoulder before ringing the bell for a servant to come and carry her travelling-bag down to the hall. When nobody came she rang again impatiently, but without result. With a sigh she picked up the travelling-bag herself, not wanting to delay any longer, but when she went out to the tower stairs she saw that the lamps in the whole wing had been extinguished, leaving no light to guide her down the last part of the flight. She shivered. It was almost as though somebody had closed up the west tower wing, believing she had already departed.

She went back into the tower room to pick up the lamp and take it down with her, not trusting herself to the flight in darkness with the bulky travelling-bag. Then she stopped, foot pointed and poised in the air. The seventeenth stair down was not there!

With extreme caution she lowered her foot on to the eighteenth step. As soon as her weight touched it there was a faint whirring of some ancient mechanism, and the seventeenth stair slipped back into place. It had been that same faint screech of the stair being withdrawn from the rest of the flight that she had once mistaken for the scratch of a fingernail – and it had been the same sound that she had heard while packing.

Now she knew why she had fallen that night soon after her arrival at the château. In the same instant she remembered how she had seen Jules look sharply over his shoulder at that step. Had he merely felt it quiver underfoot as she had done one day, or did he know of the mechanism? The misplacing of it had been an attempt on her life the first time! And this was undoubtedly a second try!

The reason was suddenly clear enough. That first time she had been the obstacle standing in the way of Sébastien and the château. Then, after Sébastien's marriage, it had been Claudine's turn to become the stumbling-block. But now the finger of doom had pointed towards herself again, simply because she was about to marry someone else and take away for ever all chance Sébastien might have had of eventually getting the château. Some person or persons unknown had made a last fiendish effort to dispose of her in a way that would look like an accident!

She reached the bottom of the flight and cast a wary look about her. Then she hurried swiftly down the long corridors to the doors that led out of the west tower wing. She left the lamp on a side table with the letter to Sébastien propped against it and hurried on again. It was very gloomy everywhere. Here and there a wall sconce glowed, but no lamps gave added brightness and the huge chandeliers were unlit. And where were all the servants? No footmen to be seen. No glimpse of maids going quietly about their duties.

The wine festival! The servants had all gone to the wine festival. It was traditional. Why hadn't she thought of that before? That was why no one had answered the bell she had rung. She was alone in the château! Why then did she not feel alone?

She tried to calm her thumping heart, walking sedately down the crimson sweep of the grand staircase to the dark hall as though trying to prove to unseen watching eyes that she felt no fear. She jumped violently when a heavy banging resounded on the great doors, but at the same time the glad knowledge of who it was flooded through her.

'Philippe!' She flew down the last stairs, sped across the shining floor and dropped her travelling-bag with a thump to shoot back the bolts and turn the key.

'Beloved!' He threw his arms about her waist and swung her around as he kissed her. 'Ready?'

'Yes.'

He snatched up her travelling-bag and held out his hand to whirl her out with him to the waiting equipage that he was going to drive himself to Paris. But in the midst of flight she halted abruptly on the threshold, dragging on his hand.

'Listen!' she said urgently.

'What?' he said, puzzled.

'A cry. I heard a cry!'

'I cannot hear anything.'

'There! I heard it again. It's Claudine.'

She spun about and darted back up the grand staircase. Philippe pushed the door closed behind him, dropped the travelling-bag down again, and followed her at a run. Neither of them noticed the hand that came out of the darkness to turn the key again and remove it.

'Claudine, I'm coming!' Rosella called, racing along the passageway. But when she reached Claudine's room there was no sign of her, although all the lamps were alight.

'Whatever's the matter?' Philippe asked, catching her up. He was completely bewildered.

'Everybody's gone to the wine festival – even the servants. I thought Claudine and Sébastien had gone too, but I heard her cry out!' She put her hand to her head. 'Am I hearing things?'

'Don't get upset. Let's listen again.'

They listened. Not a sound.

'I *know* I heard her!'

'Then we'll go back to where you thought you heard the cry the first time and try to locate it from there,' he suggested.

'All right, but you stay at the head of the stairs and see if you hear anything too.'

He stayed where she told him, leaning an elbow on the gilded newel post while she ran lightly down the flight. But when she came close to the great doors she frowned, seeing the bolts were shot and the key gone.

'Why did you lock up again?' she asked, swinging round to look up at him. Then she screamed out. He was collapsing from a blow dealt by a silver candlestick that was vanishing into the darkness in the hand of an unseen assailant.

'Philippe! Philippe!' She tore up the flight towards him and flung herself on to her knees where he had fallen, not wholly unconscious, but dazed and groaning. She cradled his head in her arms and looked with terror in the direction of the jet black shadows that had hidden whom or what from her sight.

'Get up! Oh, please try!' she implored, struggling to make him move, dragging his arm about her neck.

He responded automatically to the urgency of her voice, but having no idea why he had to obey or what had happened to him. She reeled under his weight, but kept her balance. She would take him up to the tower room. There she could barricade the door and they could stay there in safety until everyone returned from the wine festival.

A sob escaped her as she staggered along with him. She kept glancing over her shoulder, terrified that a horrifying figure would emerge from the darkness behind them to strike again, but they reached the west tower wing without mishap.

She longed to pick up the lamp she had left alight, but could not manage it with Philippe lurching and stumbling along. She decided to see him safely into the tower room and then return for it.

'Not much farther,' she urged frantically. It seemed he must pitch forward and fall sprawling with every step. 'Lean on me a bit more. That's it. Now up this flight to the tower room.'

They managed it. She helped him on to the bed and he fell back on to the pillows with his eyes closed, breathing deeply. After fetching a towel dipped in cold water from the bathroom and placing it around his head she went out, locking the door behind her, and hurried down to fetch the lamp.

She had picked it up when she heard the cry again. It

was Claudine. And she was in pain! Quickly Rosella darted into one of the salons and she took down a cutlass from the wall. With the weapon in one hand and the lamp in the other she set out again to try to locate the direction of the cry.

There! In the library. With the point of the cutlass she pushed the door open and entered warily.

'Rosella! Thank God! I thought you'd left long ago with Philippe. Or have you come back?'

'Claudine! Why are you in here?' Rosella rushed across to where Claudine lay half-sitting, half-propped against a wing-chair like some poor scared little animal seeking whatever shelter was available. Her hair was dark with sweat and her pupils were dilated with pain. She was wearing only a cambric nightgown. 'What on earth has been happening?'

'That twinge of pain I had when you were with me was the start of my labour. It suddenly became acute after Sébastien and I had been talking for a while. He helped me into bed and then went himself in the carriage to fetch the doctor.'

'Why didn't you stay in your bedroom?'

Claudine clutched her arm. 'There's someone prowling about in the château. I became so frightened that I felt I had to get outside somehow and shout for help. But the pains became so bad that I was forced to crawl in here and hide.' She buried her face against Rosella's shoulder, trying to smother a moan of agony.

'I'll take you up to the tower. Philippe is there. I don't know who it is creeping about, but it's not safe for any of us to be down here.'

'I cannot move!'

'You must and you shall. Get on your feet.'

Sobbing quietly, Claudine obeyed very much as Philippe had done, responding to the note of command in Rosella's voice. 'I'll never get to the tower. It's too far!'

'No, it isn't. Come on. A step at a time. That's right.'

The lamp had to be left, but Rosella took the precaution of pushing a box of matches into her pocket. They would have to make do with the candles in her room. Once again she set off for the tower with a burden to support, but this time with the cutlass poised ready in her right hand she felt a little braver.

When they started up the flight to the tower she struck a match to make sure that the seventeenth stair from the top was in place. Then the flame burnt her fingers. She dropped the match and at the same time Claudine doubled over, screaming out with pain. In the darkness she slithered down on to her knees, refusing to move, clutching at Rosella's skirts. Somewhere in one of the salons a door creaked.

'I cannot move another step! Don't make me! Oh, don't make me!'

In desperation Rosella knelt down and put her arms about her, feeling the girl's tear-wet face against hers. 'You'll be safe in the tower room. Think of your baby. That's all that matters.'

To her relief her words gave Claudine the strength to struggle up and lumber on again. Rosella, groping along the wall for the door, looking back constantly over her shoulder for the first hint of attack, felt the cool handle slide under her straining fingertips. She pressed it down, swung the door open, and pulled Claudine with her into safety. The door slammed and she leaned against it, taking the matches from her pocket to strike one.

'I'm back, Philippe,' she said between laughter and tears, 'and I have brought Claudine – '

Her voice trailed off. The match revealed a bed, but Philippe was not lying on it. Neither was the window there any more. And the walls were not pink silk, but palest green, the paintwork silver and not gilt. With a horror that stunned her momentarily she realized that she and Claudine, who had now thrown herself on to the bed, groaning in agony, had stumbled into a secret room that was sandwiched between her own room above and the store-room below! A windowless circular room in which the weeping spectre had sobbed night after night. They must get out! They must! They must!

She spun about to feel for the handle, but the flame burned her fingers again. Another match showed her a smooth panel like all the others in the circular room. The handle was concealed as it was in the room above. Outside on the stairway the wooden veneer had hidden the presence of a door, but between her helping Philippe into the tower room and fetching Claudine there had been hands drawing aside a certain section to disclose the secret entrance for her to stumble through by mistake in the darkness.

With shaking hands she lighted a candle that stood on a chest of drawers. In the resulting glow she examined the moulding. But it was different in design from the room above, and any one of the intricate leaves and flowers could conceal the catch. Or was it the panel next to it that had opened to let them in?

'Rosella! Help me! I'm going to die!'

Rosella flew across and smoothed the girl's tumbled hair back from her sweating brow. 'No, you are not, Claudine. You're going to have a fine, beautiful baby and everything will be all right.'

'I'm thirsty!'

'I'll see if there's any water.'

The room was exactly the same as the one above it, but the adjoining bathroom was thick with dust and had not been used for years. Returning again to the bedside Rosella paused, holding the candle high, her attention caught by a large and ancient black stain that had dried into the pale carpet. Slowly she stooped and examined it more closely. Blood! Blood had flowed and darkened in this terrible room.

Then she knew the château's secret. Murder had been committed long ago on the very spot where she was standing. And she knew the night when it had happened. Why should she not indeed, for she had been a terrified child in the room above, hearing a woman scream out when a murder weapon had taken life from another human being.

The château had been strangely deserted that night. Now she remembered. It had been the night of the wine festival too. Perhaps Sébastien had come from it when she had thrown herself into his arms on the stairs. And for the rest of that night all the château had been turbulent and astir. Had silent hands been moving the body out of the château and away? But where? And who could it have been?

Holding the candle high she went swiftly across to the nearest panel and examined it closely. Somewhere there was some kind of air vent through which that scream and the eerie sobbing had echoed. If she could find it and stand close to it Philippe would hear if she shouted. And he should certainly hear Claudine's anguished cries. If he had not lapsed into complete unconsciousness!

'Philippe!' she called. 'Can you hear me? We're in a room below you. Philippe!'

'Look!' Claudine gasped from the bed, trying to rise.

Rosella looked aghast at the spot where she was pointing. A curl of smoke had come up through the floorboards. A fire had started in the store-room below!

'Philippe!' Rosella screamed, hammering on the walls. 'Fire! Fire! Fire!'

She went on screaming and shouting, thumping on the

231

walls, and trying again and again to find the hidden handle of the door. The smoke thickened, creating a fog in the room that made Claudine choke on her shrieks of pain. Rosella, with streaming eyes, leaned against the wall, coughing helplessly, her strength going from her.

Then there was a crash and a splintering of wood. Another blow from a powerful boot sent one of the panels splitting into the remains of a door. And Philippe, white-faced, but very conscious and very much alive, thrust himself into the room to give Rosella a push out of it and then pick Claudine up in his arms to carry her to safety.

They went out of the château by way of the great kitchens, Claudine wrapped in an ironing blanket snatched up on the way. She was left on a garden seat while Rosella ran to ring the fire-bell and Philippe made a dash for the tower store-room.

He tore aside the creeper and thrust wide the half-open door. There, pulling the furniture over to the blazing pile stacked against the wall, was Marguerite, her hair tumbled about her face, her gown ripped and torn. On the floor lay the silver candlestick with which she had struck him down.

She saw him when he reached for her. With a piercing scream she stepped back and would have fallen into the blazing fire if he had not lunged and snatched her with him to the door. In the same instant that they tumbled into the open air a tremendous torch of flame leapt across the rafters, turning the whole store-room into an inferno. He saw her go darting away across the lawns before he ran for fire buckets, and by that time the first of the fire-fighters had appeared at a run in the distance, summoned by the wild clanging of the bell.

The whole of the tower was destroyed and with it most of its wing. Hundreds of volunteers, who had left the wine festival to follow the racing horses and fire-engines in a cavalcade of carts, wagons, and carnival floats, had worked valiantly all through the night, passing buckets, pumping water, salvaging valuable furniture and other goods. But at dawn the tower was a blackened heap of stones and thick smoke still rose and curled through the empty window frames of the roofless wing.

Claudine's son was born at the height of the fire in the lodge by the gates. Rosella was with her, as well as the lodge-keeper's wife, who had had some experience of midwifery. But the doctor, whose progress with Sébastien in the calèche had been delayed by the confusion of traffic and sightseers on their way to the fire, had arrived in time to hurl off his coat and deliver the child.

It was Jules who found his mother. She was lying under the willows by the lake, face downwards, half in the water, her long hair floating like rich-coloured weeds.

In the library Sébastien and Philippe, still grimed from fire-fighting, their jackets lost, their shirts filthy, turned when Rosella entered the room. She looked pale and exhausted, but she smiled gratefully when Philippe put an arm about her to take her to a chair that Sébastien pushed forward.

'How is Claudine?' Philippe asked. He had seen her being carried on a stretcher with her baby from the lodge into the château.

'She's sleeping, and the baby is in the cradle. A nurse is with them.' She turned sadly to look at Sébastien. 'Your mother. I'm so sorry. Jules told me.'

He nodded gravely in acknowledgment of her sympathy. 'Philippe has been filling in some of the details for me — of the sobbing you've been hearing in the tower, and how you and Claudine were trapped. Would you tell me the rest?'

She related all that had happened. He shook his head sorrowfully when he heard that his mother had been responsible for Marie's death and of the other attempts she had made to kill both Claudine and Rosella, which had culminated in a last effort to burn them to death.

'Now I must tell you and Philippe something I never thought I'd have to tell anyone,' Sébastien said grimly. 'My brother and sisters have never been let into the secret and I feel, for their own peace of mind, they should be left in ignorance of it.' He sat down on the edge of the library table, and Philippe took a seat on the arm of Rosella's chair.

'I need hardly say that whatever you disclose will remain with us alone,' Philippe said to him.

Sébastien nodded again and his eyes rested on Rosella. 'That night when you were staying here as a child and came running to me on the staircase was the night that murder was committed in that hidden room. I thought you had had a nightmare, but you were extremely frightened, and after I had put you to bed in my dressing-room I went to investigate. I knew the legend of the tower and I was curious.' He gave a groan under his breath. 'I've wished a thousand times that I'd simply gone to my own room and fallen asleep. Instead, I became an unwilling accessory to that murder.'

He thrust himself away from the desk and paced slowly over to the fireplace before continuing. 'My beautiful mother was spoilt and pampered all her life. She married my father for all he could give her, and the devotion that should have been his she lavished on me, her first-born child. My father's love for her became inflamed by jealousy. His business interests took him away from the château for weeks at a time, and he began to suspect that she had lovers, but what he didn't suspect for a long time was that she knew of the hidden room, which an old servant, who had been in my grandfather's confidence, had revealed to her, together with ways of reaching it unobserved. For obvious reasons the location of that most convenient room and the secret passages in the château had previously remained the exclusive knowledge of the head of the household who – in due time – passed it on to his eldest son. My father never dallied with other women, but my faithless mother made good use of that room.' He sighed heavily. 'On that particular night my father returned unexpectedly. And he caught my mother with her lover there. And killed him. Before her eyes. With the sword-stick that he always carried. It was her scream that scared you, Rosella.'

'What happened then?' Rosella asked in a low voice.

'I arrived in the west tower wing and practically stumbled over my father dragging the body down the stairs. Filial loyalty outweighed any other thoughts that I might have had about the murder. It was I who carried the body out to my own carriage, which I drove myself to Paris, timing my arrival there for the darkness of the following night. Then in a back alleyway near the Seine I tumbled the body out and drove off again. Nobody had ever known of that man's association with my mother and no shadow of suspicion ever fell in the direction of the Château de Louismont. The police believed that he had been killed where he was found.'

'Then it was the shock of the murder that brought about your mother's nervous breakdown?' Philippe said.

'That is correct. She never fully recovered. My father changed all the staff in the château, not wanting any overlooked clue or casually expressed question about that night to set off any new line of enquiry. Not long afterwards he suffered a heart attack and died. Then for a while my mother took to returning to the secret room and crying at night for hours on end, almost as though he had left her free to mourn her lover. I had the west tower wing closed up, took her away for a long holiday, and although the best doctors in France advised me that she would never wholly recover from her nervous breakdown they gave me no reason to believe that she would ever become – violent.'

'Undoubtedly it was the shock of my grandfather's will that upset her emotionally again,' Rosella said with sorrow. 'That was why she returned to her weeping in the tower.'

'It also meant that in her unbalanced state of mind she sought first to remove you in order that I should inherit. Then, after I married Claudine, she might have taken no further action, but – perhaps I should have told you at the time – she was in one of the alcoves on that day when we had signed the agreement over the income from the château with Monsieur Bataillard, and she overheard – and saw – all that took place.'

There flashed into Rosella's mind an image of herself and Sébastien held in a glow of candlelight amid the dark shadows when he had told her for the first time that he loved her. Gravely she understood the significance of what he was saying. 'How did you know she had been there?'

'She emerged after you had gone, the tears running down her face, almost in a state of collapse in her distress that I was not married to you, who could have given me everything she wanted for me.' He spread his hands expressively. 'I was in a fury that she had spied on us, but her condition was such that I had to control it. If I had been less annoyed I might have been struck then by the fact that she had been sitting in the alcove where a door leads to secret passages. It never occurred to me that she might be wandering about in them again.'

'That must have been the turning point when Marguerite decided that she must get rid of Claudine,' Rosella said unhappily.

He gave a weary nod of agreement. 'Then there followed the two abortive attempts on Claudine's life when in her unbalanced mental state my mother tried first to strangle her and later sought to smother her with a pillow. After that your maid became an innocent victim to her murderous scheming. Then yesterday evening, after your announcement that you were about to marry Philippe, poor foolish *Maman* decided to make one last effort to eliminate you before the château was lost for ever to you and your husband and the children of your marriage.'

'But there's one thing I don't understand,' Rosella said. 'When I left everybody in the salon, Louise had decided that they should all go to the wine festival.'

'Apparently *Maman* cried off at the very moment of departure, saying that she was tired and that her companion, who had been given the evening off, had returned and would be with her. Louise did not think to check, having no reason to imagine that she might be lying, and thus was my mother left without attendance. She must have decided to use whatever methods came to hand to kill you, including the use of the seventeenth stair, which was installed a couple of centuries ago by a certain cardinal under the guise of hospitality.'

'How tragic it is,' Rosella said, rising to her feet, 'that I did not know the contents of the letter from Monsieur Bataillard, which was waiting for me up in my room, when I made that announcement of my intention to marry Philippe.'

She turned slightly for Philippe had come to stand at her side, and she put her hand into his with a quick loving look, having confided already to him during the flight from the burning château what she was about to tell Sébastien. Then she turned to Sébastien again. 'My good lawyer has not been idle in trying to follow my dearest wish to be rid of the château. He has discovered the tiniest clause that will release me, but he wanted me to say nothing about it until after your child was born in order not to raise any false hopes.'

Sébastien stared at her, puzzled. 'I don't understand.'

'The Château de Louismont can only be handed on to a member of a *younger* generation, as you know, but in the event of the owner being childless it can be bequeathed — or given by deed of gift — to the eldest *son* of the next de Louismont in line. When I get to Paris I shall sign a document that will make your son the new owner of the château and all its lands. As his father you will be in full control until he comes of age. Everything is yours.'

Sébastien looked dazed, wanting to believe what he had heard, but still reluctant to accept that it was possible. 'But you will have children,' he protested. 'There is no reason to suppose you will not.'

'That is beside the point,' Rosella answered, smiling. 'I'm childless *now*. Therefore this might be the only time left to me to make that deed of gift.'

For a few moments Sébastien was unable to speak. Then he snatched up her hand in both of his, putting it to his lips. When he slowly lifted his head and straightened to his full height again he still kept her hand in his clasp and he spoke directly to her as though they were alone in the room and Philippe was not present.

'In my heart I return a thousand times over all you have given me.'

Philippe saw her give Sébastien a curious, meditating look with softness in it, and for a moment he felt shut out and forgotten. But almost as though she sensed his reaction she stepped closer to him, withdrawing her hand from Sébastien's hold.

'Goodbye, Sébastien,' she said.

'Goodbye, Rosella.'

She took Philippe's arm and they went from the room. She had said her farewells to Claudine and there was no more to be done. In the hall was her travelling-bag, which Philippe had dropped down only a few dramatic hours before. In it was all she possessed in personal effects. Everything else had been destroyed in the fire. A footman picked it up and carried it out to the carriage where it was stowed away.

Rosella stepped into the sun and felt the cool shade of the arched entrance fall away from her. The shadow of the château had left her at last. She did not get into the carriage at once, although Philippe stood ready to assist her. Instead, she took a few paces across the forecourt to where she could view the still smoking ruins of the west tower. With it had gone all her terror, her fears, and even her hatred of the château itself. She had met her destiny and emerged free to start life afresh at Philippe's side.

In those last words to her Sébastien had shown that he knew the extent of the gift she had made him. With all the evil wiped from the château she could have – if she had wished – settled there in happiness with Philippe, knowing that no dark shadows from the past would haunt her ever again. But she had chosen to give the Château de Louismont to him as a token of what she had felt for him and he had known it, telling her in reply that he returned her love a thousandfold. And she had realized the depths of his true feelings for her. In the end she had come to mean more to him than the château or anything else in the world.

Perhaps he would always love her, yearning after her as once she had yearned after him. But she had not left him bereft. Claudine would take on a new stature in his eyes as mistress of the château and mother of the son for whom he would hold it in trust, his light and hope for the future.

'Rosella, it's time to go!'

Philippe was right. It was time to go. But she knew that one tiny part of her heart would always remain at the Château de Louismont.

She turned and at the sight of Philippe waiting for her she felt a rushing lift of joy. With running steps she went to him, her hands outstretched for his, her face ardent and suffused with the sudden gladness of homecoming.

WOLVERHAMPTON
PUBLIC LIBRARIES